THE SECRET HISTORY OF MY HOMETOWN

THE SECRET HISTORY OF MY HOMETOWN

ANDREW BODEN

FREE ATTIC PRESS

Cataloguing data available from Library and Archives Canada.

ISBN: 978-1-7778223-0-9 (paperback)

ISBN: 978-1-7778223-1-6 (ebook)

ISBN: 978-1-7778223-2-3 (audiobook)

Cover design by Michel Vrana.

Typography by Scribeworks.

The story *Letters to Trotsky* appeared in Amazon's *Day One* magazine in 2017.

Visit the author's website at:

andrewboden.com

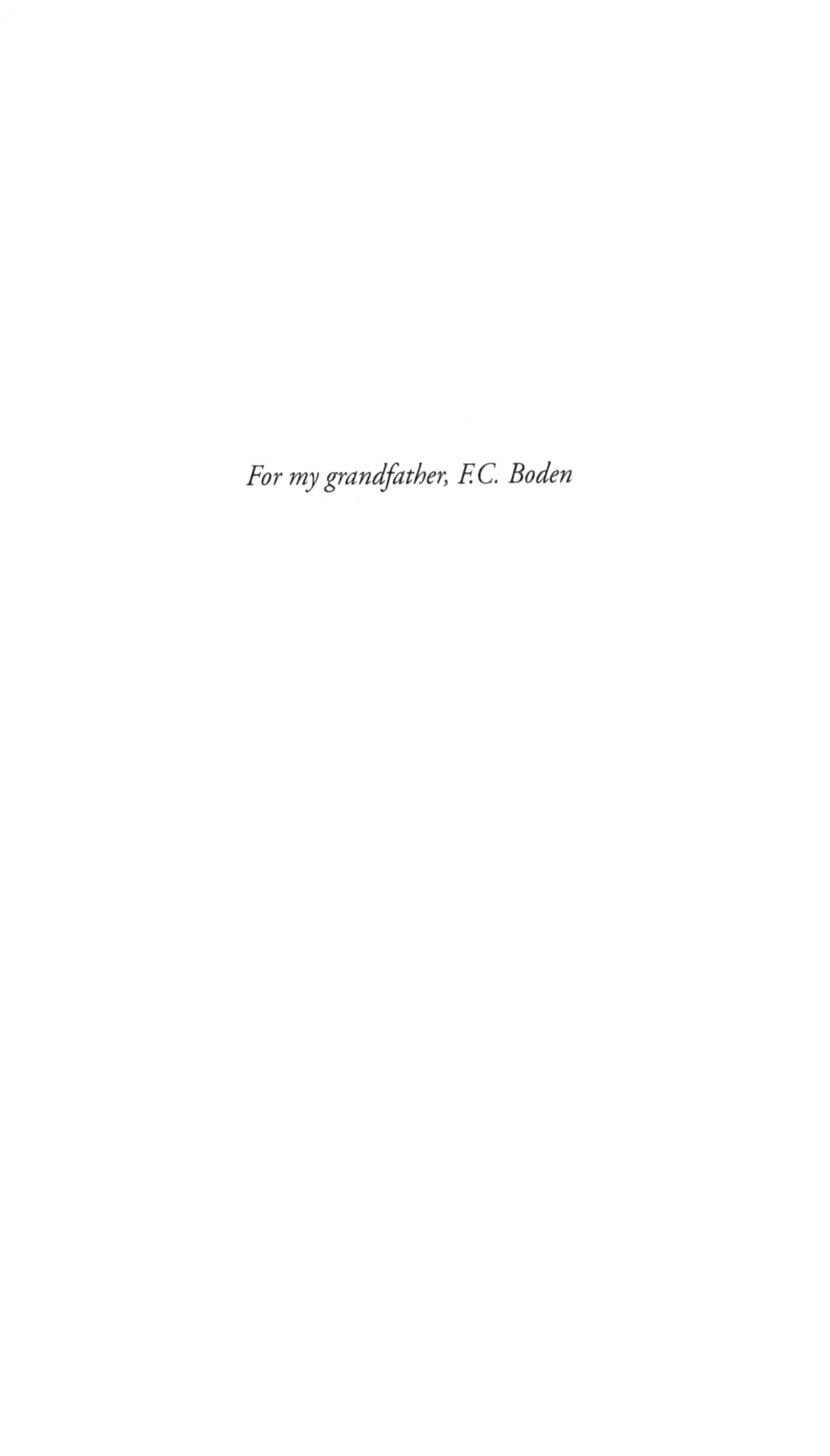

For my grandfather, F.C. Boden

CONTENTS

MARK TWAIN AT THE END OF THE WORLD

My name is Charles Cunningham Jarvis. The same Charles Cunningham Jarvis from the Sells Brothers Big Show of the World. *See the baby who refused to be born! Hear him talk! Hear him tell your future!* I could speak at age three months or one year, depending on when you started counting—when I was made in an act of carnality or after nine months of gestating came and went. Dr. Loveaster said that my long time in the belly of my mother quickened my mental acumen, though my body stayed as stunted as a fairy child. "The richness of amniotic fluid must super nourish your cells," Doctor Loveaster said. "There is no telling to what evolutionary limits your body and mind will reach." I could converse from my mother's womb before my infant peers could coo. I spoke with Superintendent Stone while he still lived at our fort. I spoke with the constables and the gold men who wanted to know the ground in which to strike the next big vein. I spoke with the Indians about the future of their race now that white men had rooted their grasping souls in Indian soil. I spoke with Mr. Mark Twain in 1895 when he detoured from Spokane, Washington, to hear the "conversating fetus of Fort Steele, British Columbia."

"Charles," said Dr. Loveaster. I had become attuned to every inflection of the good doctor's voice and in that one declaration of my name I heard the push-push of ambition. "Tomorrow, we're expecting a very important visitor. An author of the highest calibre. He wrote a famous book called *Huckleberry Finn*."

"Mother's pulse has been very quick," I said.

"I've been more tired lately," she replied.

I knew she was fibbing. I knew it in her blood because I could taste the smoke in her womb. Not like the smoke of the wood stove, but stronger—a much larger conflagration. And close.

"Has my father been here?"

"Dr. Loveaster is right here, Charles. He is standing no more than two paces from me. I am holding his hand."

"Is he my father?"

"Of course he's your father. Who else could there be?"

A week ago at night, long after Dr. Loveaster had lain with my mother for the third time that week and long after my mother had fallen asleep, my brother, Edward, came and spoke to me about his father, a blacksmith from the nearby town of Wild Horse. My father, Edward said.

"My father?" I asked. "You mean Doctor Loveaster?"

"Our father real and true. He boxed people, that's what Mother says."

And now he was dead or mostly dead, burned up in a fire, because Dr. Loveaster gave him whiskey with something sleepy in it. But he didn't exactly die and neither did our eldest brother, Henry. "They're ghosts, Charles. Fire ghosts that rides horses and burns things. I saw'd it plain as day. Father and Henry burnt up Old Senior and now they burnt up a barn just down the lane. The police has lots of guards out."

"I will not speak when Mr. Twain comes," I said to my mother and Dr. Loveaster, "unless you tell me about my father real and true."

"I don't know who put this into your head, Charles," replied my mother. "Dr. Loveaster is your father, as he is the father of Edward. Haven't you seen your brother's eyes? They're different from Henry's because—" My mother's voice filled with sorrow. "Of course, you can't see Edward's eyes. I forgot that you can't see us. Doctor Loveaster has one blue and one green eye, just like Edward."

That night, when Dr. Loveaster's member was prodding at my mother's cervix, which now seemed less likely sealed by a mucous plug than the curse of a dead man, I kicked at my mother's bladder until she told the good doctor to stop. "The child is very active, James." And then, a minute later, came a burning sensation. I could feel the heat of the fluid radiating down my mother's esophagus and then pooling beside me in her stomach.

"One more," said Dr. Loveaster, "then he will settle."

Another draught. Soon that warmth began to radiate to my limbs and my eyes— I'd like to say that they drooped, but as they'd never opened I can only report that they felt heavier and heavier, no matter how hard I stamped against my mother's bladder. My feet tingled and went numb and Dr. Loveaster's member was sliding into my mother again and I went, with mercy, to sleep.

I awoke to the most heat I'd ever felt in my life. I smiled my sleepy smile. This was the conflagration I'd seen on the canvas of my mind soon after I spoke my first words. The red flames. The orange sparks that shot up into the night sky. The billowing black soot that darkened the full and wicked moon. My real father, the spectral blacksmith, had come for me. He'd set fire to the house, where I lived. He'd burned up my mother to scorch through her skin, so that he could rescue me from the inertia of my floating, naked life.

"You're going to meet someone very special," my mother said. She hummed a waltz I'd not heard before. Water splashed. "I feel just like you, Charles. Afloat in loving warmth." I could taste the lavender soap in her lungs. "A real, live author here in Fort Steele. I don't think a word has been written in our village that isn't a report of the constabulary, the tally of a bill of sale, or a sermon to a disreputable mob of gold rushers on a Sunday morn. Did I ever tell you that I once wanted to be Charlotte Brontë? *Villette* entranced me. I used to pretend I was Lucy Snow, up there in Wild Horse living with your—"

"Father?" I asked. "And brother, Henry?"

She paused for eight beats of her heart. The break between the seventh and eighth beats lasted so long I feared water might rush into her lungs. "His name is Mister Mark Twain and he's come from his tour of the world to talk to you, Charles. I would hope that you will engage with him rather than brooding. You have been brooding so much lately. It's unseemly. Don't think Doctor Loveaster hasn't noticed it."

If anyone was guilty of drawn-out brooding, it was my

mother. She'd kept to her bed for our first four months here, after we'd escaped from Wild Horse on the back of Dr. Loveaster's horse (so said Edward). She'd hardly moved, except to weep and take a little bread and broth. And she'd instructed Edward to never mention the name *Henry* again.

I thought to starve myself, rather than speak to Mr. Twain. To pinch shut the cord between me and my mother or better yet tear it, pumping and bloody, from my belly. But I couldn't endure the horrors that visited my thoughts after even a half hour of my life without the food my mother's body so generously gave my own. What were they, these images? I saw white flashes of light over land so muddy and wasted of life—trees, grass, flowers—and heard explosions so loud I couldn't believe that those outside my mother's womb couldn't hear them. And there were great machines rolling on through the mud and sometimes the light flashed from a long, metal limb attached to one of the machines and an instant later came the explosion and the screams and the wide, rolling yellow mist that left in its wake a jigsaw puzzle of filthy bodies, human and animal, and, tottering over the horizon, a wounded elephant. I wanted my father, my real and true, to lay waste to it all with fire, so that like the forest blackened by flame, the green shoots of the new would come again.

I had told only Edward of my *sees*—as he called them. I told him two weeks ago of the miner who would come to Fort Steele with but one arm on a horse with one ear and in their tow, a dog with one eye. Three days later Edward ran into the parlour, where my mother was learning the finer art of sewing skin from Doctor Loveaster. "He's here, Charles! The man you seen, he's outside come to get a tooth pulled. Mama, Charles seen the man who's come."

That was just one of my sees. There were others, too numerous and small to mention. And they all came true and I hushed Edward into silence, because no one else saw what I saw and my existence had attracted enough attention to draw the likes of Mark Twain of Hartford, Connecticut, to travel by train and stage coach to Fort Steele.

I smelled my mother's cooking all morning of his arrival. A roast beef, potatoes, corn, and carrots. A Yorkshire pudding, because Dr. Loveaster hadn't eaten a Yorkshire pudding since he'd left his family behind in London, England. A meal so delicious I couldn't wait for its odours to make their way into my mother's lungs, so I could taste it, too. "Charles, I want you to remember just who it is who's visiting this afternoon. You will not brood on this occasion."

I hadn't said anything except to Edward for two days. Why should I, a post-mature fetus by a few years, be charming host to a continual parade of the gawking curious, so that Dr. Loveaster could not only publish his articles on my medical wondrousness in the academic organs of the day, but gain coin from the commerce of a once-a-millennium miracle? "Doctor Loveaster took us in," my mother had replied to my numerous laments of his backing-and-forthing member disturbing my sleep, "at no small expense of his own."

A great flurry of sounds overcame the house. The clop-

clop of a horse and wagon. The opening of the front door. A yelp from Edward. Greetings out on the porch. Voices. "I am most humbled to make your acquaintance, Doctor Loveaster, and you, Mrs. Loveaster. It was a full three-day trip through some of the most charming country I have seen in my travels thus far. I haven't seen mountains quite so high since—"

"Edward, your hand please," my mother said.

I wanted to laugh. I could just see Edward with his hands down his pants, squeezing his testicles in front of the Connecticut Yankee gentleman.

"Ma'am, I hope I am not too forward in observing that you appear no larger than my wife did during her ninth month."

"The circumference of her abdomen," Dr. Loveaster said, "is forty-nine inches and holding. But what is so startling is the development of the fetus at just three years old. He can hold full conversations as you and I can. It is as if each year in the womb is equivalent to ten years outside it."

I sensed Twain's head was very close to my own. "Young man, I am very pleased to receive your invitation to dine and I look forward to a discussion on many topics, which I am sure will exceed that of most of our politicians for maturity."

"He's likely sleeping," Elizabeth said. "He sleeps a lot. Don't you, Charles?"

Soon they were eating the dinner my mother had taken so much time to prepare. They talked of Twain's travels so far, his plan to go on to Portland, Tacoma, and Seattle and then cross the border back into Canada to give talks in Vancouver and Victoria, before he left for overseas. "In the first twenty-one days I've not had a blue day and I've gained seven pounds. I expect to weigh six hundred pounds by the time I return in two years. I hope at that time to be exhibited as a circus freak, which you might imagine is not a stretch from my present condition." After the roast beef came my mother's apple cobbler, which Twain declared to be the best he'd ever tasted. I could taste the cigar smoke in my mother's air.

My mother's voice grew insistent. "Charles, why don't you tell Mr. Twain something about yourself?"

"I remember how long my own daughters used to nap as infants," Twain said. "Now as I find myself returning to infancy, naps are—"

"Charles," Dr. Loveaster said. "Did you hear of Mister Twain's time in the laboratory of Nikola Tesla? The inventor? He works with electrical current to make light."

"His inventions are marvels of first-rate imagination," said Twain. "I had the honour of seeing Nikola at the World's Columbian Exposition in Chicago. I saw him light a wireless gas-discharge lamp some fifteen feet away from the terminals. A lamp I held in my hand, connected by no wires, lit up and glowed as if by some enchantment of the gases inside."

I thought of Old Senior, as Edward had described the scene to me. How that ancient ponderosa ignited at a distance of thirty feet from the spectres of my father and my eldest brother, how he'd seen the hay shed ignite a month ago, because my father was still searching for me and Edward and my mother.

"You are indescribably rude." It was my mother. I

hadn't noticed that she'd gone to the kitchen under the guise of preparing coffee. I could hear the kettle land on the stove with a metallic thud. "Mr. Twain came all this way to hear you talk and talk you will." I felt the heat of the whiskey descend my mother's gullet and her stomach begin to glow. The draught was not as large as the ones that made me sleep, but in a minute I began to feel light-headed and dizzy. I wouldn't fall for her game. I'd keep my mouth shut. All I had to do was stick my thumb in my mouth and never let go. A simple procedure I'd performed numerous times before.

My mother was moving again in the slow wobbling way she did. "I've good news. Charles had just woken up and is anxious to talk. Did James tell you, Mister Twain, that Charles can tell you your future? He's done it many times for our guests."

Mr. Twain gave an excited clap. "I thought I might be returning to my travels without a delightful conversation with this young man."

Young man? I was just three in your years out there, yet I could speak on Darwin's principle of natural selection, Mendel's experiments with peas, the novels of Henry James, and the politics of Benjamin Disraeli. Not because I could read—that came much later, when I left my mother's womb—but because Dr. Loveaster read to me about the former and my mother, whom I took initially for lacking in intelligence, read to me James and Disraeli. I had a passing knowledge of Helena Blavatsky, because Superintendent Stone read the *Key to Theosophy* to my mother, as part of the Fort Steele Book Hounds book club of which my mother was president for the first year of its existence. I also knew intimately Susanna Moodie's book *Roughing it in the Bush*, because that had been the first choice of the FSBH.

"You must tell us about your life, Charles," said Mr. Twain, "on the inside."

Words pushed at my throat. I didn't want to speak. I didn't want to be a sideshow for the born—even the likes of Mark Twain. The whiskey had begun to make my head spin. I clamped down on my tongue and then came a long draft of wine down my mother's throat. It pooled with the whiskey in my little fetal brain. "Charles?" she said. "Answer the nice gentleman."

"No," I said. "No, no, no."

"Was that him?" Mr. Twain asked.

"Very much so," said Dr. Loveaster. "Good evening, Charles."

"I must apologize," Twain said. "I am very acquainted with the works of ventriloquism. You have perhaps heard of Fred Russell of England? No, never mind. I—"

I couldn't listen to the man. The more I listened, the more I wanted to speak against him. This must be what it was like for my father, the blacksmith Jarvis, when he learned that my mother had slept with Dr. Loveaster and made Edward. The heat rose in him until he had to burn something. Torch a tree, a house, or a man.

"—and to the ancient Greek the sounds emanating from the ventriloquist were thought to be the voices of the dead."

"You're going to be very, very miserable," I said, "for the rest of your awful life."

"I would call you the Pythia of Fort Steele, Missus

Loveaster, but those words, I understand, are not coming from your mouth."

"Everyone you love is going to die."

"Charles," my mother exclaimed. "You must be pleasant—"

"You wanted me to talk and now I'm talking. Mister Twain didn't come all this way to leave without knowing his future."

"I confess I barely understand the present, Charles. So many of my own follies blind me to its comprehension. Still, you may be assured that I have left a selection of my books with your parents. I had thought that a young man such as yourself would enjoy my Tom Sawyer, but now I recommend my essays."

"They're going to die," I said.

"That is an affliction all of us will share."

I pinched my umbilical cord. Formless colours began to swirl in my brain. Red and blues and streaks of violets. They took shape. The outlines of faces. Numbers. Dates. Voices now. A young woman's voice, in agony. "Susy is the first. Next year."

"You know my daughter's name, Charles. You could learn that from any article about my life."

"Meningitis. And she'll have been only twenty-four."

Twain laughed. "Now that is more like it, Charles. Her birth date is harder to come by—"

"Olivia is next. Eight years after Susy. Olivia Langdon Clemens, 1845 to 1904. Her heart."

"Missus Loveaster, your babe has a very active imagination fuelled I think by studying my life."

"Charles, let us talk of nice things," my mother said. "You must forgive my son, Mister Twain. He—"

I pinched my umbilical cord a little closer to my belly. "Jean is next. 1880 to 1909. Christmas Eve. A seizure that leads to a heart attack. That leaves you only your middle daughter, Clara. And your close friend, Henry Rogers. Would you like to know what comes of him, Mister Twain?"

A great swallow of wine rushed into my mother's stomach.

"Charles has not been himself since the hay shed burnt down last week."

"It was my papa that did it!" shouted Edward. "And my big brother."

I felt dizzy, sick, as if I was somersaulting, twisting in my umbilical cord. "You die, Mister Twain. You die in 19—"

My mother began a fake coughing fit. "I need some water." Her voice became a hoarse rasp. "James, what's the matter with me? I can't hear. Is Charles still speaking?"

My world went horizontal. My mother had fallen, fainted. The little ocean I lived in sloshed around me, beat me against the sides of her.

"Twain, help me get her on to the settee," Dr. Loveaster said. "Smelling salts in my office."

I was upside down, twisted up in the cord, the great burning skein of it. I grabbed a handful of the thin, hot tube and crushed it in my gelatine fist. "Are you there, Mister Twain? Don't you want to know what's next? After you die? Because you die and as miserable as you leave this place, it's a relief. Tell me you want to know. You have the courage to know, don't you? A man like you must want to know things."

"Charles, your mother is very ill. Your father—"

I had the clearest images of the future I'd ever seen in my short life. "A whistle blasts and blasts. There's a burning sky filled with flying machines. Down below more machines churn up mud. Trenches are filled with bitter wrecks of men. Rifles and guns and barbed wire. Screams in languages I've never heard of. Agonies I can't comprehend and smells—have you smelled these things? —sulphur, chlorine, and the rotting flesh of the half-alive? They stink in your mind long after they're gone. You can't get rid of them. Or the images of the dead. By nightfall, there are lifeless, bloating corpses strewn across that great muddy plain. Do you understand what it is? It's an open-air factory for making dead people. Seven thousand a day. That will be the great industry of the twentieth century— making dead people."

At the head of the dead was my blacksmith father and my eldest brother on their old nag horse. The flames that leapt from their clothes and skin and hair blazed the way for the parade of the dead through the darkness that fell over the twentieth century. There was a light ahead of them and they were steering toward its yellow orange glow. But it was the wrong light, the wrong way. That real-ization came to me now as a great stabbing pain in my eyes. I wanted to cry, to cry out in agony. To condemn Dr. Loveaster for what he'd wrought in his ignorance. What had really happened on the night he and my mother and Edward fled from our house in Wild Horse? What had happened couldn't be ignored now. I saw it, I saw it as plainly as if the sun had winked out. Do you understand? I saw it plainly and I'm trying to tell you plainly, so you know which path to take. When my blacksmith father burnt Old Senior, that spectral light became the beacon for the twentieth century. When you looked at the great ocean that is time as God saw it—as I glimpsed it now in my reverie—that burning tree, that giant, burning ponderosa at the confluence of the Wild Horse and Kootenay rivers, nearly destroyed us. It steered humanity off course for a hundred years. We almost shipwrecked our whole species. We almost drowned. We almost drowned because Dr. Loveaster spiked my blacksmith father's whiskey with laudanum and my father fell asleep with the door of the wood stove wide open and he and Henry were...

"You've driven Mister Twain away, Charles." It was Dr. Loveaster. He was close to my mother's stomach. He spoke in a savage tone. "He was going to tell everyone about the miracle that you are. I would've been known, my father would've read my work. Respected men would've sought out my opinion. Do you know what it means to be unknown at the ends of the earth? To be a pioneer of nothing in this forsaken place? To know that my father seated on his throne at the Pathological Society of London tells everyone that I am best disposed of by an ursine quadruped?"

He poured something into a cup and then something else. "You're coming out now, Charles. You're coming out. Out."

The fluid burned in my mother's throat. She coughed and choked but enough of it came down. Whiskey. The burning peat whiskey. And something else. Bitter. Acrid. Awful. Laudanum. I felt sleepy.

"I see another light, Mister Twain. Are you there? No, you're riding away into the night on your stagecoach. I see another light and I must warn you not to steer to-to-towards it."

Oh God, the light.

The Cranbrook Herald, June 6, 1899
Local Notes

Dr. James Loveaster has purchased the Thomas Green Residence and has removed his office and abode thereto from Fort Steele. Eh? Looks suspicious? Don't know—the doctor is one of those quiet birds and doesn't do any unnecessary talking; may be so, however. New wife, Elizabeth, says she and baby boy Charles and his older brother, Edward, enjoy the environs of our newly minted town. "Welcome to Cranbrook, Loveasters!"

"Jarvis!" exclaimed son Charles from his perambulator. "Charles Jarvis!" Very suspicious? Come find out at the good doctor's banquet this Saturday at Colonel Baker's manor house.

The Cranbrook Herald, July 16, 1899
Thomas Green Residence Burns Down

The Thomas Green Residence ignited sometime after 1 a.m. into what one witness called an infernal blaze. "I was coming home from my train," said resident tracker and guide, Zachary Joles, "when that house leaps into flames. Like God reached down and lit a lamp." Cranbrook's volunteer fire brigade subdued the flames with water and later searched for survivors amongst the charred ruins of the second floor. Doctor James Loveaster, who recently purchased the house, and sons Charles and Edward were whisked away to the St. Eugene Hospital, where the sister supervisor reports that they are recovering from smoke inhalation and minor burns. The whereabouts of wife, Elizabeth, remain unknown. The cause of the fire has not been identified.

HEMINGWAY AND THE
ELEPHANTS

I t's a funny photo, though none of us—not even the little elephant, Charlie Ed—are smiling. My father is the one in the brown Stetson holding Charlie Ed's cinch rope, so he won't bolt for the ponderosas behind us. Beside my father is Zachary Joles, his rival in the small world of tracking big game. There's top-hatted Mr. Gardner from the Sells-Floto Circus and Luther Polk, his assistant, looking as slouched and beaten down as only an assistant to Mr. Gardner could. What's so funny is that just out of frame is me, Mary Lapointe, vomiting on a juniper shrub because of my unborn baby, and holding me a little low on my waist is Ernest Hemingway. "You're ruining good gin, Mary," Hemingway is saying. It's 1926 and he is twenty-seven to my eighteen.

Hemingway came to us between wives, between Hadley (number one) and Pauline (number two). Mid-August, as I remember, because by then Zachary and some hunter client of his had found the first of the six escaped elephants out near Wycliffe and Zachary had blown his share of the reward money on Canadian Club whiskey and Hettie Klemm. Well, it was a dusk of blood orange light and cricket song when Hemingway pulled up outside our shack on Joe Salt's buckboard. Here was this tall moustached man in a brown jacket and sweater with a fat leather suitcase in one hand and a loaf of bread in the other. He traipsed across the parched postage stamp of scrub my father had bought after the war and said, "Is this where I can hire Lucien Lapointe, animal tracker? Man at the Baker Hotel said if Zachary Joles wasn't free, try Lucien Lapointe. Zachary Joles's a rummy and in the pay of Milton Posey. Two strikes."

My hand went to my swelling belly. A man anywhere near me and my unborn baby was an occasion for fear. I drank a swallow of my tea and picked myself up from my chair. "I'm Mary Lapointe and you're on Lapointe land, Mister . . .?"

"Hemingway. Ernest Hemingway. Now Lucien Lapointe—"

"You return to wherever it is that you came from, Mister Ernest Hemingway, because it'll be dark as stink soon and there ain't nowhere for you to stay on Lapointe land."

Joe Salt's buckboard rattled away into the dim ruddy dusk. Hemingway had stopped in the middle of our yard and was admiring the roseate light as it seeped from a long row of craggy peaks—our share of the Rocky Mountains.

"Colours remind me of Switzerland. The Alps. The gloaming is what they call this time."

The mountains turned violet as the last rays of the sun vanished and wherever this Switzerland was it probably looked violet, too. And so what? They were just mountains and always would be just mountains and wherever this Switzerland was I would always never see it. "Don't matter what they call this time—time for you to leave."

Hemingway's foot tapped the busted edge of the porch. "I'll have a cup of that tea, if you're offering."

I snorted. "You got a baby in you, Ernest Hemingway? Because if you do, that Angelica tea will get rid of it."

Hemingway sat down in my father's vacant chair and his air of can-do puffery vanished with the last of the light. "Long, long country. Four days on the train from Montreal." He wiped his face with a red handkerchief and sipped something from a steel hip flask.

"So I'm going to get my father's rifle and then I'm going to ask you to leave again and probably have to shoot you."

He held out a little photograph. "This is my Bumby. Couldn't imagine getting rid of him. I would've stopped Hadley if she tried it. It'd be wrong anyway—a sin. A deadly. Keep your baby, Mary."

I went inside our shack and took down my father's Lee-Enfield from the wall, the same rifle he'd sniped Germans with in the war. I couldn't find the magazine, so I stuffed the cartridge straight into the chamber and went outside to shoot Hemingway in his face.

He'd lit our oil lamp and was writing something with a pencil stub in one of his notebooks.

I raised the rifle. I thought I should say something, but what was there to say to this bullying jackass seated on our porch in my father's chair sniffing at my Angelica tea?

"I can pay, not a lot, but some. More than you probably have. I just need to find those elephants before goddamn Milton Posey does."

"What is it with the male race?" I lined up the iron sight with his head. "I want a mountain lion or bull moose or now one of them elephants. And I want a woman for the cold nights. The last man who sat where you are made it so I have to drink that tea until I bleed again. Told my father to fetch him a grizzly. Said he loved me. He got his grizzly up there on the foot of Mount Fisher and then he up and leaves for Wenatchee without so much as saying good-bye."

Hemingway took a sip of my cooling tea. "I am a big baby. Least that's what Hadley says. But I'm tired as hell and this seat is too damn pleasant."

"Hadley your wife?"

He looked out past my rifle barrel at the first star of the evening and said nothing.

"Adultery I suppose? Seems about right from the looks of you."

His moustache vanished beneath his lower lip.

"She got a name?"

"Who?"

"That other woman you left Hadley for?"

Hemingway leaned forward so the barrel of my rifle sat in the centre of his forehead. "You going to shoot that Enfield or show me where I can sleep?"

My FATHER CAME HOME at dawn on Jig, our dun mare. He'd been guiding out Bull River way for bow hunters after elk, but once word got out about the escaped elephants and the $75 reward for each one, all the hunters went southwest to Wycliffe, where Zachary Joles and this Milton Posey had caught the first elephant. My father said he'd never seen an elephant—he knew bear, elk, deer, moose, cougar—an elephant might as well have come from Mars for all he knew about tracking one.

"That isn't me in my bed, I hope," he said. He spoke in French. He hardly spoke in English anymore, since the years he fought in the war, at Ypres and, later, at Passchendaele. The butcher show he'd suffered in the trenches came to him in English words and if he didn't speak them, he wouldn't ache from the gunfire, the artillery, the chlorine gas, the dying men, and the dying horses.

"That's Ernest Hemingway," I said. I explained that Hemingway wanted to see the elephants and was going to pay—handsomely. He was some sort of writer, a journalist maybe.

My father stooped over Hemingway, who was still asleep on his side in a fetal curl. You never heard my father coming, even when he walked with his hobnailed boots on the creaking planks of our floor. It was as if he never touched the ground or at the last minute the earth pulled away from his tread. "Why do they all look in pain when they sleep?" he asked. "This one looks worse than the one hunting grizzly." He lay down on my cot on the other side of our one-room shack, behind the blanket I'd hung up. "Tell him to go back home. Tell him elephants aren't in my nature." Soon I couldn't even hear my father's breathing. His sleep was a succession of short and long silences.

A Morse code I hardly understood beyond the first few words—*please, please, no.*

It was another hour before Hemingway woke up. He came onto the porch and I gave him a cup of tea, but not the Angelica tea I was drinking to make me bleed. I gave him my father's Jacksons of Piccadilly Earl Grey, which was all he'd drunk for most of the war.

"My father is back," I said. "Sleeping."

"When do we leave?"

"My father doesn't know anything about elephants. None of us have even seen an elephant or their tracks or their shit or smelled their piss. Not too many Lapointes get into town for the circus."

"How hard can it be to track a three-ton pachyderm?"

Pachyderm wasn't a word I knew back then. I'd heard a man in a moth-eaten bowler hat use it at the Chinaman's store in Moyie, which was where I had to buy the Angelica tea so my father wouldn't find out from any locals that I was pregnant. "Those pachyderms are in an ugly mood," the man in the bowler said to Mr. Sun whose store it was. "Tore up Neufeldt's orchard and took down every fence the man had. Nothing left but to shoot the lot of them." I knew they were talking about the elephants, but I thought *pachyderm* was from another language not English. I pronounced each syllable as Hemingway had—*pack-ee-derm.*

Hemingway wrote the word down on a piece of paper from his notebook and gave it to me. "Pachyderm means elephant, rhino, or hippopotamus."

"Don't read," I said.

"Don't or can't?"

"Didn't go to school. Everything I know is from out there—the bush. Or my father." I almost added the name of the hunter—John Stiles—who'd made me pregnant and left for Wenatchee to hunt mallards. Surely, I'd learned something from him?

"There's that Catholic school I came across."

"You want to know about that school? A constable comes with Father Louis one day. Knock, knock, knock. 'We're here to educate Mary in the ways of the Lord. Here's a piece of paper that says we can.' I'm barely six, you know, and my mother was still alive back then. My father hides me in our guiding hut out on the west arm of the St. Mary River. Then he's off to war, leaving my mother alone. She dies from tuberculosis in the winter of '16 and I didn't know for half a year. She just stopped visiting the hut one day—I thought she was angry with me. I was alone until 1918. That's when my father comes back with his Victory Medal and his shell shock. My father said my living alone in that hut was better than having priests and nuns for teachers."

Hemingway looked away at Mount Fisher. "Is that why you don't want your child? It'll get taken because you're beggared?"

"Don't you understand anything, Ernest Hemingway? The thing that John Stiles put in me is as good as dead."

He drew a picture of an elephant beside the word *pachyderm* and then a rhino and then a hippopotamus, little black ink squiggles, yes, but I knew them for animals of the world, even though I'd never laid eyes on a single one.

"This is for you," he said. I traced the word and then

the elephant, back and forth a few times, until both had entered through my index finger and coursed along my blood stream to my little brain.

"Two dollars a day is what I'll pay your father." It was a lot more than my father made guiding, almost double. "More than enough for you to see a doctor about your baby. But we leave today, because I'm not losing to Milton Posey."

I went to my father's cot, as quietly as I could. I'd been drinking Angelica tea for a week and using parsley pessaries for almost as long and each day I checked my shadow in the morning sun for signs of my belly mounding up with John Stiles's beast. The tea wasn't working. I'd not had a single spot appear. Nothing. I'd had a jackass's baby clinging to my insides for almost three months and the tea wouldn't make it leave like Mr. Sun said it would.

"Where you going, Mary?" my father asked me. His words didn't sound as if they came from the cot, but all around me in the gloomy shack.

"Hemingway will pay two dollars a day. You know we need the money. I'm taking your Trapper Nelson. You coming or not?"

My father rolled over. "I lied to you, Mary. I saw an elephant once. On the front. All our horses were dead, so we pulled our 18-pounder with mules. Then all the mules were dead, so what do we pull the big gun with? There's people to kill with it, you know? Sergeant Roberts comes back next morning with a circus elephant he found somewhere. It's got shrapnel in the hip, but it pulled the big gun all by itself. That elephant dragged our 18-pounder for two weeks, dragged our gun until it found a land mine to step on. I never forget how that thing screamed for its life. I emptied my rifle into it and still it's screaming."

I SADDLED up our two horses under a hot afternoon sky. I took Jig, my father's mare, and I put Hemingway on Leo, her one-eared, piebald colt. I slid my father's Enfield into a leather scabbard and climbed up on Jig.

"Not going anywhere without Lucien Lapointe," Hemingway said.

"My father is the number one tracker 'round here. Zachary Joles is number two. And me, Mary Lapointe, is number three. You can wait for my father to come around to liking elephants, which'll be never. Or you can come with me. Either way, the price is two dollars a day to hire a Lapointe."

Hemingway jumped down off Leo and strode at the front door of the shack with his fists balled at his sides, as if the door had just insulted the size of his manhood.

"You can go in there, but when you come out, you'll be alone and I'll be gone. And then what? You know where the number four or five or six animal tracker is? Tracking those elephants to get that $75 a head."

I started riding away and called to Leo and he trotted after his mother. "Good-bye, Ernest Hemingway. Say hi to Bumby from Mary Lapointe. I'll say hi to Mister Milton Posey."

I was glad my father wasn't coming. I wouldn't have to spend all my day trying to hide the baby growing in me.

The random vomiting. The Angelica tea. The hiding in the bush to stuff a pessary in myself and then retrieve the wilted mess hours later.

Hemingway was suddenly alongside me. He looked like he was marching off to a war below a ticker-tape sky. His right hand walloped down on my thigh and then his left grabbed at the reins in my hand. I thumped Jig with my boots to get her moving faster and in another second Hemingway was skipping alongside me, refusing to let go.

"Another story," I said. "Number one fighter 'round here is Lucien Lapointe. Number two is Cecil Grass. Number three is, well, you get the point, I'm least five or six." I punched Hemingway right between the eyes with my gloved fist. He stumbled back into a cloud of withered horseshit and looked up at me like he was going to charge me again. "We can keep this up, but my next trick is with my skinning knife."

Hemingway swore at me. Words I'd never heard before arranged in a way I couldn't even marvel at because of my lack of schooling. His curses came down on me like a swarm of hungry crows and for a dim minute I felt my throat tighten. And then his words fell away and the sky brightened again and he fell back behind Leo like a spent child. We walked like this for a good mile. Though the sun was August hot, it was Hemingway's eyes I felt heating my back.

"We can go this slow all day," I said, "but we're not getting to them elephants any faster."

Of course, Hemingway's letter about this incident to F. Scott Fitzgerald told it different: *I wish to hell you could've seen it, Scott. The little pregnant girl high atop her Daddy's mare, as I the great swearer of English (tell Ford about my new title) reduced her to mute tears. Don't think she didn't have it coming. The girl may not have had the words, but she had a bone-handled skinning knife and her Daddy's Enfield and the nature of a wounded bull. You didn't pull your punches with this girl. You didn't turn your back. You brought the axe down.*

Well, the "great swearer of English," the great conqueror of little girls climbed up on Leo and in a second was beside me. Out came a single grunt: "Which way?"

"South for a time. Then west towards Wycliffe."

He sped in front of me on the wide dirt road and that was where he stayed. He hardly looked at me except to throw a glance over his left shoulder just to make sure that he was still leading me through country he barely knew. He was a passable rider though. He told the colt what to do with a click of his tongue or a little jerk of the reins and sometimes a whisper in his horse's one good ear. By the time we hit the main junction, Hemingway let me come alongside him. His eyes roamed the hot, balding, tawny hills, as if he expected to find something there. His face was a darkening sky of passing moods for which I didn't have words.

"You need to put up a better fight than that," he said. "I mean with words." He passed me one of his little notes as if we were kids in a schoolroom. The note had three single words on it: *H-O-R-S-E, B-R-I-D-L-E,* and *C-R-A-Z-Y. Horse* and *bridle* seemed like obvious words to learn to read, to trace with my finger and repeat to myself. But why *crazy?*

"Listen," he said.

I was too used to hearing the shots. The hills had echoed with rifle fire pretty much every day since Mayor Roberts had declared open season against the "pernicious pachyderms." They started up again, not long after Hemingway and I left our land. There were more rifle shots than there could possibly be live elephants.

"This town is crazy," Hemingway said. "That's your first sentence of the day. Simple, direct, and true—that's how you should write. No ornaments."

C-R-A-Z-Y. I traced the whole, hammering landscape around me in looping squiggles. Hemingway pointed at the shallow, green northwestern slope of Baker Mountain and said that it looked like an elephant lying down. My other hand went to my stomach, because to me Baker Mountain looked like a pregnant woman lying on her back and maybe the hunters were shooting at her for getting herself pregnant. For wanting love.

We rode along the outskirts of Cranbrook until we came to the road north to Kimberly. Four brown chickens pecked at the dust beside the road. A cow lowed for her calf to come and drink milk.

"That way go to Wycliffe?" Hemingway asked.

I nodded. "We're not going there."

"We're going where the elephants aren't on the chance they are?"

"They'll go west for water. Perry Creek maybe. Them hunters will be crawling all over Wycliffe."

Right on time, a mud-spattered black sedan with four men inside it sped up the road to Kimberly. Their rifle barrels half hung out of the windows.

"I'm for following them."

"Couple lakes in the hills to the southwest. Don't think the elephants stuck together. They're scared."

"I need to get these damn elephants before Posey does," Hemingway said. He said it with such force that Leo whinnied and backed up. Hemingway took out a silver flask and drank from it—he offered me some. "Better than that damnable tea you drink."

"What's this Posey to you?"

"Ever read his columns in *Field and Stream*? Too many fucking words come out of his pen."

It'd be years before I could read Posey's article on the elephants. Ernest Hemingway, let alone Mary Lapointe, didn't get a single mention in all two thousand words. Zachary Joles got half a sentence. Posey said he found the elephants. Posey said a lot of things about Posey without mentioning a word about the tragedy. Even the water-colour of him looked perfect—stubbled jaw, thin, curving nose, opal eyes, light brown wash to the perfectly clear skin.

I turned Jig south and began to trot away. Hemingway didn't move.

He called after me: "Why'd you let that hunter have you anyway if you're so handy with that skinning knife?"

John Stiles had said he loved me. John Stiles had said that he wanted to marry me. Take me with him because the local churchgoers would call me a whore for giving birth outside of holy wedlock. I could travel the world with John Stiles, the great hunter. "You'd like Africa, Mary. You could track lions and impalas and ibexes. Me and you on the trail of the great Nubian ibex. Or how about an oryx? A Scimitar-Horned oryx?" Those words had enthralled me: *impala, ibex, oryx.* They sounded like something I'd searched for all my short life, but I didn't know what. Something fleeting, something I'd tracked and tracked and the trail had gone faint. John Stiles had laid out his honey trap for me and I'd believed him and I'd let him just about every night right under my father's nose in John Stiles's canvas tent, on John Stiles's canvas cot. I'd cleaned and polished his rifle every time he shot it at a grizzly too far away to shoot. I love you, he'd say.

Hemingway was suddenly beside me on Leo. "He was your first, wasn't he? He said nice things, didn't he? That's how it is for you, they say nice things and you open up. If I said nice things I'd have you. But I'm not about to say anything nice to you. And I damn well wouldn't have you."

I kicked at Jig to go hard. I burst ahead until I couldn't take carrying the words welling up in me anymore. I jerked at the reins—stopped the goddamn horse. I looked back at Hemingway with the sun shining right on his squinting face under his brown fedora. Behind him was this whirling breeze of dust that I wanted to be a tornado that would suck him up into the dark heart of it and then spit back him at the rejecting earth.

WE RODE IN SILENCE, but I don't know why. I was pretty sure we hadn't finished with the hateful things we wanted to say to each other. We followed the road southwest up into the hills, until the beaten-down dust turned into the crushed shrubs of a logging trail and, some miles after that, narrowed again to the width of an animal path. I saw deer and elk sign everywhere. Tracks and shit and broken branches that said this way, go this way. I saw an antler rub on a tamarack too high to be anything else but a bull moose. What a bull moose was doing in this dry country I didn't know. I expected them farther south, soaked up to their shoulders in the little sloughs out Creston way. I plucked a tuft of deer hair off a dead snag and smelled it for sex.

"Nothing," Hemingway said. I ignored the half-snort that went with the word. "Less than nothing."

The light had begun to dim and the hot air had cooled like a fever cooled when the body beat down sickness.

"We need to make camp. Second lake is another three miles."

A couple dogs bayed over the hills and then went quiet and all there was was the drone of the crickets in the dry grasses. The air smelled of pine and, from somewhere distant, alfalfa—someone had cut hay and the scent of it had travelled on the breeze to caress the lake. I picked an open spot above the lake to make camp, so I could easily go down and get water.

I couldn't find the rhythm of my camp self. I felt dizzy and cramped in my guts and I thought it must be the Angelica tea finally eating at John Stiles's baby and the baby hitting back against my insides with its little jelly fists. I took three Bayer aspirins with a little tea and got down to work. I took the piece of canvas I'd packed and staked it down over two aspens I'd cut for poles and in a few minutes I had a makeshift shelter—not that it was going to rain, but because that's what my father always did for our clients. I laid out our bedrolls and went down to the water and took back a potful for tea and thought how stupid I was for not getting a fire going first before it got too dark. I found a broken-up piece of red cedar, so I cut kindling with my hatchet and used a hunk of the dried bark for tinder. And then I thought how foolish I was for not setting up a hook in the water for trout and went down and did that and came back and started the fire and, two breaths of cedar-smoke later, vomited right beside the ring of rocks. Oh yes, I thought, I should hobble the horses. I should check the fishing line. I should stand up. I should have bed rest. I should admit I had no place in the world and hide for the rest of my life, because I, Mary Lapointe, the number three tracker in these parched hills and valleys, couldn't find a three-ton elephant.

The whole time I worked, Hemingway had stayed seated on a big stump and written in his notebook and drank from his hip flask. When I finally had two trout frying over a bed of cedar coals, he condescended to look up from his notebook.

"If you loved someone, wouldn't you write to them?"

I had my back to Hemingway and closed my eyes and tried to push down what I still had in me while the smell of the fish tried to pull it up. I presented trout and half a bowl of beans to Hemingway and a toasted slice of the bread he'd brought to our shack.

"Can't write, remember?"

"But say you could and you were separated by half a continent and you loved this person more than anything else, wouldn't you write?"

I thought of how in the first few days after John Stiles

left for Wenatchee, I'd talked to him in my head, like my father and I talked to each other over distances. I'd told him what I'd done during my day. Swept the shack and plucked three grouse and harvested a whole basket of dandelion greens for salad and ground their roots with a little burdock to make this drink my father liked. How I thought of John Stiles holding me in his little cot, how I'd missed the smell of his coal tar soap, missed the pigeon bump of his chest. But there'd never been any reply from him. He didn't think of me. Or if he did, he didn't send his thoughts loud enough. When I'd finally gone into Cranbrook and dictated to the CP man my telegram —*Me, Mary Lapointe, I am having a baby. Sincerely, Mary Lapointe*—he'd asked me where to send it. "Wenatchee while there's duck hunting," I said. "After, try Spokane. He has a mine there. Lead." The CP man said the funniest thing as he crumpled up my telegram: "Sometimes you love people and no words come back."

Hemingway scraped at the ground in front of the fire with the heels of his boots. Two parallel wounds formed in the earth, but no blood burbled out, not yet.

"Written Pauline three times and not a single damn word. Hell, Scott Fitzgerald's telegram got to me at the Baker Hotel. Pound wrote back and the old master's been sick as a dog. He's in Fascist Italy for god's sake. You know what I did?"

It was dark now. Beyond the reach of my little fire, the night was so black you'd drown in it. I nodded my head. I didn't know what Hemingway had done, but I knew what drunken men do.

He stood up, teetered a little from whatever was in his

hip flask. He stared at me. "I said do you know what I did?" He lurched back and forth between the walls made by the darkness.

He told me about his first wife Hadley and their son Bumby and then Pauline Pfeiffer—Pfife in his letters—who met them in Schruns, Austria, last January. And then the affair. He was fucking (his word) Pauline and right in the pleasure of it, like a fly in his vanilla sundae, was this goddamn pain. How he'd left Hadley with the sin of his adultery and Bumby without a father and Pauline with—what had he left Pauline with? Why didn't she write him? He told me all this while I lay back on the ground and could barely stop from vomiting and the whole time he was pacing he was sucking from his hip flask that never seemed to run out. His Pfife, his goddamn Pfife, why wouldn't she write? If she left him he'd kill himself. He'd had a dream that she'd dropped him and he'd woken up screaming at the ceiling of the train that brought him here. And goddamn, why did he accept Hadley's deal? She wouldn't grant him a divorce unless he and Pauline remained separated for three months—to learn if they really loved each other. Where was she? Piggott, Arkansas, in her parents' white-framed house.

Hemingway gave me the most twisted sick look I'd ever seen on a man. I'd left my skinning knife on Jig. "Why can't you be Pauline?"

John Stiles, in his half-sleep after having me, had called me *Helen* once. "No, it's me, Mary Lapointe," I'd said. Helen must have been in Wenatchee or Spokane, where John Stiles had his lead mine. Helen and the kids. Mary and nobody.

Hemingway loomed right over top of me beside my vomit. My hand reached for the knife I'd forgotten on Jig. "Right height to be Pauline. Hair colour is the same."

"It's me, Mary Lapointe."

"Mary Lapointe and her other man's baby. Lord, why can't Mary Lapointe be Pauline?"

"Can't write, remember?"

"Won't write. Won't—"

"Don't—"

He snatched up my arm. "Then find me Pauline. Find Pauline if you're such a damn fine tracker. Go on, find her before Milton Posey does."

"Pauline ain't no elephant."

My arm ached where he'd grabbed me. He leaned in close to me and I cursed myself because I closed my eyes.

"Find her."

He stumbled beyond the fire light, crashed into the darkness. Swore. Branches snapped and something large flew up into the canopy and flapped around and away. He called out for Pauline. He called out for her with such yearning I thought of a wolf baying at an eclipsed moon.

I lit the little oil lantern from my side bag and went after him. All I could see was broken branches and kicked-up pine needles and a scrap of his white shirt dangling from an upturned tree limb. "Pauline! Pauline!" It sounded as if he'd travelled miles in only five minutes. I went on into the cold night and everything felt like it was hitting me. The branches and the shrubs and the name Hemingway kept calling—Pauline! Pauline! Pauline!— because it wasn't my name.

When I looked back, the fire I'd made was a little slash

of light way off in the forest. I couldn't hear him anymore. The forest felt hungry and lean, as if it itself was hunting me. "Hemingway?" I called. I had my knife and the lantern and nothing else. I should've brought my father's Enfield. "I'm going back to camp." I held the lantern high and scanned the dry forest floor for the least sign and turned around and around.

"You can rot out here, Ernest Hemingway. You hear?"

His boots stuck out from behind a ponderosa snapped off about mid-trunk. His white shirt had slipped off or crawled away from embarrassment, because he was down to a torn undershirt. He was on his back with his left arm splayed out making these little patting motions as if searching for someone who should be in bed beside him. His eyes were closed.

Beside him, just out of reach of his probing hand, was the biggest mound of dung I'd ever seen in my life. It looked like a pile of horseshit, except from something far bigger than even the tallest Clydesdales I'd seen out at Fort Steele. It was maybe a day old at most.

"Hemingway," I said. "You know what that is?" In the morning, I'd come out and search for an elephant footprint like the one Hemingway had drawn for me. A circle with four toes. A track. A trail. "It's not far away." When I was calmed down enough, I'd widen my awareness as far as it would reach across this dry forest and see if I could touch the mind of the elephant. That skill was what my father had taught me and not taught Zachary Joles and I would never divulge to anyone not my blood. It would be hours before I'd calmed down enough to use it.

I bent over Hemingway and went through his leather

billfold and took out a two-dollar bill for today and took a quarter as tip to make up for pretty much everything up until that moment.

"Pauline?" Hemingway moaned. "Pauline?"

I took off my shawl and covered him with it right over his head, like a shroud.

"You shouldn't've had that baby with Hadley. You never really wanted it and now look what you've done."

I DREAMT the smell of burning cedar. In our guide camps, my father was always up first and had the fire going and that had been my signal to slip out of John Stiles's tent.

Jig whinnied low and quick.

"Getting up," I said.

I'm sure my dream would've become a forest fire, except I rolled on my back and felt the blood between my legs. It had to be the Angelica tea finally working. The end of the baby—the beginning of what I took for me again. But it hurt, you know? I vomited on the ground beside my bed, because of the pain of that dead, unwanted child. I wanted to tell my father, but how could I? Who could I tell? The Chinaman who sold me the herbs with that almost sly smile on his face? What did he care about what had been done to me?

Jig whinnied louder.

"Where's your boy?" I asked.

Leo's hobble lay beside the grey powder of last night's fire.

"Hemingway?" I called.

His bedroll was still beside mine under the shelter I'd made, but his rucksack was gone. Leo was gone, too. I ran out into the forest, where I'd left Hemingway last night by the bent-over pine. He'd left my shawl hanging from one of the ponderosa branches. The goddamn gentleman left me a note, too, stuffed into the weave of the fabric. I ran my fingers over his few words, as if I could absorb their cold meaning through my fingertips. No, those aren't words, I thought, they're the trail of some little insect that began its life on the left side of the page, travelled for a time through the bends and twists of its little existence, and curled up into a period and died. What did Hemingway mean that he should bring to life this little creature only to kill it a few words later? I read the only sign that I could. Right beside the elephant scat were two of Leo's hoof prints headed southwest.

Blood oozed down my leg. I ran back to camp and rushed down to the water's edge and yanked off my wool trousers and tried to clean the blood. The blood wasn't coming from my sex, but from a nice gash high on my right thigh that I must've got when I'd chased after Hemingway. I thought I should drown myself, it was the only way to kill the baby, because I had two dollars and twenty-five cents and that wouldn't pay a doctor to do it and my goddamn paying client had taken off to find the elephants without me because I wasn't this Pauline.

"Hear who's coming, Ernest Hemingway?" I called out. "Me, Mary Lapointe, number three tracker and number four skinner. I'm gettin' my money, you hear."

I threw the note he'd left on the surface of the lake. Even the water wouldn't wash his words away.

A White Hunter: A white hunter is nearly crazy. Gertrude Stein.

Good-bye, Mary.

I BROKE down camp inside twenty minutes and sped Jig up the trail after Hemingway and Leo. I didn't have to cut sign. If there was one thing the great, white writer didn't know how to do it was ride a horse such that he didn't leave a path as obvious as a yellow brick road through a pine forest. The tracks went elephant-horse-elephant-horse in a looping trail toward the upper lake. I could smell Hemingway's whiskey on the cool breeze, the shit-airs of his general disposition toward women and life. The stink of his arrogance dragged over a forest floor of rust-coloured pine needles and wheatgrass. I rehearsed what I'd do when I found him—bullet in the gut and then, after a time for my enjoyment of his suffering, a second in his pretty, moustached head. I'd take his wallet and his note-book and bury him six feet deep in the dry clay under a ponderosa. And maybe I'd have me the reward of a Sells-Floto elephant. I could buy us a real place in town. A real place with decent soil and water.

The sun roasted like a winter stove, so I shaded myself with this scarf John Stiles had given me a week before he'd left. A white thing with a monarch butterfly knitted on the back of it, the best thing a man had ever given me. I don't know how long I rode like that. The passing of the animal tracks and Jig's trotting rhythm put me in a state of mind I'd rarely known. I felt warm and buzzing in my head and a strange calm came over me. Hemingway was as good as caught. He had a head start of maybe a couple hours, but all there was to this chase through the arid forests and grasslands I knew in my blood was the obvious end of two gunshots and a couple lies. I was about to be a confirmed murderer at age eighteen, but I wasn't without my decencies. When it came time, I would tell someone that Hemingway had run off. The C.P. man at the telegraph office would help me with the simple, true sentences of my report. *It's me, Mary Lapointe, and I am telling you that Mr. Ernest Hemingway up and left and the last words on his lips were that he loved all of you—Hadley, Pauline, and Bumby. I will send on his notebook, suitcase, and all his money (less the balance owed to me) to your address or the address of your agent. Yours sincerely, Mary Lapointe, Cranbrook, British Columbia.*

I hinged over in my saddle and hiked up my skirts to change my pessary. The wound on my thigh looked crimson and grim and every part of me throbbed as if I'd been struck over and over by a nun's rod. My short-term debility didn't change a thing. In the coming end for Mr. Ernest Hemingway was the true beginning of Mary Lapointe. *Freed of the twin burdens of a vain American writer and an unborn bastard (half-American), Mary Lapointe would go on to become the number one guide and tracker of the Kootenay region. She was courted some, but never married on account of her formative years with the male race.*

I clicked my tongue at Jig. I rode not more than fifty feet when the elephant tracks went northwest and Leo's tracks went southeast.

I cut back and forth between the two tracks to read the sign. Hemingway's boot tracks went after the elephant —he was on foot—and he'd sent Leo off in the opposite direction, because he knew damn well a Lapointe couldn't afford to lose a horse. I could run Hemingway down inside half an hour, but Leo would head straight back to our place via the road through town and I knew damn well if someone found him he was as good as gone. I tried to push my mind out, to tell Leo to stop where he was, we were coming, but my head was a whirlwind of cusses. I rode hard for five hours and along the dusty train tracks at the edge of town, I spotted Leo in the hands of a man I didn't know.

I thought now is the time to be the polite, young woman that John Stiles found so—these are his words—*so sweetly enduring.* "Hey, mister," I said to the man with Leo. I already had my skinning knife out. I already had my thumb picking at the notches on the back of the blade. Before this fat man in his dirty derby hat could even glance at me, I snatched Leo's reins from his fist. I had Leo's hackamore in one hand and the skinning knife in the other and down the front of my shirt this drying run of vomit and somewhere under my skirt half my pessary falling from my underwear.

"I am obliged to you for saving my horse. His name is Leo. That's his mother right behind me." He lurched toward me and his hand reached out for what was not his and I waved my skinning knife. "Now, I have to be after an elephant. Have you seen him? He's got a moustache and a hip flask and fancy ways with words." The man's hand clamped on mine and then on Leo's bridle. I slashed lightly with the knife, one way and then the next. I cut nothing but the man's suspenders, which flew off into the air like bolting grouse. I was still heaving and the man's hand was still on mine and he was saying, "Idjit bitch, lookit what you done." I felt this hot agony on the side of my head—no, no, I heard it, I heard the pain as a screech so loud my ear exploded outward. The man struck me again and I lashed again at what I don't know, because I was falling and John Stiles's baby was laughing his death rattle laugh at me, his murderess mother.

"You stole them horses. Didn't you? Little cunt thief. I'm gittin' the constable." The baby kicked at me and the man kicked at me and Hemingway I'm pretty sure was kicking at me too from up there in them hills.

THE WHISTLE of the train woke me. The air was cool with dusk and my mouth was hot with blood. The hawk wheeling above me looked so far away I couldn't imagine that this creature belonged where I belonged, this land of horses and elephants and Hemingway. I slapped at the mosquitos suckered to my cheek. The train whistled again. I rolled off the track and lay in the creosote stink of the rail bed. I called out for the horses. Jig whinnied back, but not Leo. "Leo? Where'd you get to now?" Jig was right where I'd left her beside the track, but Leo was back in the bushes a ways. "Leo? Who's that you riding for?"

The man in the derby was mounted on Leo, not bolt upright like an alert rider, but slumped forward against his mane. The train went by us slow and rhythmic like a light rain on a drum. "Hey, mister?" I called. The inside of his left pant leg was red and wet. My skinning knife was edged with drying blood. The man still had a faint tambourine shake to his heart.

I cut off a good half yard of my wool blanket and wrapped it as tight as I could around the man's leg and towed Leo behind Jig all the way down King Street to the St. Eugene Hospital.

"Found this wounded man," I said to three nurses who were sharing a cigarette in the dark courtyard. "Out by the train tracks. Help me get him down."

None of them moved. I was soaked with blood, vomit, and I'm pretty sure the coal stink of the railway tracks. I lowered the man's body across my shoulders and eased him to the ground against a lamppost. "Artery is nicked some, but he's still got a heartbeat." I wasn't so sure of myself. That I had a heartbeat.

I went up to the nurse with the cigarette and extended my hand.

She examined me as if I was the most pitiful, crazy thing she'd ever seen. "You sure you're not pregnant?" she asked. "I remember how sick I was."

I had a little puff on her cigarette.

"You should have an exam. You look anemic."

"Is it bad, anemic?"

"It could harm a baby."

"Seems fair. Baby's been eating at my insides like a woodworm for weeks now."

"Janey, don't talk to her," said the youngest of the nurses. "There's blood on her knife. Her hands."

I gave back Janey the cigarette and she said, "I'm going to ring the constables."

"Tell them I went Creston way. Down into the United States. Idaho." I felt their eyes on me as pelts of hail as I went back to the horses. "I could use a bar of that hospital soap, if you got some."

I sped back through the dark of King Street and back out onto the railway tracks and then as far up into the bush as I could see by the light of my lantern. I made it to the creek that comes down from the lake Hemingway and I had camped at the other night, maybe three miles from where he went one way and I went the other. I tore off my clothes and waded out into a pool with the soap the nurse gave me and scrubbed at every stain in my dress until I couldn't see them anymore. I washed myself. I washed my knife and I washed the gash in my leg and washed at my hands until my fingertips felt puckered and sore. The bush around me watched me with three pairs of green glowing eyes. Coyotes, maybe. "Ain't you never seen a woman clean herself before?"

And then I waded with Leo into the pool and washed the man's blood from his side and scrubbed the saddle blanket and when I looked up there were three more pairs of eyes. "It ain't my blood," I said, "and it ain't my fault he bled so. He was going to—" Even as I thought it I knew it wasn't true. He wouldn't've raped my unconscious self, because I knew from the look of him he'd just wanted to take Leo. Under a little cascade coming over the rocks, I soaked my head where he'd hit me. I cleaned out the blood from my left ear and in a little while I could hear again. Inside me, the baby shivered like a trembling fawn.

I lit the biggest fire I could and hung my clothes and the saddle blanket to dry and ate a supper of Hemingway's bread and some dried venison. I brewed up a big pot of Angelica tea. "You want to be warm," I said to the baby. "Well, here you are." I drank so much I had to pee four times. When my clothes were pretty much dry, I saddled up the horses. I had enough oil in the lantern to go hours yet. Goddamn if I was going to let the night stop me from murdering Hemingway.

I CAME across the first sign of him again around midnight. A single boot track about ten inches behind an elephant print. His boot heel was sunk back in the soil, so I knew he wasn't running. He was pushing east toward the second lake at a good walk or had been hours ago. I snuffed out the lantern and slowed my breathing and listened to the night and when I heard nothing that wasn't the stars or moon or crickets, I took the darkness in through my nose. I divided the smells as they came to me from the base-note scent of the life around here—the dry, sweet half-desert air. I smelled the sleeping ponderosas and the scent of an exhaling juniper and the old, spent flowers of a silky lupine. Breathed in some more—the fescue and blue bunch grass and, somewhere beyond the next hill, the faintest trace of an old camas meadow. And something acrid, something eaten. Burnt, stale bread maybe. I could smell the hint of an old fire upwind, maybe a couple hours away. If I was my father I could tell you what kind of wood that fire was and how long it had been out and how long it had been since the man who sat near that fire had bathed or been with a woman.

My father came to me right then. I felt his awareness at the edge of mine—his knock on the gate into the meadow of me. Then flowed the images, which was how we talked over a distance, no matter how far. You cannot talk in words over a distance, he'd said years ago. He tapped on my head—they're too big to fit through the mail slot in there. You talk in pictures like in dreams. You can send and receive, like a telegraph. You have to tune out the static, which is what most of your thoughts are anyway. His first pictures came to me at the end of his time in the war, when I was alone in our guiding hut on the St. Mary River. The translation was simple. He missed me. He loved me. He was coming back home. Over and over—*missed me-loved me-coming back home*. It was years before I could send images back. I had to learn to tune. I couldn't tell him that my mother had died and I had been alone for over two years. But he'd known about my mother, because she'd stopped sending to him. *Missed me-loved me-coming back home.*

"You're hurt?" he asked now. "Sick."

I sent back a picture of me falling off Jig and then me smiling.

"Constables came looking for a girl covered in blood. Stabbed a man almost to death."

"Been in the bush the whole time."

"Seen one?" He sent me a picture of an elephant against a blue sky.

I sent back one of the elephant shit and tracks.

"Who's that with you?"

"Jig and Leo and Hemingway."

"No, smaller than them."

My skin stung with a sudden chill. The baby was old enough to have a pinpoint prick of awareness. A little picture voice.

A hare. That's the image I sent. A scrawny, grey-brown hare and me about to butcher it.

"'Bout the smartest hare ever caught," he said.

"Good night."

I drove Jig and Leo on after the scent of that old fire. I kept the lantern out, except to check now and again for one of Hemingway's tracks on the trail.

"What hurts most of all," I said to the baby, "is that you think you get to live. You just wait till I get that reward money and the doctor lets the air in. You're gonna roll out of there on a little cart straight up to the hang-man's noose."

The baby didn't kick or punch or scratch. He didn't bite or head-butt or jab with his elbow or spit his baby venom into my stomach. He sent a goddamn picture. The little fucker sent a goddamn picture right out of my womb into the wide world. A picture that he'd seen right out of my eyes—my bone-handled skinning knife slashing that man's thigh and then the spray of blood and then the hammer fist coming straight at my skull.

"You think anyone but me heard you?" I asked. "You are about the stupidest collection of whatever it is that you're made from." I choked down the last of my Angelica tea. "Try and send something from underwater now. Blubbering little fool."

After about three hours of riding, I could smell

Hemingway was close—the whiskey'd, inky sweat of his permanently rutting self. I tied the horses to a thin tamarack and unsheathed the Enfield. I took off my thick blanket and left it on Jig and shoved a bullet up the spout of the rifle. I crawled down low from tree to tree, maybe two hundred yards. There was the little orange ember of his fire and beside it, in the dim moonlight, the heap of his drunkenness beside the fire. He lay under a blanket on his right side. I could shoot him from here, but what was the fun of that? The whole point was that I wanted him to see that it was me, Mary Lapointe, just before I shot his balls off. I crawled at him from behind, inch after inch, on my elbows and knees. When I was ten feet away, the fire popped and I sucked in my breath and did not move. I waited for a count of one hundred. I thought it would be more personal with the skinning knife, but if I just shot him in his rumpled foreskin, I could still go in with the knife. I knelt down over him and raised the rifle to my shoulder. "Mister Ernest Hemingway," I said. "It's me, Mary Lapointe."

He didn't stir. "Hemingway?" I said a little louder.

I jabbed him in the back with the rifle barrel. The barrel pushed into his body as if nothing was there. I eased the blanket back. What was supposed to be Hemingway was a mound of spruce boughs.

This was when the barrel of a pistol pressed into my back.

No, that's what I wished happened, that he'd deceived me and then rammed his famous Colt Woodsman pistol with its five-inch barrel and magazine of 40-grain hollow points into my spine, that he'd snarled, "Time's up, Mary," that he'd at least tried to take me on. No, I whirled around, not because he'd stepped on a branch or cocked his pistol or choked down a cough, but because he was pissing at the dry-dog earth. He had his infamous tool out and his other hand held the high branch of a bull pine and his stream rained down the bark of the tree and, when he turned slightly to the left, it sprinkled a steaming clump of junipers.

"Mary," he said, "I've been waiting for you to catch up. Somewhere around here are some leftover beans."

"Why'd you run away?" I said. "Could've found that elephant by now."

"Who ran away? Virgil sleeps in and blames Dante for forging ahead?"

"I don't know what them names mean. You tricked me. Sending Leo back to town like that."

Hemingway was still pissing as much or more than a horse. I reckoned that a bullet hole or two would speed up the leak.

"You've got the jumps of a fifty-year-old divorcee, Mary. It'll be sunrise in a moment, so let's make some coffee and catch Milton Posey. Now put that Enfield down."

His stream stopped. Started again and then he was shaking himself.

"Okay, you want the word of the day. How about *urinate*: u-r-i-n a-t-e. Or if you want to be more highfalutin in the scientific sense *micturnate*: m-i-c-t-u-r-n-a-t-e. I like good old *piss*, one word that sounds like what it is. I mean those two esses, like the leak of a tire. P-i-s-s. Pisssss. Scott Fitzgerald picked up some slang from an

Englishman outside Paris and now he uses it all the time. Got to take a slash, Hem, he says. Can you believe that? Debonair Scott Fitzgerald saying something that doesn't sound like a saxophone from a record?"

He buttoned himself up and pulled his suspenders over each shoulder. "Well, which will it be, urinate, micturnate, or piss?"

"Now you're letting me choose?" I levelled the iron sight of the .303 over his heart. "I'd use none of them words. Unlike you, I don't talk about it, I just do it. Like now. By the way, your story is a crock of shit."

I pulled the trigger. The valley echoed with the thunderclap of a rifle, but it wasn't mine. My rifle let out the awful click of a goddamn dry fire—a dud bullet. I pulled the bolt back, ejected the shell, went to jam the next one up the spout, but Hemingway had charged at me. I flung the .303 at him and grabbed for my skinning knife.

His letter to Fitzgerald again. *Oh she was savage, Scott. She knew I'd tried to trick her again, she knew she had me dead to rights. She would've shot me if it wasn't for that dud shell. You should have seen the look on her face when I went at her. Surprised as hell to be defeated in her own country by an American hunter. I know that if I were her I would've felt the shame of it.*

Defeated? We rolled around in the grey dawn beside Hemingway's old fire. Me on top and then him on top and suddenly both of us beneath the great weight of the reddening sky. I couldn't get my skinning knife off my belt and he couldn't pull his fist back to hit me square. I kicked and punched and scratched and bit and he slapped back because I was pretty sure he didn't think I could take a full-on punch, so I clawed at his eyes. Inside my belly, my baby punched not at me, not to hurt me, but outward at Hemingway.

I don't know which of us heard the wailing first. It sounded like the siren I once heard in town, when the forest fires threatened to burn down everything. *Get out!* that siren said. *Run for the hills!* The wail was as loud and as insistent as that. But it sounded otherworldly. And judging by the closeness of it, the animal wasn't far away at all.

Our hitting stopped, not for lack of desire, but because we were both scrambling after the horses.

"North," Hemingway said.

"East," I said.

I took off on Jig and headed east and didn't much care where Hemingway went. The shriek of that beast hadn't let up for a single heartbeat. My eardrums felt about to burst with blood. All I wanted to do was silence that terrible wail. The baby thrashed inside me, like some animal drowning in an icy river. I had this feeling, just for an awful second, that I should fold forward against Jig's neck and protect my abdomen. I write *abdomen*, but I mean the baby. Goddamn, Mary, I thought, you're a sick daughter of a whore if you want to protect that pot-licking baby. Let the death throes of whatever horror you're racing towards be the instrument of miscarriage. Hold yourself up!

I crested a hillock and there it was. A great grey, tusked beast collapsed on its side, its two enormous ears flapping like wings. Zachary Joles was pulling at what I thought was its leg, but when I drew in closer, I saw it was a man's leg, a man pinned beneath the enormous abdomen of the creature. A man whose own wails couldn't be heard over the trumpet shriek of the elephant. I got down off Jig and unsheathed the .303 and started on after Zachary. Hemingway was suddenly beside me. I don't know how he'd got here so fast, after he'd taken off north. I didn't care to answer. He had out his Colt Woodsman and I said, "That .22 is going to do shit against that thing's skull. I'll do it with the .303."

"Just watch," Hemingway said.

"Goddamn," I said to Zachary. "Why'n't you finish it?"

Zachary looked up at me in his whiskey'd bleariness and said that if I wanted to know why I could go look at the ass end of the thing. "And where's your father, eh, Mary? Scare't of the little elefint?"

The elephant had a great bloody bullet hole in its right rear hip. The man pinned underneath the elephant had a .455 Webley revolver in his thrashing, blood-smeared hand. There was a gold ring on his left finger, which looked three sizes too small, because his finger had swollen up from the pressure on his body. It was the famous Milton Posey and his famous pistol here to make Ernest Hemingway smile his hateful smile. I couldn't smile. The elephant had two tiny elephant legs kicking out of her enormous vagina. The torso of the calf looked streaked with blood and half-sheathed in a pale exploded balloon.

Zachary's mouth widened on his white, white teeth. "Two elefints, Mary. Two times the reward. Now yank on the baby's legs. Do it. An' you, big man, stop the bleeding."

Hemingway stared at the shrieking elephant. He held his Colt straight down at the ground in his white, ugly fist.

"Big man, you want her to die? You hear, two times the reward?"

With half that money, I could buy five doctors.

I had both hands on the greasy leg of that baby elephant. It felt like I was pulling on a warm, wrinkled table leg. I pulled as hard as I could. I'd helped my father give birth to a cow or a horse, but never something as big as an elephant. The more I pulled, the more that baby pulled against me. It wanted to go back inside. I said no, now is the time for coming out into the world. If Mary Lapointe has to be in the world, so do you. The calf pulled its leg out of my hand. I grabbed at it again and it kicked at me with the other leg, so I clutched it behind the hips and yanked with all the hateful strength I had left. The thing rolled out on its side in a lake of mucous and blood. Its legs thrashed at the air. The mother wailed and kicked and tried to get up but she was never getting up again. Hemingway had my father's .303 in his hands. He put the barrel just shy of a spot behind the elephant's ear and pulled the trigger. I saw the muzzle flash, but I didn't hear the sound. I fell backwards into the dust. All that was moving on the baby elephant was the steam coming off the thing's grey, wet body. Everything else had the look of a sudden paralysis. Hemingway with the gun bent over the elephant's ear as if whispering a secret name. Zachary pulling on Milton Posey's thrashing leg. Me, Mary Lapointe, on my back looking at the sky as if it should be the earth upon which I walked and now I was hurtling face first towards it.

Zachary was the first to say something.

"Now we got to chop off the horns of these things. Sell them to the Chinaman. You got the axe, Mary?"

I DON'T KNOW how they found us this far out in the bush.

We stood in the morning sun around the dead elephant and Milton Posey's unconscious famous self and the earth steamed up all around us and I argued with Zachary about chopping out the ivory. "Chinamen'll make art out of it," he said. "An' it's good for the falling sickness. An' it makes it go up," and he stuck out his index finger from his groin.

"They should be buried." That's all I could say about it. "One beside t'other."

"Can dig that hole by yourself."

"He needs a hospital," Hemingway said of Milton Posey, as he splashed a drink from his hip flask across his rival's mouth.

"Wanted to git up close with that Webley," said Zachary. "Think an animal like that wouldn't go down so fast, but it did. Oh boy, it sure did."

The flies found us. And then Mr. Gardner from the Sells-Floto Circus and Luther Polk his assistant and a dozen circus labourers with axes, crosscut saws and a heavy logging wagon drawn by four Clydesdale horses. Then came Sergeant Fanning from the BC police, two constables, and the pinched-cheeked coroner, Mrs. Cable.

"I want no pictures, you hear?" Mr. Gardner said. "I

want no newspapers. No one speaks of this. No one saw this." He looked at the three of us. "If you want your reward, that is."

"Din't see it," Zachary said. "You see it, Mary?"

"Not me you got to worry about," I said.

Mr. Gardner turned to Hemingway. "Stewart Gardner of the Sells-Floto Circus. You are . . .?"

"Hemingway, Ernest Hemingway."

"Reporter?"

"Was. I'm a writer. Stories. Novels."

"We won't see any elephants in one of your stories, now, will we? I could make it worth your while. Shall we start at seventy-five dollars? Too low? One hundred then? Wife and kids? I can see from your face you do. Think of what one hundred dollars could do for them, Mister Hemingway. Nice dress for the wife, bat and ball for the kids. Maybe you don't have to scrape so hard for a while. Mister Hemingway?"

There was a second where I thought Hemingway was going to slug Mr. Gardner of the Sells-Floto Circus. Slug him back to town. Hemingway said nothing and walked back toward Jig and Leo.

I don't know how he found us this far in the bush. Maybe the screams drew him in. Maybe the smell. Maybe the ravens.

Over the hill came the little elephant, which Mr. Gardner called Charlie Ed, and behind him on our neighbour's horse, my father. My father would say later that I was calling to him—I was sending pictures of the dying elephant and her dying baby and there was nothing he had to do but follow the warm breeze for a half a day's hard ride down the main road to the northwest. Follow the wagon and the Clydesdales and, later, Sergeant Fanning.

I'd sent no such pictures. It was the baby. He'd sent those pictures to my father. If I let my baby come out into the world, I don't know what picture he'll send his father down there in Spokane. Maybe a picture of me, Mary Lapointe, his mother, with the tiny newborn crawling up my body for my milk. Maybe one of me waving good-bye to Hemingway's train. Maybe the first name I wrote with my finger across the warming blue sky: *E-r-n-e-s-t.*

You see, Scott, I would never tell the girl this—but after we finished burying the two elephants, I looked over at her with the only feeling I had. Respect.

LETTERS TO TROTSKY

L eon Trotsky <u>did not</u> try to settle in rural Canada in 1936—the Norwegians had already deported him to *Mexico.* So wrote V. Kristoff for the Wikipedia Arbitration Committee. The committee banned me from editing the Trotsky pages for one year—longer if I *conducted further vandalism of Wikipedia articles.* I have, of course, no written evidence that Leon Trotsky lived in Cranbrook, British Columbia, in the fall of 1936. The fire that levelled our family home in 1953 blackened my two letters from Trotsky with broad, sooty strokes. The one photo I still have—Trotsky reading *Fly Fishing for Trout* in the shade of a ponderosa pine—can't be authenticated. *Looks like the high plateau around Mexico City,* wrote Kristoff, *which was where Trotsky was in late '36, the esteemed guest of Frida Kahlo and Diego Rivera. The book proves nothing—even revolutionaries have hobbies.* The only surviving witness to my story is my older sister, Jean, who lives in the F.W. Green Memorial Home in Cranbrook. She believes that I am our father and that Leon Trotsky wrote *Uncle Vanya.*

"Poppa, Trotsky died in 1904," she said to me over the phone last week. "Too-burk-u-losis."

Trotsky was very much alive in 1932, when I wrote my first, secret letter to him. I wrote it because Mayor Roberts gave Jimmy Leask's father the Key to the City for being nothing more than a rich sawmill owner and I thought someone important in communist circles should know how hard my parents fought for people and permanent revolution. My parents were so self-effacing about their political work that if they'd known about my letters, they would've burned them. So I lied to them. I was practicing my typing, I said. I didn't know to whom I was writing that first letter, so I typed *Dear Mr. ________* and began with my father's usual opening: *I trust this dispatch finds you well.* My mother called from the kitchen, "What are you practicing with, Thomas?" When I was seven, she had insisted that I learn to type by copying page after page from Lenin's *The Tasks of the Proletariat in Our Revolution* and Marx's *The Manifesto of the Communist Party*, because typing was the way of the future—no one would handwrite anything in twenty years. Well, I blurted out the first thing that came to my eleven-year-old brain. "Mister Stalin's book. *Marxism and the National Question.*"

My mother rushed into my father's study, where I sat at his Underwood, and reminded me that our household hated old Comrade Walrus-face for his seizure of the Russian Central Committee. She pressed her wooden spoon against my shoulder until my fingers tingled. "Never mention his name again, Thomas."

There it was: I couldn't address my letter to Stalin and, as for the other twentieth-century revolutionaries my parents had made me read about, Pancho Villa and Emiliano Zapata, both were long dead. I settled on *Dear Mr. Trotsky*. My mother had tacked up a world map from *National Geographic* in her sewing room that tracked where Trotsky had lived after Stalin exiled him from the Soviet Union. She used sewing pins labelled with the year and Trotsky's most current city always had a tiny red flag taped to the pin. In 1932, I addressed my envelope *Leon Trotsky, Büyükada, Turkey* and, in 1933, *Leon Trotsky, Barbizon, France*. In 1935, when Trotsky had been exiled yet again, I sent my correspondence to Oslo, Norway, and for my final letter, which was returned blood-spattered but unopened, Mexico City, Mexico.

My letters were always less than three pages long and typewritten on the lightest onionskin paper. My mother believed that anything beyond three pages required too much commitment from readers—when I was a famous revolutionary I could write as much as I wanted. I sent Trotsky reports of what happened at my parents' meetings of the Cranbrook Communist Party (CCP) of which my father was first secretary and my mother secretary of the three-woman ladies' auxiliary. My first letter was a simple transcription of the March 16, 1932, meeting held in our house:

Mr. Walczak, our town's butcher, gave us a talk about bringing permanent revolution to Cranbrook, as he'd tried to do in Poland. He said that we shouldn't make the mistake that the Communist Worker's Party of Poland did when it supported the Soviet invasion of his former country. When the Soviets invade Canada, oppose them! Always be patriotic! Love Canada, but help communism flower! Mr. Crimsey said that we should teach the miners at Corbin and the loggers who work at Cranbrook Sash and Door how to strike. It was agreed to invite men from each group to our next Wednesday meeting. Mrs. Paquette and ~~my mother~~ Mrs. Gilchrist will write pamphlets for the miners and loggers using selected quotes from Mr. Lenin. ~~My father~~ Mr. Gilchrist, an elementary school teacher, will print them on his school's mimeograph machine. Mr. Walczak played "The Internationale" on his Victrola and the meeting was adjourned at 9 p.m.

I signed my letter *Mr. Thomas V. Gilchrist*, stuffed it in an airmail envelope with our return address, and, on the way home from school, went to the post office with all the money I'd earned helping shovel snow from our neighbours' front lanes. I held my four Canadian pennies tight in one fist and the letter to Trotsky lightly in the other and asked Mr. Chittick, our head postal clerk, for international postage.

"Tommy, do you 'ave a pen pal then?" asked Mr. Chittick.

I nodded and Mr. Chittick dipped his fountain pen in his bottle of blue ink and said, "You've made just one error in your address." He wrote "Master" in front of Leon Trotsky, because he assumed that I was writing to someone my own age and, maybe, the way ideology can take hold of a person's mind, maybe I was. I didn't correct him about Trotsky's age, because I didn't want Mr. Chittick, whose politics my parents had said were to the right of Mussolini, to open my letter, as he'd opened the mail of the CCP and reported my parents' secrets to the police and the Canadian government.

"You'll want a five-cent King George V," he said.

"Mister Chittick, I've only four pennies."

But he was already telling me the story of how King George V removed all the German titles from the British monarchy in the Great War, as if even a king could cover up the stink of sauerkraut with a little sprinkle of Yardley talc.

I smiled at his story, even though I had no idea what he meant. Mr. Chittick took a penny from his waistcoat pocket and placed it beside my four coppers. "An advance, Tommy. You understand my meaning?"

I shook my head.

"It means I've paid you before you've even done any work for me."

"Yes, sir," I said, though I'd never worked for Mr. Chittick before. I didn't know anything about the internal workings of a post office. Or Mr. Chittick.

"Next time your parents 'ave one of those meetings of theirs, you come pay me a visit. Understand?"

"A spy like Baden-Powell in the Boer War?" I'd also been a boy scout until my mother found out that Baden-Powell had admired Mussolini.

"No, not a spy, a storyteller. I like stories and I'm sure you'll 'ave plenty to tell."

I nodded—mostly to get away from Mr. Chittick before he figured out who Master Leon Trotsky was.

Mr. Chittick let me stick the blue King George to my envelope, then cancelled it with a slap-slap of his rubber stamp and dropped it in a canvas bag labelled *International.* I hung around outside the post office until closing and peeked through the window, to make sure he was too busy with other customers to open my letter and read it to Sergeant Fanning of the British Columbia Provincial Police. Sergeant Fanning hated disorder and nothing caused disorder in his universe like uncensored, socialist words.

That was my first letter to Trotsky and, likely, my most true. By 1935, when the membership of the CCP still remained at ten and revolution seemed destined never to come to Cranbrook despite the agonies of the Great Depression, I began, as my father would have said if he knew, to "tart up" my letters. I'd been sending them every month since 1932, with never a reply from Trotsky, so what did it matter? I wrote that *Mr. and Mrs. Gilchrist were jailed for two months for leading the strikers at Corbin to violent protest. 150 strikers and protesters marched on the Cranbrook jail to demand the release of the Gilchrists and when Sgt. Fanning of the BC Police refused to release them, the protesters broke into the jail and freed them. Later that week, Mr. Paquette was shot at from the cab of a logging truck when he delivered a rousing speech in the style of Lenin to the men of Cranbrook Sash and Door. He emptied the buckshot from his overcoat, straightened his tie, and continued his speech to the cheers of the fallers, buckermen, chokermen, chasers, and riggers. All in all, a good month for advancing the cause of Cranbrook's miners and loggers, our exploited working men, our unemployed left to slave for twenty cents a day in federal relief camps; their wives and their children fallen into abject poverty. Mr. Walczak, once again, played "The Internationale" on his Victrola and the meeting was adjourned at 9 p.m.*

None of this was true. The Corbin Strike happened, but without the help of a single CCP member. No one shot at Mr. Paquette, but he did take an apple core to the head when he delivered a pamphlet opposing General Franco to Mr. Chittick's house.

When my parents asked me what I was writing so furiously at the typewriter and I said, "I'm writing another letter to Mister Trotsky," they laughed.

"Wish him well, Tommy," my father said. "Quisling's thugs have been hounding him and his wife for months now. There's nothing Nygaardsvold's Labour government will do to stop it either. Stalin's behind it all. "

And so in my next letter, after I lied that the CCP was conducting manoeuvres with Mauser rifles to fight the Spanish fascists, I wrote that *each member of the CCP hopes that you can overcome Quisling's thuggery, which as everyone knows is Stalin reaching across borders to persecute the one, true successor of Mr. Lenin. Enclosed for your pleasure is a copy of* Roughing It in the Bush *by Mrs. Susanna Moodie of Ontario, Canada. We hope that it provides you and your family with hours of solace.*

Of course, my parcel containing my letter and Mrs. Moodie's book were far more than a five-cent King George —thirty-two cents, in fact. And when I showed Mr. Chittick that I only had seventeen cents, he shook his head. "Now, Tommy, I've been paying you a stamp a month for nothing more than little dog scraps. Fifteen more cents for this 'ere parcel. That's a lot of money."

I'd been telling something true to Mr. Chittick about my parents' CCP meetings each month for the past two years, without any concern that I was betraying them— their meetings amounted to nothing more than boring talk. The CCP's stagnant membership promoted communism through means of the unread pamphlet, the unattended speech, and the out-of-tune labour song. There was no chance that the CCP would ever spark a revolution or even a tiny blaze in a cold hearth. So, I told Mr. Chittick about the CCP's declaration in favour of the march on Ottawa, Mr. Walczak's song against the re-election of Prime Minister Mackenzie King in 1935, and a letter the Paquettes had written to the Canadian Parliament to oppose Canada's participation in the Berlin Summer Olympics.

I leaned across the postal counter and said in low voice, "The CCP is marching in the summer parade."

Mr. Chittick's eyes did a little loop in their sockets. "As they do every year."

"Mister Walczak wrote a song against Chancellor Hitler."

"So? I don't buy my meat from Walczak anyway. Or let your father teach my son or, if I get 'urt or my son gets 'urt, will I let that nurse mother of yours succour our wounds."

I looked down at the worn wood floor. I could go on and on with such little tidbits, but they'd never add up to the fifteen cents I needed for my parcel to Trotsky.

Mr. Chittick pushed my package back across the counter. "Now run along, Tommy, 'ere's Missus Leask for 'er stamps." I could already smell Mrs. Leask's French perfume, bought by her husband's immense logging fortune. The sleeve of her sable coat abraded my face as she stepped in front of me.

"A sheet of one hundred King Edward the Eighths, if you please, Mister Chittick," Mrs. Leask said. "The five cents. That man's reign won't last long, you know. Has his eye on an American divorcee. You know how that'll cook his royal goose."

Mrs. Leask was buying five dollars in stamps she'd stuff in her stamp album and I couldn't even afford one thirty-two-cent stamp.

"Mister Chittick," I said. "There's something else."

"Go 'ome now, Tommy. Missus Leask is a very important collector."

"Who is this one?" Missus Leask asked.

"James Gilchrist's son," Mr. Chittick said. "Leaving for 'is supper."

"Gilchrist? The teacher. I've a good mind to slap you, young man. Your father leaving those communist pamphlets on my husband's trucks. Half the homes in this town are made from our trees."

"Revolution." I was looking right at Mrs. Leask and her sable coat when I said it. "Violent overthrow."

Mrs. Leask snorted. "Violence. The trouble with you poor is you don't know how to get what you want behind a closed door."

Years from then, I would know how to get what I wanted behind a closed door: my first wife would be Mrs. Leask's youngest daughter. But I didn't know that back then, so all I could do was sputter my hatred.

"Here I am being presumptuous again," she added. "These ones can't even pick the right door to be behind."

"Too late for all that," I said. "My parents are planning a rebellion."

"What's that, Tommy?" Mr. Chittick asked.

"Fifty men being trained out at Old Town. They've got Mauser rifles. More on the way."

Mister Chittick's face went as pale as his fists. "Very good, Tommy," he said. "Very, very good."

EARLY IN SEPTEMBER, after the start of my grade nine school year, the old brass school bell outside our front door clamoured. There, wet from the heat, was a CN Telegraph man.

"It's for you, Tommy," my mother said.

I'd never received a telegram in all my fourteen years and couldn't imagine who'd sent it. It was addressed to *Thomas V. Gilchrist.* I read the two lines of text in one glance and then read it again as if I couldn't believe what I was reading.

"Tommy?" my father asked. "Has someone died?"

I looked at my parents and Helen and Jean, my sisters, as if I'd never met them before, as if I'd stepped on to the stage of a school Christmas play and hadn't been given any lines.

The telegram read:

He thought Ms. Moodie's book about you Canadians was the cat's meow. We're in Montreal, to tell the truth. Been twice to Schwartz's Deli already. See you next week. L. Hellman.

The telegram couldn't be referring to anyone else but Trotsky, because that's to whom I'd sent Susanna Moodie's book. Unless, of course, my letter had been intercepted by the Norwegian version of Mr. Chittick, turned over to the authorities and now through this dirty trick of sending a false telegram, I would be turned over to the police for sympathizing with a "red bastard," as I'd once overheard Sgt. Fanning call men like my father.

"I have a guest," I said. My voice faded like a dying radio.

"Is that Bobby Ferrante coming over?" asked my mother. "He eats so much, doesn't he, John?"

My father shook his head. "His father can't work since the mine collapse. We help class friends."

"Helping is one thing. Refilling a barren cupboard every time he leaves is quite another."

My head felt as if it was going to fall off my body and roll away. "Not Bobby. A pen pal."

"A pen pal?" my mother asked. "When did you get a pen pal, Thomas Gilchrist?"

I regressed to about age seven. I held up four fingers. "That many years ago. He's coming from back east."

"Has he a name, this pen pal?"

I nodded.

"Well, say something."

I looked down at the telegram. "L. Hellman."

"L. Hellman have a first name?"

I closed my eyes and struggled to think of one: Lawrence, Leonard, Levy, something else.

"Could be a young woman, Tommy," my father said. "Louise Hellman looking for a Canadian lad to marry."

My sisters laughed. "Will Bobby Ferrante be the maid of honour?"

"L. Hellman is a he, okay?" I said. "We talk about things like fishing and camping and bear hunting."

"If he brings food into the house," my mother said, "he's welcome to stay for as long as he likes."

For the next week, I felt nauseous each time the telephone rang or the front bell jangled. My bedroom was on the second floor and overlooked the front walk, so I could watch the wide road in front of our house for signs of Trotsky or L. Hellman—whoever that was. Mostly, I started seeing Mr. Chittick walk by with his weepy-eyed English bulldog, Bohort, or sometimes he was seated across the street in his green Buick convertible. Twice I spotted a black Ford parked there with two men in suits seated in the front. They smoked and ate the whitest sandwiches in the world and generally looked bored, which is as you would expect when they watched a house of do-nothing-but-talk-in-circles socialism. Now if they or Mr. Chittick spotted Trotsky with a little suitcase sauntering up our walk, the police or whoever those men in the car were would descend on our house so fast I wouldn't have time to cry out that I was sorry.

I stood on guard for a week and heard nothing more from L. Hellman. My mother quit asking me about my pen pal and my sisters stopped bugging me about having a girlfriend or a boyfriend. My parents had their second September meeting of the insipid CCP and it was time for me to write another letter to Trotsky. It hadn't occurred to me in my week of anxiety to write and tell him not to come, to make up some excuse to keep him away. I ran to my parents' Underwood. I wrote that the entire CCP was off to join Canada's Mackenzie-Papineau Battalion to fight in the Spanish Civil War. As I typed, I imagined my parents and Mr. Walczak fighting Nationalists in the hot

Iberian sun while in the skies above them German pilots of the Condor Legion loosed bombs from the bellies of Ju 86s. The Spanish would wipe out Mr. Walczak and his Victrola and likely my parents, too, but at least I wouldn't have to suffer the shame of having lured a famous revolutionary to a nowhere town of lumbermen, ranchers, and—to quote my mother—half-baked, Sunday-suit-wearing fascists. Scratch that: Trotsky might still come to Cranbrook, but at least not to my parents' house with my parents in it. *So, in conclusion Mr. Trotsky, while you can't visit with us, please do enjoy the mountains around our little town. And don't stay at the Mount Baker Hotel—it's owned by the Leasks.* I signed the letter and smiled. Where in the world should I send it?

The phone rang and rang. My mother called up from the parlour.

I could send the letter to Norway and two more copies to Schwartz's Deli in Montreal and one more to the railway station in Calgary, all care of L. Hellman. Total cost in postage nine cents, which between the seven cents I had and the tiny two-cent lie I would tell Mr. Chittick was very little indeed.

My mother's voice steamrolled through my reverie. "Come down, Thomas. We're off to the train station to pick up L. Hellman."

At first, I didn't notice the black Ford following our Durant down 11th Avenue. I was preoccupied with dying before my mother discovered my lies. I leaned out the passenger window and tried to suck in the soot the trains spewed into our wide valley. There was no way that I would inhale enough sulphur to kill myself before we reached the train station. There was no way my mother would kill us in a car crash. She always drove our car as if she were being followed by one of Sgt. Fanning's constables. My mother was one of the few women you saw around Cranbrook driving alone: to get groceries or deliver CCP pamphlets or take my sisters and I to Fort Steele in the summers. My father said that it was right and proper and to hell with what the Leasks and Chitticks of the world thought—if she can vote, she can bloody well drive. Unfortunately, not very fast. She rarely made it out of second gear and there was no way she would outrun the Ford tailing us downtown.

"Mum, they're following us again," I said.

"We've nothing to hide."

"But L. Hellman—"

"Your pen friend has nothing to fear from the police."

"*Are they* the police?"

For the first time ever, my mother took her eyes off the road. She looked at me as if I alone possessed the answer to a deep riddle. "Well, who could they be?"

I shook my head.

"Tommy, who is L. Hellman?"

"Not someone those men should see."

"You haven't been writing to a criminal, have you?"

"He's kind of a communist. From away—from Europe."

We were a block away from Baker Street when my mother rolled to a stop in the middle of the road. The black Ford had stopped about ten feet behind us. I could see the two men inside it trying to look anywhere but at our car.

"Stay here," my mother said.

I'd seen the way she walked towards the Ford a thousand times before. It was how she walked when she was angry with my sisters or me. Careful, measured steps that betrayed no hint of rage until she was upon you with harsh words and sometimes slaps. The engine of the Ford gunned and roared. My mother took step after step at the wall of engine noise and smoke. "Excuse me," she said, the same "excuse me" she used before she indicted me for teasing my sisters or for forgetting to deliver the latest CCP pamphlet. My mother knocked on the Ford's window and the man behind the wheel stared at her as if she were insane and, then, for some weird reason, he began knocking back against the inside of his window each time her knuckles struck the glass, as if they were both trying to get a stranger's door to open. "You will kindly stop following us, or I'll report you to the authorities," my mother said, in a loud voice. And the man—I could see his lips—was repeating my mother's words back to her over and over again with the most twisted look on his face, as if she were talking to a funhouse mirror. "You will kindly stop, you will kindly stop—"

The black Ford lurched backwards and spun around in the middle of the road and shot off back up 11th Avenue. It was then I realized that the three cars that made up Cranbrook's downtown traffic were bleating their horns at us and that the men and women on the sidewalks looked just as crazy as the man behind the wheel of the black

Ford had. Out from the side door of the Mount Baker Hotel stepped Mr. Chittick. He cupped his hands around his mouth like a megaphone and shouted, "Commies, that's what they are!" just as loudly as if he'd yelled at a newsreel of England taking in Haile Selassie, exiled Emperor of Ethiopia. "Godless commies. The parents, I mean. There's still 'ope for the lad."

My mother walked straight at Mr. Chittick. This was a walk I hadn't seen before. Her fists were balled low on her stomach and her torso leaned into the only source of wind there was right then: Mr. Chittick's lungs. He was yelling every vile thing he could think of about my treacherous parents and how much they despised Canada and the postal service and King Edward and those pillars of the Cranbrook economy, the Leasks.

I ran from the car and yarded at my mother's coat. If news of the dispute reached the spiteful little mind of Sergeant Fanning, I knew he'd arrest my mother and question her about the lie I'd told to Mr. Chittick—my parents' armed plot against the Canadian government.

"Philip Chittick," my mother hissed, "you bollocking shit, I've a good mind to—"

My mother had never said anything nasty about anyone. I'd never even heard her swear when Mrs. Leask had sent us a Christmas ham with a label that read *To help feed your poor socialist waifs. God bless us everyone, Edna Leask.* My mother was as dull and as polite as Pope Pius. "You will kindly stop," she usually began when she confronted enemies and then you could fill in whatever grievous action had been thrust on her or us: the letters (*Reds beware—We're watching—KKK*), our slashed car tires, the firebrands being thrown at our house and car. But there was no "you will kindly stop" coming from her now, so I made myself a wall between her and the little postal clerk.

"Watch it, Tommy," Mr. Chittick said. "You know she's got her Mauser 'neath her coat. A little bang-bang at the truth. You know it's coming."

"I wouldn't waste a bullet on a gin-paranoid clerk like you."

"Who is it who wants to take down this glorious city with 'er rebellion out at—"

"Think of the CCP!" I yelled at my mother.

"—Old Town?"

My mother looked down at me. "The CCP?"

"The meetings? You run the Ladies' Auxiliary. Mister Walczak plays the Victrola. Dad—You said words would be our victory over the bourgeoisie. Never violence."

My mother's face softened.

"Words, Mum."

"Mister Chittick," my mother said, "forgive my—"

"You've poisoned that boy's mind," Mr. Chittick said. "I'll save 'im yet from you Marxist—"

I pushed my mother back, barely a foot. She stood there rooted to the sidewalk again and gave Mr. Chittick such a hard look I thought she might slap him.

"Words, Mum," I said. "Words. Please."

I couldn't breathe. The car horns bleated around us again. We were back in our Durant. My mother turned the car down Baker Street and I exhaled everything I had souring in me. There was no sign of the black Ford or the police or Mr. Chittick's nasty words on the cool breeze.

"Mister Chittick," I started to say, "drinks in the morning and—"

"I shouldn't have said those things, Thomas. I'm not that person anymore. She shouldn't exist. Forget what you saw."

We turned down Van Horne Street and the dark red planks of the train station came at me like a matador's cape. I struggled not to look at the sickening, motionless train. That coal black engine had arrived from the world of my lies. Two men with brown leather suitcases stood outside the front doors of the train station. Both men wore heavy woollen overcoats even though it was a warm October morning. The younger man was easily a head taller than the smaller, older one. The older man had a grey moustache and goatee beard and round, chipped spectacles that gave him the general air of being the sort of psychiatrist who rarely let his patients interrupt him. He looked nothing like the little leader of the fledgling Red Army who once strode about in a gleaming black leather coat and commanded who lives and who dies.

My mother asked a nearby baggage clerk where she might find an L. Hellman.

The younger of the two men had overheard her request and asked, "Help you, ma'am?"

"I'm Joan Gilchrist," my mother said. "We're here to pick up my son's pen friend, L. Hellman."

"Must be some mistake," said the younger man, "'cause I don't write to children."

"Excuse me. Master Hellman must be inside. Come along, Thomas."

Trotsky's gaze couldn't settle on me, as if his myopic

eyes couldn't focus on the page of a book. "You are Thomas V. Gil-chreest?" he asked. He spoke in a high, halting voice with a thick accent I hadn't heard before, like Mr. Walczak our Polish butcher, only different somehow. "You wrote letters?"

"What letters?" my mother asked.

"Reports of the . . . Lewis, what is name again?"

The younger man took out a small black notebook. "The Cranbrook Communist Party. Also called the CCP. This is Cranbrook, ain't it?"

My mother looked at me, through me, and in an instant had recalled all the times she saw me at the type-writer the day after the meetings of the illustrious CCP. "I'm afraid my son has taken it upon himself to act as our secretary."

As my mother was talking my eyes fell on Trotsky's leather shoes. They looked worn and scuffed and cracked next to Lewis's black work boots, my mother's black flats, and even my grey socks. I'd left the house without putting on my shoes. Trotsky had left the Russian revolution behind without taking his gleaming black jackboots.

My mother stopped talking as abruptly as if Mr. Chittick's god had taken her voice, her vote, and her driver's license. She couldn't stop staring at Trotsky. Her face took on the colour of a wet bed sheet. She said to me, "All those letters you were typing were to this man, Leon –?"

The younger man hissed at my mother, "Don't you ever say it, okay, lady?"

She switched to French, so the baggage clerk, who was still standing beside us, wouldn't understand her. "I, I—

Sir, it is an honour to meet you. My husband and I have followed your flight across Europe. Despite my son's error, you are most welcome to stay with us. There are no Russian agents here."

"*Et lui? Cette greffier?*" Trotsky said in French of the baggage clerk.

My mother looked at the clerk. "He wants to know if you're a spy for Stalin."

The clerk laughed. "Me? A commie? Leafs fan through and through, lady."

"When does next train leave for coast?" asked Trotsky.

"Right now."

"There's no place safer," my mother said to Trotsky, "than a little town in the Rockies."

Trotsky and the younger man, Lewis, looked at each other. "Norway's pretty much done," said Lewis in a low voice. "It's here or Mexico. It's the boy and the housewife—"

"Nurse," said my mother.

"Sorry, ma'am. Or Rivera and his brunette."

The waiting train shrieked two long notes good-bye and hissed and shuddered to a slow roll. Trotsky turned north towards the Rocky Mountains and stared at them as if trying to read a distant sentence. I don't know what he saw there or hoped to see there, because he offered his hand to my mother. "Here I am Paul Eberstark. This one is Lewis Hellman."

"How do?" said Lewis. He sounded like the American actors I sometimes heard on newsreels at the Star Theatre or on *Gang Busters* on the radio.

"Sir, this is my son, Thomas," said my mother.

"Sir is for tsars," said Trotsky. "We must be equals in our fight, yes? We remain united or the fascists shoot us one by one." He patted my shoulder. "Little secretary, we need more like you for revolution."

Lewis loaded Trotsky's suitcases into the back of our Durant and then searched through the interior of the car as if he'd lost a quarter. He pulled up the seats, peeked under them, even peered under the car. I knelt down and watched him from under the opposite running board and he waved at me. "See any dynamite, bud?"

I shook my head.

"Know what's next?"

I shook my head again.

"We call out all clear! One, two, three—" and together we called out that phrase, as we would most days.

My mother sat behind the wheel and Trotsky leaned towards Lewis and said, "Perhaps you drive?"

"I drove a tractor at thirteen," my mother said. "Rest assured I can drive an old Durant across town."

My mother turned left even slower than she usually did and took us north on Van Horne at a crawl.

"Your village reminds me little bit of Germany," Trotsky said. "The *frischluft*, the high peaks, the high snow. Where are your peasants?"

"On reserves" my mother said. "They're a little like your gulags."

"Lewis, write in book—you know, after the revolution —we open gates of these reservations. Let peasants out."

"They're Indians," I said. "They go to a different school than me."

"School in gulag?" asked Trotsky.

My mother nodded.

"Not even in Russia was there such a thing."

"It works," my mother said, though I didn't know what she meant at the time. Not until years later, when the St. Eugene Residential School had been converted into a hotel and casino could I wander the halls as an old man and look at the greying photos of the unhappiest children in the world.

"What is that mountain?" asked Trotsky.

"Fisher Peak," my mother said. "The Paquettes planted the CCP flag on its summit this August."

"It was first climbed in 1865," I said. That much I did know.

"I did not exist then," Trotsky said. "But I do not exist now either. Lewis laughs at old man's folly, but it is true. Who am I? Bronstein, Eberstark, another? Stalin has sentenced me to death. I have no country, my wife and child have no country. But your country gives me hope I can exist once more. When do I meet your revolutionaries, Missus Gil-chreest?"

MY MOTHER INTRODUCED Trotsky to my father, on the back porch. He was hanging laundered bed sheets—at that exact moment, my sister Jean's favourite southern belle pillowcases. He had a long row of red, blue, and yellow clothes pegs clipped to the front of his white shirt and in his mouth a big red one, and when my mother whispered into his ear that this was, you know, Leon Trotsky, the red clothes peg dropped from my father's lips and struck the galvanized laundry tub with a loud clang.

"Of course it is," he said in a testy voice. "I'm not blind." And then to me: "Tommy, pass me my leg, would you?"

I passed my father his prosthetic leg, but he was already pumping Trotsky's hand, at first in mute shock, and then more and more excitedly, as if he'd met Basil Rathbone, his favourite actor. My father had marvelled at newsreels of Trotsky in the twenties and raged when Stalin had forced his favourite revolutionary into Turkey and then across Europe, followed by Stalin's agents and, years later, my letters.

My mother made a lunch of poached trout, boiled potatoes with butter and parsley, and green beans. My sisters, Helen and Jean, joined us and Trotsky noted to my father how fine they looked, as Lewis picked through the plate my mother passed to Trotsky, just as he had picked through our Durant looking for bombs. He cut off the smallest piece of trout to which he added a piece of potato and green bean. "You hungry, bud?"

"Is it not to your taste, Mister Eberstark?" my mother asked Trotsky. "The fish was caught just this morning."

Lewis passed me the fork of food. "Go on."

"But it's Mister Eberstark's," I said. My mother nodded and smiled at me.

I swallowed the food and then Lewis said, "Now, I want a boy like him. Obedient. My own kid don't listen to nothing I say."

When it was apparent that I would go on living, Trotsky inhaled my mother's fish as if he'd not eaten in days. "Food on train was not fit for starving Kulak. Not since Norway have I had fish so moist." He looked at my mother when my father wasn't looking at him. "Already I like your country, Gil-chreest."

"What brings you to Canada, Eberstark?" my father asked.

"Something like—how you say?—nostalgia. In 1917, I was on ship back to Europe from New York, when I was imprisoned. I spend one month in . . . Lewis, where was this place? New . . .?"

"Nova Scotia," Lewis said. "The Bolshies had just over-thrown Tsar Nicholas."

"What a good memory you are, Lewis. Yes, Nova Scotia. I could not understand anything they say there, but they fed me most beautiful fish every day. I was ready for fighting revolution." Trotsky laughed and my mother laughed along with him. "I am needing more fish."

"If it's fish you want I can show you our lakes," said my father. "St. Mary, Moyie, and Premier are all fine for trout. But you've come a little late in the season. August through September are the best months. Do you know fly fishing, Eberstark?"

"I sit in boat on ocean with fishing rod with my son in-law and this fisherman from Cyprus—Haralambolos—and ghost of Lenin, because even dead, Stalin exiles him, too. Haralambolos throws the net and up come the fish. Lenin and I would laugh at them as they flop on bottom of boat. I miss those years. The peace."

"You'll like the fly then, Eberstark." My father held up his right arm to simulate fly fishing and snapped his arm forward. "Nothing can compare to it if it's contemplation you want."

Trotsky's eyes looked so far away it was as if he'd left as abruptly as he'd arrived. "Stalin is on the other side of the world. I can bring revolution to Canada. Your letters give an old man hope."

"Letters?" My father looked at my mother.

"You remember the letters you dictated to Thomas? Which Thomas so kindly sent to Mister Eberstark, year after year?"

"It was as if," Trotsky said. "I sit in this very house and overhear your meetings. How Paquette gave speech on truck to lumberjacks. How Walczak your Polish butcher played 'Internationale' on Victrola. But we are not here for idle talk, Gil-Chreest. A revolution must come to Canada. I meet your Central Committee of the CCP. Tonight."

The moment Trotsky said *tonight*, my father looked as pale as my mother had at the train station. My mother's complexion fared no better. She looked down at her fork stuck fast in a mound of green beans that would never make it to her mouth. It was as if, at that exact moment, in the presence of this revolutionary who had achieved the unimaginable, both my parents realized that the CCP was nothing more than a glorified book club with an occasional published pamphlet or leaflet that no one not a communist or stone drunk would ever bother to read.

"Eberstark, you've come at an awkward moment," my father finally said.

"Awkward moment?" asked Trotsky. "Awkward moment is when you have to leave children behind and flee with false passport with the NKVD in—what is phrase, Lewis?"

"Hot pursuit," said Lewis.

"Hot on heels."

Trotsky waved to Lewis and the younger man passed him a black leather valise. Trotsky rooted around in it and there, in his hands, was the canary yellow onionskin of one of my letters. Trotsky read from the second page. "After the rally on Baker Street, the numbers of the Central Committee surpass fifty. What is awkward?"

My mother looked at my father with the purse-lipped horror she reserved for the funerals of people she liked. The meetings my parents held for the entire CCP, let alone the Central Committee, numbered never more than the Paquettes, Mr. Crimsey, one or two unemployed miners, and Mr. Walczak, especially if my father promised to serve vodka.

"Dad," I said, "don't you remember what you said about Spain? It was in the letter."

"Spain?" my father asked.

"The fighting?"

"Fighting?"

"How many of the CCP have joined the Mac and Paps to fight the fascists?" It was the lie I'd written in my last letter to Trotsky, which he'd likely not yet received, but it was the only thing I could do to save my parents from the humiliation I'd brought to our house. "That's what you told me to type? Remember?"

My parents stared at me, as everything became clear to them: my typing, the letters, Trotsky's presence here. My imagination's constant need to improve reality with lies, fibs, fictions, and half-truths.

"Yes, yes," my father was saying, "most of the CCP have gone to Montreal to join the Mac and Pap battalion."

"Our ranks are rather depleted," my mother added.

"What is Mac and Pap?" asked Trotsky.

"The Mackenzie-Papineau Battalion," I said. "Canadians going to fight fascists. We learned about it in school." Which was, of course, another lie. Cranbrook Central School couldn't stop talking about the origins of ice hockey in Canada. What was going on in Spain didn't happen on ice, so it didn't happen at all.

"How many remain?" asked Trotsky.

"A handful," my mother said. "David Crimsey, the Paquettes, Mister Walczak. Those with children or too old to shoot a, a—"

"Mauser rifle," I said. "You should have seen everyone at the shooting range, Mister Eberstark. Learning how to shoot the Mauser rifle. Right, Dad? You were pretty good, because you fought in Ypres. Dad shot Germans with the Ross rifle. .303 calibre. Bam, bam, bam." And he'd kept shooting his Ross rifle for days after his shrapnel-shattered knee began to ooze lawn-coloured pus. "He got the Victoria Cross. Bam, bam, bam."

"Thomas," my father said. "We don't want to bore Mister Eberstark."

"He has passion," said Trotsky. "I was like him as a young man in Odessa, full of ideas about making Russia great. Our revolution needs passion. He comes to CCP meeting tonight. We will talk about bringing revolution to Canada." Trotsky's hand was suddenly tussling my hair.

"You will be my Commissar of Military Affairs in the town of Cranbrook."

I saluted Trotsky and smiled. "Yes, sir!"

Trotsky rose. "I like this country more and more, Lewis. Such passion in the people. It gives old man hope. But now I must rest for meeting tonight."

TROTSKY WAS asleep in minutes behind the closed door of our second-floor guest room.

"He talks in his sleep," Lewis said. "Pretty much always in Russian. His wife says he talks to Lenin. Lenin complains that Stalin is ruining everything. And then my boss wakes up yelling '*Nyet! Nyet!*' Sometimes he just talks fishing. That's on good days."

Lewis said all this seated in a wooden chair he'd taken from the desk in my room, so he could sit on guard outside Trotsky's bedroom. He chain-smoked Player's Navy Cuts. "In Norway I could only smoke Aladdins. Turkish. You ever smoke Turkish cigarettes? Like sucking on burning cow pies."

I slunk downstairs. My parents had returned to the parlour to rally the CCP. My father was on the phone to the Paquettes, telling them that they had a very important guest who wanted to attend a meeting tonight. "Babysitting?" My father looked right at me. "Thomas can look after little Cynthia."

My mother looked at anything but me. "Your father can't reach Mister Walczak. You will go down to his shop and tell him of tonight's meeting. And purchase two pounds of sirloin. He can put it on our account."

"Mum," I began my apology. "I—"

"There's no point, Thomas. You've made it very clear what you think of your father and I. And yourself."

When I left the house, the black car that had tailed us in the morning was parked again across the street. Cigarette smoke seeped through the windows. The man in the passenger seat had a newspaper spread across the dashboard. The man behind the wheel watched me as I walked down 11th Avenue. As soon as I could turn out of their sight, I ran towards 10th Avenue. I didn't understand why I was running. What had I done that was so wrong? If permanent revolution was going to come to Canada, it wouldn't happen because the CCP talked and talked and wrote endless unread pamphlets. There had to be action and protest and, probably, fighting—maybe even dead people in the streets. The revolution had to look more like Eisenstein's films, like *October* and the *Battleship Potemkin*. As I ran, I took swings at the air. People like Mrs. Leask had to take a punch or two, give up their furs so poor people could eat. They had to wake up to what had been done to us.

I'd not run more than a block when I ran pell-mell into Mister Chittick out for a walk with Bohort. I apologized and tried to run past them, but in a second both had some part of me: Mister Chittick my arm and Bohort a slobbery piece of my pant leg. "Thomas, you're just the boy I wanted a word with."

Mister Chittick's grip tightened as I tried to pull away.

I could feel the nubbins of Bohort's worn teeth grinding on my tibia.

"Now, you gave me a piece of information for which I gave you a lovely thirty-two-cent stamp. Isn't that right?"

"Mister Chittick, I've got to get some sirloin," I said. "For supper. My mother—"

"Except, Master Thomas, your information turns out not to 'ave been true. There've been no plotters training out at Old Town. No Mauser rifles. Nothing. You were telling me a fib. A little fib so you could get your stamp."

"They moved. Old Town became too dangerous. They've been going to Bull River. They'll be there tonight."

Mr. Chittick looked at me as if he was examining the hull of a canoe for cracks. "Tell me about those guests of your parents."

"Mister Eberstark and his cousin? Friends of my father's from the War."

"Which side were these friends on?"

"Ours, Mister Chittick."

"Eberstark sound like the name of one of ours, Thomas?"

I shook my head.

"Sounds rather Hun, doesn't it?"

"No, Mister Chittick. He's from Norway. Can Bohort let go now?"

"Here's what you're going to do to repay me, young Master Thomas. You're going to get your sirloin from Walczak's and then you're going to get Eberstark's and this cousin's passports and you're going to bring them to me. Tomorrow. Or maybe Sergeant Fanning will come in and get them for me. And we'll get your parents', too. And we'll 'old them for a very long time."

BY 8 P.M. THAT NIGHT, the entire membership of the Cranbrook Communist Party sat in my parents' living room. Mr. Crimsey, Cranbrook's librarian; Mr. and Mrs. Paquette, Cranbrook's token Francophones and once members of the Montreal Labour college; Mister Walczak, whom you know; and a man I didn't recognize with a long grey moustache, brown coat, and a stained wool cap.

"This wot-ka," Mister Walczak said to the man in the wool cap, "is like piss of old goat. I will assist." He took the man's tumbler of vodka and gulped it down. "Walczak," he added and held out his hand for a handshake. But the man whose vodka he'd just snatched sat taut and stiff-backed and glared at my father, as if Mister Walczak, like the vodka in his tumbler, no longer existed.

"I don't know who he is," Mr. Crimsey said to the Paquettes of the man in the wool cap. "But he looks just as bored as I am." He, too, glowered at my father. "Gilchrist? When is this so-called emergency meeting going to begin?"

My father stood up from his chair with the help of a cane he sometimes used when his amputated leg bothered him, but it was my mother who spoke. "I realize that notice was very short for all of you, but we're waiting on a very special guest. He's just delayed. Please have some more trout. Jack smoked it last week."

"So special 'e isn't coming?" It was the man in the

wool cap and he spoke in the kind of deep, world-weary grumble that if it was an earthquake would level buildings. "You called Arthur and tells 'im this meeting is so fucking important it'll change the lives of us proles forever. Send your man Kells, you tells 'im. Well, 'ere he is 'is man Kells after five hours driving from fucking Trail an' so far Kells 'as wasted 'is time."

No one breathed. Everyone knew the name Patrick Kells, Arthur "Slim" Evans's right hand man in the interior of British Columbia. Kells was head of the Mine, Mill, and Smelters Union in Trail, after Arthur went to organize the Vancouver shipyards and raise money to fight the fascists in Spain. These were men who'd done in one day more than the CCP would ever do in the rest of its tedious little lifetime. Walczak offered Kells his own glass of vodka and said, "Brother Kells, I —"

"Mister Kells," my mother said, "I assure you that you'll be very justly rewarded for your trip when you meet our guest."

But Kells was on his feet. "Lenin 'imself could walk in 'ere an' kiss me fat on the lips and I'd not give two shites. I've two little ones just born an' I'd rather be there with 'em if you want to knows the truth." And he stuffed the tumbler of vodka back in Walczak's hand and strode in his little stiff-backed way across the living room and out into the foyer.

"Kells," my father said, "you'll miss—"

The front door opened and closed and there was a cry of surprise and then a shout. "Who are ye then!" Kells yelled from the foyer. "Yer not 'im! Yer nothing! Get away from me!"

Kells rushed back into the room with his cap tumbling from his hands. "Kells 'as seen dead men before, but never a spirit. Translucent 'e was but solid like this 'ere wall. I could touch 'is arm."

Lewis Hellman walked into the room and behind him, Trotsky. "We had most terrible beer in the world, right, Lewis?"

"A real stinker," said Lewis. "Not since Jacob Ruppert started watering his ale has there been such a stinker."

"There was man shouting in foyer. But my glasses, how do you say . . .?"

"They was fogged up. You go from cold to warm, you get fog."

Trotsky pointed at Kells. "This was man?"

Kells looked down. "I did not realize it was ye, Mister Trotsky."

Lewis jabbed his index finger on the little union organizer's chest. "Never repeat that name again, okay, bub? In this country with its stinking beer, this is Paul Eberstark." He glared at the rest of us. "All you got that?"

Kells threw himself at Trotsky and hugged him as if he was gripping a mast in a hurricane. "If only Arthur could be 'ere to see yiz."

Everyone closed on Trotsky in two steps. Yes, the boring old CCP was on their feet chirping like birds drunk on old berries.

"Mister Eberstark! So good to meet you!"

"What do you think of our chances in Spain?"

"Oh, Mister Eberstark, you must come for dinner!"

They struggled to shake Trotsky's hand or touch the sleeve of his coat or just get him to notice them.

"Not so close, bub," Lewis was saying. "That better not be a knife, lady. Yeah, yeah, okay it's a fountain pen."

I'd spent so long in so many tedious meetings and now, suddenly, to see the CCP come alive after years of comatose talk—well, it reminded me of the resurrection, not that I knew much about the resurrection at the time thanks to my parents' insistence I shun the Bible. But not everyone had got to their feet. Mr. Walczak hadn't budged from his chair. He looked down at his lap, as if he was reading from an imaginary book only he could see. His deep voice came low and soft: "Zis is not Trotsky," he said. "I see Trotsky in Minsk in 1920 while Poland and Soviets fight in Warsaw. I was prisoner but I cook for Soviet officers, because I know Russian food better than Bolsheviks. Who comes one day to visit Marshal Mikhail Tukhachevsky in dining room? Leon Trotsky in black leather coat and gleaming black boots. I never forget face. Like little psychiatrist with pince-nez glasses and air of professor who knows God's politics. That is real Trotsky. No, this man in living room is imposter. Let us drink to imposter. *Na zdrowie!*"

I credited Mr. Walczak's words to the three tumblers of vodka he'd already drunk. Not Leon Trotsky? This man looked and sounded just like the Trotsky I'd seen in newsreels at the Star Theatre with my parents. He walked like Trotsky, he spoke like Trotsky, he looked at my mother like only someone such as Trotsky would. And he'd brought more energy to the CCP in five minutes then Franco, Hitler, or the Winnipeg general strike had over the course of years. Mr. Walczak was beyond drunk, he was an old fool.

We were in our seats again. Trotsky hadn't moved from the centre of the warm room or even taken off his coat. He spoke for two hours about his plans for Canada. The first revolution to come to the American continent since the Mexican revolution in 1910. We needed to organize. We needed to gather workingmen and -women into a fist to pummel the old order. We needed to open the gates on the Indian gulags to free this oppressed people—we'd need their strength, their blood. We needed, most of all, to stop thinking like pacified victims of the Canadian bourgeoisie. "I see bourgeoisie in Montreal," Trotsky said, "in *rue Saint-Paul Ouest*. Bourgeoisie in hat and coat tails, with no care in the world, while outside train station family of Kulaks begs for crusts of bread and asks who wins hockey game? Who wins hockey game? Stomachs are empty but head wants to know winner of foolish game. Slogan of workers cannot be who wins hockey game? It must be what it was in 1905 in St. Petersburg—Death or freedom!"

"Death or freedom, bubs," Lewis repeated.

My mother and father murmured death or freedom as if they were mumbling song titles in a pleasant dream. No, I wanted to yell, no. Mr. Trotsky sacrificed everything to come all the way across Canada and my parents could only just sit there and mumble slogans with all the heart of tired, old drones. I was on my feet, alone. "Death or freedom," I said in a loud voice.

"Yes, yes," said Trotsky. He took my hand and raised it above my head. "Yes, Thomas, you will be on the barricades soon enough and that will be your cry!" He looked at the rest of the room. "Now, who else?"

Mr. Kells rose. "Aye, death or freedom, it shall be."

And then Mr. Crimsey and the Paquettes cried out in unison, "Death or freedom!"

I looked at my parents—no, I yanked at them with my eyes, to get them to stand up, to shout out. They looked like they'd woken up in the wrong house in the wrong country. Death or freedom? They had three children and jobs and a house, only half-owned. But so what, my fourteen-year-old brain concluded? What did any of that matter when one of the greatest revolutionary leaders of all time called for revolution from their 11th Avenue living room? The uprising began here in little old Cranbrook, right now! Throw up the barricades on Baker Street! Man the clock tower! Light the fires! My father pressed his scarred hands into his legs and leaned forward as if he was about to stand. My mother put her hand on his good knee. They perched on the edges of their chairs over an open abyss. The clock struck nine. My parents looked one last time at each other and rose tottering like ancients rising from their deathbeds. They opened their mouths, but no sound came out. Surely, there was only one thing they could say? Everyone in the room was waiting on them. History was waiting on them. "Death," I whispered, and after that, "freedom."

"Yes?" Trotsky asked them. "What is it?"

"Mom, Dad," I said, "say something."

Mr. Walczak had started up his Victrola. "The Internationale" blared out of my parents gaping mouths.

"*Da, da*," Trotsky was saying. He shook my father's hand. He hugged my mother, as if she was a wayward child and kissed her on the cheek. "Death or freedom."

I almost wept when I saw the smile widening on my mother's face. "Yes, yes," she said. "Death or freedom. Anything."

"Death or freedom!" I cried.

"Long live imposter," Mr. Walczak said and raised his vodka glass. "*Na zdrowie!*"

I WAS TOO excited to sleep. My mind whirled with scenes of our coming revolution. Spraying bullets into a charging phalanx of Sgt. Fanning, Mr. Chittick, Mrs. Leask, and the two men in the black Ford. As soon as we'd shot them, they'd rise up again and we'd have to shoot them over and over, until it occurred to Mr. Walczak to douse them in vodka and strike a match.

I typed up the minutes of the greatest meeting the CCP had ever known, every last shimmering detail. I changed nothing. Well, almost. In my version, Mr. Walczak sobbed in Polish and embraced Trotsky and called him the one true revolutionary and my father too had cried, "Death or freedom" just as my mother had. I left out the whiskey and the dancing to Duke Ellington, Mrs. Paquette with Trotsky and then my mother with Trotsky and me with my sisters. Revolutionaries shouldn't dance, should they? I laughed as I typed up the last paragraph. I wouldn't have to send the letter to Trotsky or lie to Mr. Chittick to get a stamp. I wouldn't even have to leave our house, because the greatest revolutionary in the world was here, a floor above me, asleep in our guest room. I would write a book of my observations, my collected letters. My heart stopped—I could hardly breathe. Yes! I would write down the history of the Canadian revolution just as Trotsky had written his history of the Russian one. An eyewitness account of how Canadian workers seized state power, beginning in my hometown, in my parents' living room, on a cooling October evening to the music of Mr. Walczak's Victrola. *The History of the Canadian Revolution* by Thomas V. Gilchrist. I would borrow my father's reading glasses for my dust jacket photograph, so I would look as intelligent as I sounded in my mind.

A bang came from the kitchen. A piece of cutlery rattled to the floor. I stopped typing and turned out my father's little desk lamp. I wanted to cry out. Sgt. Fanning had already discovered Trotsky, before our revolution had even started! I snuck into the dark living room. Mr. Walczak snored in a low, rumbling gurgle on my parents' settee. I took one step and stumbled over a piece of clothing, someone's coat, going by the thick wool of the fabric. A second step and my feet were tangled in a skirt. I stifled my cry. The truth of what had happened came at my skull like a police truncheon. I'd been so captivated by my typing that I hadn't heard Sgt. Fanning arrest everyone except our Polish butcher, strip them of their clothes, and march them through the cold, cruel night to the Cranbrook jail. It was up to me, Thomas V. Gilchrist, and Mr. Walczak to rescue them—the boy and the butcher, the climax to my memoir of—

Voices came, low and breathless, from the kitchen.

I crept up against the far wall and peered around the corner. The squat outline of the icebox and the wood stove emerged from the gloom. Then a third shape. A figure bent over our butcher block, as if inspecting a slab of beef. The figure was naked from the waist down, dressed in what looked like a white bathrobe.

"Listen," someone said.

"*Da, da.*"

"Quiet."

It was the unmistakable "quiet" of my mother, the same "quiet" I'd heard most of my life as a young child. *Quiet, I'm not buying you Sugar Daddies, quiet or they'll be no supper, quiet they're playing "The Internationale."*

"*Da, da, da.*"

What was my mother doing on the butcher block with my father wedged between her dangling legs? I'd almost said, "Dad?" when I realized that the figure in the robe had two good legs, unlike my father. He turned slightly towards me and in the diffuse moonlight outside the kitchen window I saw it was Trotsky. His crinkled hair stood on end as if he'd been electrocuted, his glasses looked ready to fall off the tip of his nose, his goatee jutted from his chin like a goat's horn. And I asked the question again, what was my mother doing with her rump on our butcher block and Trotsky bent over her? Mr. Walczak, after all, was our official butcher, but he was too drunk to do butchering of any kind and Trotsky was a revolutionary, not a tamed man of flank steaks and Polish sausages. I still had the three sheets of typed onionskin in my hands—the minutes of Trotsky's rallying cry to the CCP. They rustled like autumn leaves in a stiff wind. I'd begun my letter, as I always had: *I trust this dispatch finds you well.* Did that letter find me well? Alone in the dark with Mr. Trotsky struggling to embrace my mother in our kitchen? And where was my father, speaking of tamed men? Upstairs, no doubt, in bed, crawling between fetid trenches in Ypres with both legs still attached to what was unmistakably him. That was the father I was proud of, not the man who hung laundry on our clothesline and wrote pamphlets fat with staid and sober socialism. Whose very idea of a revolution was a collection of pickets outside City Hall on a Sunday afternoon. Death or freedom. Something in me died at that exact moment and something else, something weeks older and wiser than my fourteen-year-old self, had been freed. I felt close to my mother, proud of her, whatever it was she was doing with Trotsky to a rapidly increasing rhythm and a long, drawn-out moan. The old revolutionary collapsed onto her belly —the race was over. The taut, glistening muscles of his pale back relaxed. He sighed as if everything in his revolutionary universe had become the stillness of a Chinese vase.

My mother was suddenly off the butcher block and close enough to me in the dark that I could touch her. She was re-tying her robe. "This is quite impossible," she said in a low voice. "You're—"

"Alone," Trotsky said. "Without country. Family is dead or exiled."

"I am not this, this person anymore."

"*Da.*"

"No."

My mother was gone. She'd left behind the dissipating heat of herself, her smell, a new, earthy, acrid scent I'd never known before. I reached out with my hand to touch it, because if I did I could preserve part of the glorious moment I'd just seen.

Trotsky leaned against the butcher block. His robe had fallen to the kitchen floor. It was as if a flag had been discarded, but I didn't know for what cause. Death or freedom? Or something else? I wanted to say something to him—how proud I was, how glad I was that my mother could help him with the pain of his exile. No, I thought, I will be silent. I will let Trotsky savour this moment in the stillness of the Cranbrook moonlight. I will add my thoughts to my letter: *Addendum—Later, after Mr. Trotsky's speech to the CCP, ~~my mother~~ Mrs. Gilchrist consoled him, as Mr. Trotsky expressed great personal difficulties with his flight from Norway and having to leave his family behind. Over and over, Mr. Trotsky hummed "The Internationale."*

My PRIDE in my mother hadn't worn off in the morning. She served my sisters and I fried eggs and smoked trout and milky Darjeeling tea and vanished back into the kitchen. She'd washed her hair and tied it back in a loose bun with a blue ribbon I hadn't seen before and left coiling in the eggy air a scent of rose water so powerful I assumed she'd emptied half the bottle in her bath.

"Where's Mister Eberstark?" I asked. "And Lewis?" I should've asked about my father, I thought, but here was his leg still leaning against his chair, so he couldn't be far off. He was never far off even when he was away: the tired menace of his broken body was always with us. I grimaced. If he'd known about Trotsky and my mother would he have done anything? Or would he have been his great, conciliatory self? "Be reasonable, Thomas. That was Leon Trotsky. Privilege to be cuckolded by a revolutionary."

My mother didn't reply to my questions. She scraped the cast iron pan as if she intended to put a hole through it.

"Dad's leg is still here."

My mother put a thick triangle of scorched toast on each of our plates.

"Isn't he eating?"

"It was bothering him," she finally said. "You know how he is when is leg bothers him. Impossible. They're at Premier Lake. Fishing. After everything last night, they've gone fishing. Mister Walczak went with them."

"Maybe Mister Eberstark has to talk with the ghost of Lenin? Something is on his mind?" My mother looked at me as if I was crazy. "Don't you remember his story of fishing in Turkey with Haralambolos, the Cypriot? Lewis told—"

"Is everyone impossible this morning? All night your father moaned about pain in a non-existent leg."

My sisters piled their toast on my plate and giggled at me.

"Dad was a war hero." I said it without feeling.

"And what am I, Thomas? Nothing, that's what. The wife who doesn't get to sleep because the war hero's phantom leg hurts."

"You're a hero of our revolution. Just in a different way."

My mother laughed. "There's no revolution coming to

this backwards town or any other. Of all the stupid things, they're fishing after a night like last night. Fishing. The revolutionary and the war hero."

A night like last night. I thought at first my mother meant Trotsky's speech to the CCP and our pledges to fight. But then I thought she meant what had happened with Trotsky after everyone went to sleep. The panting jactations of that shadowy beast on the butcher block. But what had become of the excitement after last night's meeting? And what had come of death or freedom? The end of the Leasks. Their fur coats and contempt for everyone beneath them. Their make-believe noblesse oblige. All they had was money.

"'Course there's going to be a revolution. Mister Trotsky is here. And Mister Kells. And even old Mr. Walczak." I belted out the first lines of "The Internationale."

My mother looked at me as if I was the stupidest, most contemptible creature in the universe. "He's leaving the day after tomorrow. Mexico. It's too cold here. The man hails from the deepest, darkest Russia and Cranbrook is too cold. Frost has hardly touched my begonias."

"You're lying," I said.

"He's already bought train tickets to Vancouver."

I felt dizzy and sick. I took up a piece of burnt toast and mindlessly took a bite. Trotsky was going to Mexico, the land of Pancho Villa and Emiliano Zapata. I wanted to scream. Mexico had already had their revolution over fifteen years ago. What about ours? We had to have ours. We deserved ours. What would become of Canada without a revolution? The Leasks, that's what. The Leasks and all their contemptible brood. Mr. Chittick. The two men in the car. Trotsky had been with my mother—she'd given herself up for revolution—and now he was leaving?

The words welled up out of part me I didn't recognize. "I want five cents."

My mother's look was so cold I expected to die from hypothermia.

"I have to mail a letter."

"What about the money you made from next door?"

I shook my head.

I followed my mother into the kitchen and she opened the snap on her little leather purse. Placed the five-cent King George V on the stained butcher block right where her buttocks had been.

"Well, go on, take it."

I went upstairs with the nickel clutched in my hand and when I couldn't stand the thing being in my palm any longer I shoved the coin in my pocket. I put my hand on the doorknob to Trotsky's room. The door opened with a little metallic click. Light seeped around the heavy curtains. The room was a mess of clothing. Jacket and shawl on the floor. Shoes and books scattered from corner to corner. The bed was a stale mound of blankets, pillows, and sheets. The smell—it was like that earthy smell of last night in the kitchen. I tiptoed to the window and opened the curtain. I needed more light to search the room. Trotsky couldn't go anywhere without his passport. He'd have to stay, destroy the old contemptible Canadian order that had bubbled out of the east like a leaking sewer pipe and flooded the rest of the country. I was quoting my mother's words from years before, when I was ten. I believed them. I believed everything my parents had drilled into my head—Trotsky had to stay.

I began in the little writing desk in the corner. I lifted the roll top, pulled open the drawers, pawed through the stack of illegible papers. Nothing. I went through Trotsky's suitcase, his valise, his jacket pockets. And when I still hadn't found his passport, I went through the shoes and books on the floor and the bloomers and lady's blue dress. Perhaps the passports were in Lewis's room—it would make sense that the bodyguard held the key personal effects. I stared at the dress on the floor. What was a dress doing in Trotsky's room? It was too big to be one of my mother's.

A dry moan came from the lump of bedclothes in Mr. Trotsky's bed. It came louder, as if someone was in the beginning of long, enduring agony. I pulled back the bedcover. A plump, naked woman lay face down in Trotsky's bed. I hissed out what air I had left in my lungs. I struggled to cry out, but my throat was as dry as crackers. Trotsky had been with my mother last night on the butcher block and here, in his bed, was this second woman? She began to roll over and I wondered, what if Mr. Walczak was right, but on a grander scale? Trotsky was an imposter and the woman who made me breakfast was also an imposter? This creature ravelled in the twists of Trotsky's musty sheets was my real mother then? She moaned a second time, long and low, as if she had her foot pressed on the sustain pedal of her voice. It was something in French and I thought of the day that my mother had spoken in French with Trotsky at the train station. The woman sat up. Her dark hair tumbled over her face and fat breasts. A deflated balloon was stuck to her ribs.

"Thomas," she said. "Some water."

She knew my name and I stared in hypnotic disbelief at her pale, penduluming breasts and, in another breath, I remembered her name. It was Mrs. Paquette. Mrs. Paquette who, last night, had sat on one of our dining room chairs beside Mr. Paquette and looked at Trotsky as if he were nothing exceptional, as if she didn't know who he was, this man who looked too much like a disciple of Freud. It had been *Mr.* Paquette who had beamed at Trotsky from the moment he walked into our salon, as if he were the second coming of a favourite childhood school teacher. Trotsky had been with my mother and then Mrs. Paquette and, for all I knew, Mrs. Leask, too. What else was there to do? I wandered into the upstairs bathroom and lifted an empty glass of water to my dry lips and there on the little mahogany washstand was Trotsky's brown leather bag of toiletries. I emptied it into the sink. Toothbrush. Razor. Shaving brush and soap. Four brown paper packets of Cold Crest Prophylactics. His passport.

"Water, Thomas," Mrs. Paquette croaked again from the bedroom.

I presented the empty drinking glass to Mrs. Paquette and took Trotsky's passport, my letter and my mother's nickel for a walk. I went the long way, south up our street for several blocks, maybe west for another several, the most roundabout way possible to try to convince my aching, trembling self that what I was about to do at the post office was wrong. So wrong that my neck ached from the rope I imagined should cinch around it.

"Master Thomas," Mr. Chittick said. "You're up early on a Saturday morning. You've forgotten your shoes."

The post office was empty but for Mr. Chittick and Bohort.

"I'd like to mail a letter," I said.

"To your pen pal? What was 'is name now?"

I had to use my left hand to help my right hand drop Trotsky's passport on the counter in front of Mr. Chittick.

"What's this you've brought old Chittick?" He cracked open the passport. "Paul Eberstark. As I thought—a Hun name."

"That's not his real name."

"Not his real name?"

"It's Lev Davidovich Bronstein."

"A Yid? Your parents are keeping a Yid? This is a good town, Thomas."

I knew what a Hun was but not a Yid. Whatever it was it couldn't be as bad as a womanizing Leninist.

"His real name is Leon Trotsky."

"Wasn't 'e your pen pal?"

I suddenly thought of Mr. Walczak's drunken declaration that Trotsky was an impostor, an actor. It didn't matter. Real or not, he was an impostor. Not the man I wrote letters to for five years. Not a revolutionary for any social upheaval of which I wanted any part. Not, not, not.

"'e writes those plays. Wot's that one all the kids are reading? *Uncle—*"

"He's a Communist revolutionary not Anton Chekhov." I summarized Trotsky's role in the Russian revolution in half a dozen violent sentences.

"In our town, Thomas? A Yid Bolshie? You posted

letters to 'im from my post office?" He shuddered as if vermin had crawled all over the scale and counter and nested in the pigeon hole cabinet where he sorted innocent, newborn letters. "I've 'alf a mind to put you over my knee."

"He's planning—"

"It doesn't matter what 'e's planning. 'e's in our town. A Yid Bolshie is in our fucking town. We 'unt deer and we fish trout and log everything that can be logged that isn't cedar. That's the order of things. Did you want all that thrown to 'ell when you sent your letters, Thomas? Chaos in our town like in Spain?" He put one arm through his short navy winter coat. "Now I've got to go out into this rain and call on Sergeant Fanning and tell 'im that family of yours has imported a God-hating Yid into our town. I don't even like trout—give me a good salted hake any day —but I know to defend them for the people that do."

THE BLACK FORD outside our house was gone when I edged up to our little front gate. I didn't know how I could live with my parents again. I'd get my things, beg Mrs. Leask for a job as a chokerman, and take a room in the Byng Hotel. I'd never type again or read another socialist tract or go to another communist meeting. I would be like Trotsky, forever an exile. I'd drift into middle-aged loneliness. I'd die beneath the crushing silence of a barren rented room. I'd—

I could hear the music even where I stood outside our front gate. Not faintly, but so loud that our front door rattled in its hinges. Our Victrola was blaring Stravinsky's *Rite of Spring*. Our Victrola hadn't blared other than "The Internationale" in years. Our house had been the model of post-War tranquility, because all classifications of noise—rhythmic, romantic, or incidental—reminded my father of artillery, bombs, and gunfire. He would sweat and fidget by day and, at night, would cry out that he'd been shot. My father, of course, would sacrifice himself for a few minutes to endure "The Internationale," but other than that display of loyalty, my parents had enforced a strict code of silence, of low voices and becalmed laughter.

I followed the stamp of horns and strings to our dining room. My mother and Mrs. Paquette swayed in the centre of the living room in a pair of my mother's long, blue bathrobes. They held each other's hands and wavered back and forth as if buffeted by an invisible breeze. Their hair hung loose and unravelled and their eyes were closed, not tight, but as if they were dreaming a lovely dream. I could smell sherry and Mrs. Paquette's French cigarettes. The necktie belt of Mrs. Paquette's bathrobe was half undone and, once, again, I could see her breasts. Plump and ovular like pin-less hand grenades. I thought for the first time in my life that I should do something with breasts that I hadn't done as a child. Hold them or stroke them—something more than stare at them while a Stravinsky horn section pounded against my pubescent body.

"The music will hurt Dad," I said. But I hadn't said it loud enough. I raised my voice as loud as could possibly still be considered polite. "Dad will be home soon from fishing. The music."

They hadn't heard me. I was afraid of Dad coming home to all this noise and my mother out of her mind and Mrs. Paquette's breasts out of their fabric paddocks. Not to mention that Trotsky and Lewis would see my mother in this embarrassing—I wanted to write *state*. But what state? I'd never seen any such behaviour from my mother before, assuming she was still my mother. And where were my sisters? I hadn't done more than thought this question when my mother said, "They're next door at Missus Rainer's. You should be there, too, Thomas."

"If you see Alain, *mon chouchou*," Mrs. Paquette said in a loud, boozy voice of Mr. Paquette, "I will not be home tonight. Not ever."

I thought of what Mr. Chittick had said about what we do in Cranbrook—hunt and fish and log. The order of things. I imagined a stack of fresh cut logs, like the ones I'd seen at the Leasks' sawmill, when my mother or father had tried to deliver CCP pamphlets to the Leasks' non-unionized workers. A stack of dead trees as high as the clock tower on Baker Street, the sawmill pungent with the sweet, acrid sent of dying pine. At Mr. Walczak's butcher shop had been little shimmering stacks of trout or beefsteaks or pork loins. A log or a steak or a loin put in their rightful places, on top of their respective heaps. This was an order, a hierarchy, and for all my desire to upturn my parents' political lives, I couldn't live without tidy symmetry: things as they should be. I couldn't live with my mother on the butcher block with Mr. Trotsky slapping his thighs against her and then, later, doing the same with Mrs. Paquette. Mrs. Paquette! I wanted to be on top of her, my beefsteak against her pork loin, my head rooting around in the glistening space between her breasts. My groin tingled with pulsing energy. Stravinsky's horn and string section was in me, flowing like an unstoppable torrent of warm water. I wanted to cry out. I didn't know what was happening to me. I smothered my wool cap against my hardening groin and closed my eyes and prayed in the darkness of myself that I wouldn't die. There was only Stravinsky's music and Mrs. Paquette's little susurrated moan: "*Mon chouchou, mon cochon, mon mon mon*" and my buzzing, tingling testicles.

I don't know when the knocking on the rear door began. Somewhere between the snarling brass and the sledgehammering timpani came knocks. "Let us in, bud. There's been a fucking accident." I didn't want to move from my place in front of my mother and Mrs. Paquette. I felt so wonderful, as I hadn't ever felt before in my fourteen years. The door jumped again in its frame. I ran to the back door and listened. Breaths, moans, the door knob rattling in place. I pushed the bolt open. It was Lewis with Mr. Trotsky half-hanging from his arms, like an old overcoat. A bloody overcoat, because Mr. Trotsky's hair and beard were matted with great bloody gobs.

Lewis lay Mr. Trotsky on the kitchen table. "I need water and bandages and—" He let out one momentous sob. "Goddamn, just put on the fucking kettle, bud, alright? Orange pekoe."

I'd no more than turned to grab our great copper kettle from stove, when the whole world as I knew it pushed into the kitchen. My father on his crutches and Mr. Paquette and Mr. Walczak and Mr. Chittick and the two strange men from the black Ford outside our house.

And everyone had something in his hands. My father, an oak fish club, and Mr. Paquette, a claw hammer, and Mr. Walczak, a meat hook, and Mr. Chittick, nasty old Bohort, and the two men in their long dark coats, revolvers. Stravinsky's music clamoured into the kitchen on great, torturous waves from the strings and it—the music—had something in its invisible hands, too. My mother and Mrs. Paquette and her pale, brown-tipped breasts.

"Is Mister Trotsky—?" I asked.

"He's impostor," said Mr. Walczak.

"Womanizer," said Mr. Paquette.

"A Yid Bolshie fifth columnist," said Mr. Chittick.

Bohort barked and the two men with the revolvers growled that they were with the government and this man was an enemy of Canada and everything for which our great country stood. Maybe they'd arrest all of us for violation of Section 98 of the Criminal Code.

Mr. Trotsky groaned and burbled. His face was swollen with bruises and cuts. There was an inch-deep indentation on the left side of his skull, which oozed blood and what looked like minced beef.

"Bandages, I need fucking bandages, Jesus!" shouted Lewis.

It was then that I realized that there was blood on everything the men in the kitchen held—the fish club, the meat hook, the hammer, the dog, the pistols—as if everything had struck or stabbed or bit Mr. Trotsky at once. The weapons disappeared into pockets. Everyone's hands were suddenly on Mr. Trotsky's broken body. We moved him to the upstairs guest room and my mother washed and bandaged the wounds in his skull and sent Mrs. Paquette for Doctor Severn.

"We were fishing," my father said to my mother. "I was showing Trotsky my fly rod—how to let out line—when they or he leapt from the pines and struck him from behind. And Alain said, 'Well, do you know what Trotsky did with your wife and my wife and a lot of other wives in Cranbrook, including Missus Leask?' I couldn't believe any of it, could I? And then Walczak was denouncing him as an impostor and these two and Chittick were trying to arrest him. Everyone had suddenly leapt on poor Mister Trotsky." My father held up the bloodied fish club. "Where did this come from? What've we done? He's the most heroic man I've ever met and he comes to Cranbrook and—"

Doctor Severn strode up the stairs with Mrs. Paquette right behind him still in my mother's blue bathrobe. The door to Trotsky's room shut against me. I put my ear to it and listened, but there was only a profound, painful silence. I thought of the times I'd sat at the typewriter and wondered what lie to write to Mr. Trotsky next about the boring old CCP. The silence outside our guest room door just then felt like those quiet pauses between the blossoming fiction in my head and the moment before my fingers rested against the keys and I began to type my lies on onionskin paper. I tried to imagine what was to be written about the CCP and Mister Trotsky now. He survived his mortal wounds? He was murdered on the shore of Premier Lake? He slept with my mother and Mrs. Paquette and, for god's sake, bourgeois Mrs. Leask and her collection of fur coats? I pulled my ear from the door and stared into the gloom of the hallway. Wasn't it up to me as the unofficial secretary of the CCP to determine what happened to him? Typed and preserved as neat meeting minutes would be the official history, wouldn't it?

An agonized yell came from behind the door. It was Lewis. "I was in the outhouse. The stinking outhouse of all places. I'm tellin' ya I've been in this town two days and I can't stay from the toilet. This water is poison. I should've been with him. I could've stopped this. Jesus, I should've shot you all. Should've listened to that voice in my head. Shoot 'em all. Bam, bam, bam."

I was already at my father's typewriter. I rolled a sheet of paper into the carriage and rested my fingers against the cold keys. I'd send Trotsky back to Norway. No, back to Montreal for a ship to Mexico, because he and Lewis had mentioned Mexico on their arrival at the train station. No, no, I liked Mr. Walczak's theory: this wasn't Trotsky, but an impostor to trick Stalin and his assassins. The real Trotsky was already in Mexico City with Diego Rivera and Frida Kahlo. The real Trotsky would never have slept with other men's wives. Yes, that's it—the members of the CCP would bury Trotsky's double in the abandoned gold mine out at Old Town.

As the last shovel full of soil went into the impostor's grave, Mr. Walczak played "The Internationale" on his portable Victrola.

THE MONKEY KING

The news about Pearl Harbor came during Ye Ye's morning mahjong game with his oldest friend, the Monkey King. Each morning for the past forty years, the two friends had played mahjong for a gold nugget the Monkey King kept in a leather pouch around his neck and each time Ye Ye lost. The war in the Pacific came as a secret relief to my grandfather. That morning's game was number 15,000 and Ye Ye let himself think that he could postpone his milestone loss to the undefeated monkey god.

It was my grandfather's turn to play and you could feel his defeat about to plunge from the clouds. His fingers lingered over the wall of green and white mahjong tiles. He wore his wool gloves cut off at the fingertips so that you see the ugly ochre of his long nails beside the brighter colours of the playing pieces. "Crazy snow outside, huh?" he said. "White piled up to the roof." He stared at our radio. He'd heard something in the soft static we hadn't. His eyes widened enough to suck in the half-empty shelves of our family's general store.

"Hear that engine?" he asked us. "Japanese bomber. Nakajima B5N. Hirohito is up to no good."

"Quit stalling and lose again," Ma Ma said from behind the front counter. "Customers soon."

"Turn up my radio," Ye Ye called out to me. "Good war this time." And when I didn't move, he said to my mother, "Your silly daughter is always so brooding."

I had been thinking of Miyuki Yoshida, my only friend in Central School. It was Monday and I wouldn't see her in class today because of all the snow mounding up as high as the tops of the cars. I wouldn't get one of the twenty notes we passed back and forth each day—

Edith! John Allison said hi to me today at recess.

Why are you so quiet today? Listening to the bad war again?

What's 9 x 12? John wants to know.

I wouldn't smell the scent of her father's sawmill on her clothes and in her hair—pine and spruce and cedar. Miyuki smelled like a dismembered forest, not like war at all.

Ma Ma shouted my name. "Ye Ye wants—"

I turned up the volume of our radio as high as it would go. Fighter planes droned overhead, bombs whistled—in my mind the quilted layers of Miyuki's accents (Japanese and English, her hint of my Chinese one) died in a crescendo of bass explosions. The voice of President Roosevelt filled my family's store—yesterday, the Japanese attacked the American naval base in Oahu, Hawaii, by air. Everyone cared but me. Miyuki and I were safe in our town, far away from Hitler and Hirohito. I wanted to shout out my heart at President Roosevelt: I have a friend in this ugly Canadian town and that's all that matters to me!

A gust of frigid wind shot snowflakes through the cracks in the door jamb. Ye Ye's cigarette snuffed out between his pursed lips and Ma Ma's stick of sandalwood incense went cold. All the fire in the world had been recalled to Pearl Harbor. No, not all, President Roosevelt. I shielded a little blaze inside me. Just large enough to warm Miyuki and me.

None of us said anything in the crackling silence after President Roosevelt finished his speech. There would be more war, more rationing, more—whatever it was we could all feel it lurking near us. Testing the air with its long black snout.

"Someone's at the door," Ma Ma said. "Edith, let them—"

"There's no one," I said.

"I see his shadow."

"Snow fell off the roof just now. That's your shadow."

"Look."

"Everyone knows we don't open for half an hour."

"With this news, people will come early. More rationing, you watch."

I rubbed the frost-thickened glass with the sleeve of my sweater and peered into a swirling white void. I wanted Miyuki to step from the blizzard, to rap on the window pane, to take me skating on Elizabeth Lake, to get me away from Ye Ye and the Monkey King and the war. Miyuki and I took turns with her skates, because our feet were the same size and Ma Ma wouldn't buy me a pair. Sometimes we each wore one of Miyuki's skates and held each other shoulder to shoulder and tried to make it across the lake without falling. Mostly, we fell into a giggling heap and told each other that there wasn't anything better in the world than our friendship.

"There's just a black dog," I said to Ma Ma. "He came from the moon and brought his ration card. He wants one old monkey."

Ye Ye ignored my slight against his friend. "Old Yoshida will come tomorrow, maybe the next day. *Ye Ye, Hirohito is killing Americans. Hide my Miyuki before the Canadians take her. Ye Ye, here is so much money. Please, Ye Ye. I shouldn't have fired you and Monkey from my saw mill. Those things we did, I'm very, very sorry.*

"Yoshida can beg all day, I'm not lifting one finger for his so ugly ass."

I didn't know what my grandfather meant. Why would the government take Miyuki? She'd been born a half mile away in St. Eugene Hospital during the same week in March that I had. She was as Canadian as I was.

Ma Ma pointed to the Red Ensign she'd pinned above the jars of bubble gum, liquorice, and lollipops war rationing had kept mostly empty. "This isn't America. The government here doesn't take people."

"Look around—we are a British ally, American ally. You'll see—many arrests are coming."

Ma Ma slapped nickels and dimes into the drawers of the till. "Your ape is waiting for you to move. Go on, lose a bit more of yourself like you do every day."

"Just because people are born here," Ye Ye said, "doesn't mean they stay here. Japanese killed us in Nanking. Now punishment is coming. Yoshida—"

My mother shoved the till shut with a mechanical click. "Edith, the door. Someone's there."

I went to throw open the door and show my mother the snow piled up to the roof and the black dog sniffing at our picket fence, but Ye Ye had already turned on me. "Prison is coming for that Yoshida girl friend of yours. Yoshida and all the other Japanese from here to Steveston —jail."

I pressed my hands against my ears. Ye Ye's cruel voice spat from the crackling radio in my head.

"You could've stopped Hirohito," Ye Ye said to the Monkey King. "Made the wind blow away his bombers. Big waves drown his battleships." Ye Ye blew a wheezing breeze at his mahjong tiles, but not one of them fell over. "You're our secret weapon, okay? Win the war in one day. Start with that traitor Yoshida."

"Monkey couldn't stop a squadron of flies," I yelled. "Look at his arm? Turning back to stone." The Monkey King's left arm was grey limestone from the elbow down to the tip of his curled-up index finger and most of the day it hung at his side like a weighted fish hook. If I'd found the Monkey King in a taxidermist's attic, I'd have mistaken him for a large, disfigured rat and not the conquering ape Ye Ye had kept in our store for all these years. "He stinks worse than the outhouse."

Ye Ye pounded the card table. Mahjong tiles clattered to the floor. His bowl of congee spilled on its side.

I'd heard all my grandfather's stupid legends countless times before. "The Monkey King is the greatest warrior in the world. His staff weighs 17,000 pounds and it took the

Buddha to defeat him. He can cast spells and turn his hairs into twins of himself."

I yanked at the frigid deadbolt. The wooden door, warped by winter cold, sprang inward and snow tumbled over my thick boots. "There's nobody, Ma Ma. There never was. See?"

But there were his footprints. They started in the middle of the walk as if he'd parachuted there. He'd trudged a few short steps to our door and stopped— listened and lurked. I peered around the yard. No one. I couldn't tell my mother that she'd been right, that there had been a customer. She'd swat me with her broom and make me clean out the Monkey King's chamber pot. But as I was the only one who'd seen the tracks, I said, "It was that dog. I'll shovel the walk."

The door shut behind me. I pushed snow over the boot tracks with our shovel. When I came to the middle of our walk, I saw that a trail of dog tracks came up from the road and where the man's tracks began in the middle of the walk, the dog's ended. Dog tracks then a man's tracks.

His tracks hadn't disappeared at the door. He'd crept along under the overhang of our roof and around to the back yard. He'd crept—his back was to me. He wore a long, brown wool overcoat that came down almost to his ankles and a grey fedora dusted with fresh snow. He'd propped his right rubber boot on a round of our firewood and was peeing into a pile of snow that had fallen from the roof of the outhouse. He peed a little here and then a little there, left to right—yellow ink on a white page. He peed for the longest time, longer than I'd ever heard the Monkey King pee at night. "Breathe," he said. "In one,

two, three, four, five, six, seven. Out one, two, three . . ."
He counted to eleven. His breath whirled around his head
like a little cyclone. "Use your magic. You've done this
before. You can do it again. Make the sale. These people
love you." He picked up his leather brief case from the
snow. "Ready, Mr. . . .?" He looked down at a piece of
paper in his hand. "Lascelles?"

He spotted me, my blank look.

"Sorry, honey," he said. "Snow's blocking your
outhouse door. I'm early or is it late? Came from Creston-
way, last night, on the train and didn't change my pocket
watch. You going to show me around? It's Edith, right? I
heard someone shout Edith and I knew that a pretty name
like that had to belong to a girl like you. My own daughter
is your age. Merry is her name, but I call her Plum. My
Merry Plum."

"Merry Plum Lascelles?" I asked.

"Keen of hearing, aren't you, Edith? Bet you can hear a
snowflake fall at a hundred yards. Let's listen for one.
Ready?" Before I could say anything, he said, "Hear it? See
that big pine across the street? A snow flake just fell from
the top branch and boom—the whole valley shook."

"Why is your name on that piece of paper?"

"How about I call you Charlie Chan? The Charlie
Chan of Cranbrook? Thing is, I have memory problems
since the war. Which war, you ask?" He unfolded the sheet
of paper again and showed me a long column of words I
couldn't read, because his writing was small and crabbed as
if he'd written it with a hummingbird's beak. "See here?
This time it was the Spanish civil war. Yours truly fought
in the Mackenzie-Papineau Battalion on the side of the

worldly righteous. I took a bottle of cava to my noggin. See that bump?" He lifted his fedora and then pulled up a clump of oiled brown hair above his right ear and there, like a rogue patch of snow on a grey summer peak, was an egg-shaped scar. "Oh, but she could throw!" The piece of paper disappeared into his pocket. "Now, you were going to introduce yours truly to your parents, Edith. Mr. Willard Lascelles of the Canadian Western Life Assurance Company."

"Were you a dog before? Your tracks started out like a dog's."

He laughed. "The best imagination is right here in Cranbrook, isn't it? In my new friend Edith."

"I already have a friend, Miyuki Yoshida. We do everything—"

"Did everything."

"Do everything."

"I'm sorry, Edith. Haven't you heard? No? I can explain it to your parents. Someone should, before . . ."

"Before what?"

"Now, it would be wrong of me to say anything without having spoken to your parents first."

"There's only Ma Ma and Ye Ye and the Monkey King. My father—"

"Tuberculosis, wasn't it?"

I'd never met Willard Lascelles in my life and I didn't know how he knew that my father had died.

"Your father had a small life insurance policy with us going way back. That's why your mother could keep your store."

I didn't know anything about it. I didn't want to talk

about it. When I let Willard Lascelles through the front door, Ma Ma peered at him, as if she wasn't sure who was coming over a distant hill.

"Your breakfast sure smells good," he said. "Soup, if I'm not mistaken."

"You want Campbell's? Chicken noodle? Cream of mushroom?"

"Take a bowl of that rice soup you've got there, if you don't mind? One of those steamed buns, too? Is that green tea?"

"Twenty cents."

"Sounds like a premium, ma'am, but these are hard times. Have you lived in town long?"

My mother left Willard Lascelles and his question at the front counter and went into the kitchen.

Willard Lascelles took in our store. The short, sparse aisles of canned and packaged food, flour and rice and beans. The little galvanized tubs of root vegetables—potatoes, beets, celery root, carrots, and radishes. The shelves of everything you might need in Cranbrook through the decades: pick axes, gold pans, shovels, and storm lanterns. Cork boots, playing cards, and pull saws. And high up on a shelf near the front counter sat a little soapstone Buddha laughing at the joke of the modern world that felt like no joke to anyone alive. Last night, I'd put two apples, a steamed bun, and a bowl of condensed milk at the Buddha's feet. Our calico had lapped up the milk on behalf of the little god. There was no dust on anything in our store. No cobwebs. Everything gleamed as if it had just been unwrapped at Christmas. Except, of course, for the mangy fur rug that was the Monkey King.

"Hello, gentlemen," said Willard Lascelles. "A little mahjong this cold morning? Mind if I take a seat?"

There were, of course, two empty chairs at my grandfather's mahjong table. One for the Jade Rabbit and one for the ghost of the dead monk Xuanzang—the Monkey King's friends from another time. Mahjong, after all, was best played with four players, even non-corporeal ones and Ye Ye insisted on reserving seats for them.

"Edith?" Ye Ye said.

I dragged over my mother's chair so that Willard Lascelles could sit at my grandfather's mahjong table.

Willard Lascelles glanced at the tiles in front of Ye Ye and whistled. "Tough nut to crack that hand. Hope you're not playing for high stakes."

"My gold nugget," my grandfather snorted, "hanging around Monkey's neck!"

I'd heard Ye Ye's story a thousand times. He'd found the Monkey King drunk and defeated in the Klondike, after the Qing Fish Demon lured him back to earth with promises of gold rush riches. Ye Ye and the Monkey King hadn't found gold on the Klondike, but they did on the Wild Horse, twelve miles north of our small town. Or rather the Monkey King did—a ten-ounce nugget he wore around his mangy neck, the gold prize that Ye Ye played for each day.

Willard Lascelles's laugh was soft and teasing. "Now if only the Canadian Western Life Assurance Company insured mahjong losses. But I am saying too much, in front of your hairy friend there. Can't insure him with an arm like that. Rest of you is going to calcify real soon judging by the progress of your disease. God, this is a fine store. I like it. It gives me a good feeling. Like being at home. Like something you don't want to lose. Isn't that right, Edith? Something you don't want to lose."

My mother put congee and a bun in front of Willard Lascelles. "I could eat the moon," he said and drank from the bowl like a hungry beast and then sopped up the dregs of the soup with the pork bun and then gulped down his tea and said that it was the best he'd ever had in all his travels across our large country. Earlier he'd said he'd come from Creston and I pictured him as the black dog I'd seen in our yard, running along the cold highway. Lean and hungry and near death until he sniffed out my mother's cooking in the pale blue light before dawn.

"Well, ma'am, I didn't just come here to eat your fine cooking." He gave my mother a quarter and said that the nickel was a tip and he would be sure to tell all his friends about our little store. "I wanted to tell you about our new insurance policies at Canadian Western Life."

Ye Ye pointed at the Monkey King. "The Lum family's insurance is right there. Fire—he summons rain. Thieves —he catches them with his magic staff. I die—he becomes the man of our store. He dies—we sell that gold nugget."

"What about war, Mr. Lum? You thought about how war can affect a family?"

"The war is so, so far away. Yes, rationing is here, but we eat. Like you eat."

"Now, you heard the radio this morning, didn't you, Mr. Lum? This new war with Japan? What do you think is going to happen to Japanese nationals in our fine country?"

"All the Yoshidas will get arrested. All the other Japanese will get arrested, too. About time. In Nanking—"

I started to put my coat back on.

"Where are you going?" Ma Ma asked me.

"To use the phone at the train station. To warn Miyuki." Unlike us, the Yoshidas could afford a phone. Miyuki's father had paid himself to have the line routed out to their house.

"Now Edith," Willard Lascelles said, "my next stop this morning is the Yoshidas. They'll be just fine. Why don't you sit down?"

No one else in grade seven liked me but Miyuki Yoshida. I had the wrong eyes and the wrong hair. I smelled of congee and incense and fried vegetables. The smell of fresh-cut lumber masked Miyuki's scent of dashi and gyoza. John Allison, Miyuki's crush, smelled of bacon and alfalfa and fresh cream. He liked Miyuki but not me. He was drawn to her scent of fallen trees. I didn't mind. When Miyuki and I held each other and skated on Elizabeth Lake, we were one person and John Allison could never be us. He couldn't know what it was like when we parted, to feel so raw and alone you wanted to lie down in the snow and let your blood freeze.

"Will you help her?" I asked.

"I don't know if I can, Edith. And that's the sad truth. It's going to take some work from her parents. I can only promise that my employer and I will do our best." Ma Ma poured Willard Lascelles another cup of tea. "There is an unfortunate fact about our country for which I must apologize. We're an unenlightened people in some ways. You see it in the treatment of our Indians. Why, just this morning, I met an old Indian tracker face down in a snow bank and I thought, why isn't anyone in this town helping this poor fellow? Well, I helped him up and gave him ten cents and said find yourself a cup of coffee and a warm bed. That's what my father always said to me. Willard, we're all one on one planet, no matter what colour we are. But my father isn't most men. You know what it's like, don't you, Mr. Lum? Fifteen years ago, could you go into Hurry's restaurant for the White Lunch? Or what if you wanted a restaurant job? *White Help Only* sound familiar? Or how about this charming quote: *The Chinese can remain in one position an indefinite time, having no consciousness of monotony, can do without exercise, are impervious to noise, can go to sleep at any time and in any attitude —all because they have no nerves.* You see the problem is people in this country don't see Chinese and Japanese. They see Orientals and now—you heard it in Mr. Roosevelt's speech this morning—they see enemies. Oriental enemies."

Ye Ye laughed. "Ye Ye is a friend of Mr. Roosevelt. Ma Ma, Edith, and the Monkey King, too. Yoshida—" My grandfather spat at the floor. "—is enemy number one."

Willard Lascelles saw that my mother didn't look half as sure as Ye Ye. "You see, Mrs. Lum, the government, they'll round up the Japanese and the Chinese and the Koreans. All of you. They'll deport many. They'll jail more. They'll take everything you've worked for. Your store. Even Mr. King's gold nugget. It's an unfortunate fact, for which I'm sorry."

Ma Ma looked at Ye Ye. "You know this is true."

My grandfather finally took a tile from the Mahjong

wall, but didn't turn it over. "Ye Ye looks like Yoshida? Edith looks like that Yoshida girl? Ha!"

"People still don't come to our store because we're not white," Ma Ma said. "I hear them on Baker Street, when I go to the bank. Lum's general store—don't go there. Chinese—they'll rip you off. They say our food makes them sick. I was born here. Edith was born here."

"It's called risk," Willard Lascelles said. "And you can manage risk even in times of war. Protect your family and your store. In the event that the government arrests . . ." His voice died away in the cooling silence of our home. The wood in our wood stove snapped and popped but gave off little heat. My mother looked at Ye Ye, as if to say that everything Willard Lascelles had said was as real as the bombs we'd heard explode over our radio.

"You can help us?" Ma Ma asked.

Ye Ye swore at my mother in Mandarin. He started to rise to his feet with such a look of contempt on his old face that he even frightened me.

But Willard Lascelles already had his sheaf of papers in front of my mother. "Our basic policy for comprehensive protection in the event of government seizure of your assets and/or relocation to detention facilities. About $350. You would be indemnified—say, you and your father in-law couldn't work. You would receive income supplementation for—"

"The demon is after—the demon is after my gold." It was the rasping croak of the Monkey King. The Monkey King hadn't spoken since 1937, when the Japanese had invaded and occupied China. We didn't think that he could speak anymore, because his eternal life had been so corrupted by over forty years of life in this town. He set his eyes on Willard Lascelles.

"I beg your pardon?"

"L-leave, demon." The Monkey King's good hand went to his neck, to the pouch with the gold nugget in it.

"Mr. King—"

"You call him the Monkey King like everybody else!" roared Ye Ye.

"Mr. Monkcy King, this is a very important issue for your family and Canadian Western Life. We merely wish—"

"Where do we get $350?" Ma Ma asked. "We have the store and nothing else. Ye Ye worked hard, we worked hard all these years." She threw her arm out toward our dust-coated Red Ensign. "We're Canadians. The Yoshidas are Canadians."

"Mrs. Lum, the government is going to take everything you own, Canadian or not."

My mother's face took on a pale sheen.

"There's no need to get upset. This is a problem with a rational solution." He offered my mother a black silk handkerchief from his coat pocket and, when my mother didn't take it, he seemed relieved. "Caucasian or oriental, we're all a little on edge, after this morning's news." My mother changed her mind. She tried to tug the handkerchief from his hand, but Willard Lascelles wouldn't let go, until my mother snatched it from him. She dabbed her eyes with the black fabric and passed it back to him and he, somehow appearing to take the handkerchief, but not touching it, let it drop to the floor as if a leper had used it to wipe at her sores. It was then I realized that Willard

Lascelles hadn't touched any of us since coming into the store. He'd shaken Ye Ye's hand and rubbed my hair without taking off his black gloves. "You may not have cash on hand to pay the premium. But you seem like very good people. We could arrange for Canadian Western Life to own a percentage of your store to cover your premiums—"

The Monkey King's staff was in his hand and when he couldn't hold it steady with one hand, he grasped the shaft with both hands as tightly as if he was clinging to a cliff. His lips moved but no sound came from his mouth. He snorted out a stream of silver dust. He touched Willard Lascelles on the shoulder with the staff and croaked, "Vanish!"

"Mr. King, may I help you?" Willard Lascelles asked.

The Monkey King's face fell and then he got the idea to turn the staff over in his hand and touch the salesman again.

"Mr. King, please don't—"

The insurance salesman looked as if a hot poker had touched him. He stared at the Monkey King and then at my mother and finally Ye Ye. His eyes opened so wide it looked as if he was about to fall into a deep well. His tongue hung from his mouth like a slobbering dog's. His eyes somersaulted in their sockets. His lips turned black.

"No more!" Ma Ma snapped. "We need the insurance."

"The Yoshidas need insurance, too!" I shouted at the Monkey King.

Ye Ye began to smile, that cruel smile he'd had earlier when he'd spoken so terribly about the Yoshidas. "Monkey

King magic is very strong," he said to Willard Lascelles. "If you're lucky, he turns you into a frog. Maybe an ugly bird. Maybe a dog. Once he turned Yoshida's foreman into a fat cherry tree. Very funny and very terrible. Yoshida got a Japanese witch to turn him back."

Willard Lascelles closed his eyes. His lips trembled. His hands shook so hard the mahjong tiles began to topple.

We'd all been watching him so hard, none of us noticed what had happened to the insurance papers on the table. They were covered with black flies. Not because our store ever had a single fly in it (my mother killed them all), but because the very words on the documents had begun to transform into those awful insects. I watched the word *indemnify* compress itself into a little black splotch that in the next moment sprouted eyes, legs, and translucent wings. And where the flies had been born, the word it had hatched from vanished from the page. *Guarantee, vesting,* and *the*—all these words flew up as flies into the cooling air of our store, hundreds of them swirling around us like black snow. In another minute, the papers before us were as white as the winter outside our door.

The transformation of Willard Lascelles was only slightly less shocking. The pain that the touch of the Monkey King's staff had caused vanished from his face. His colour turned back to tawny white. The shakes and jerks of his limbs eased into a minor palsy and then nothing. He took from his briefcase a second copy of the papers that he'd shown my mother and placed them on top of the now blank originals. "My offer," he said, "is good until tomorrow at sundown, which I hear is pretty early in these parts. After that, I go on to the next town. Kimberley, isn't it? Hear it's good for skiing up there."

At the door, he turned one last time and said, "I want to help you, Mrs. Lum. All of you."

My mother stared at the closed door and then at Ye Ye. None of us could believe what we'd just seen. This strange salesman had defeated the Monkey King's magic.

"Don't take his deal," Ye Ye said to my mother. "We're fine. The whole world is fine." He finally looked at the mahjong tile he'd taken as if he'd seen a portent of death. "You'll see. Everybody can relax. Play mahjong. Sell to our customers." He waved at the flies buzzing around his face. He crushed three of them against the table with the heel of his fist and slapped the tile he'd chosen on its back with the piles of discarded tiles. It was the nine of bamboo. "Soon comes a myth about me. How Ye Ye Defeated the Monkey King. How Ye Ye Defeated the Monkey King after Pearl Harbor. How Ye Ye—"

It was the Monkey King's turn. He reached for the tile wall and then he glanced down at the row of thirteen tiles before him. He took my grandfather's tile from the discards and added it to his own hand and grinned from one old ear to the other—he'd won again.

My grandfather smashed a fly against the table so hard that his mahjong tiles jumped two inches into the air. "We're fine. Everyone is so fine. You'll see."

Even on the ugliest Mondays, we had customers— perhaps not many, but they came. Farmers and railway men and miners, their wives, because my mother prided herself on having the best root vegetables all winter every winter—the beets, potatoes, carrots, turnips, celeriac, taro, and rutabagas Ye Ye grew in the large field behind our store or bought from Mrs. Zheung in Creston at a discount. By noon, not a single customer had come to our store.

"It's the winter," Ye Ye said. "Who comes through deep snow for turnips?"

But the truck with the snow plow had scraped a path wide enough for two cars to drive side by side down our street. And I had shovelled our walk and a path through the gate, so anyone could come without a lick of snow touching their boots. Our store was along the southern entrance to town—nobody driving north could miss us. In twenty minutes, eight cars and the empty milk delivery truck had driven by our store.

"It's the war," my mother said. When she said war, we all knew she meant what Willard Lascelles had said about all of us looking the same to the government, to our country.

"You'll see," Ye Ye said. "Customers will come. Mrs. Prior, at one o'clock. Mrs. Hearn, at three o'clock. Just like every Monday."

I'd packed small sacks of carrots, potatoes, beets, and four eggs from our chickens for each of Mrs. Prior and Mrs. Hearn. Ma Ma had added a little bag of rice and a little bottle of soy sauce to Mrs. Hearn's basket, because Mr. Hearn had taken to eating rice with his pork chop and apple.

At 1:30 p.m., Mrs. Prior still hadn't come and at 3:20

p.m. there was no sign of Mr. Hearn's blue Ford truck with Mrs. Hearn at the wheel.

"Maybe the snow truck didn't come to the other side of town," Ye Ye said. "Maybe there was an avalanche. Wiped out the whole town." He looked at the Monkey King, who was asleep in the rocking chair beside the wood stove. "Maybe Monkey King magic will bring back spring."

"I can walk to Mrs. Prior's," I said to my mother.

"It's dark soon."

"It's dark now."

I trudged along towards the turn for Third Street. It was cold enough that I could feel the dry, frigid air pinch in my nostrils and if I squeezed my eyes shut, I was pretty sure that any tears that I made would freeze. I walked for twenty minutes through the empty streets, passed darkened houses. I didn't know where everyone had gone. I was relieved to see Mr. Simes, the mailman, across the street. By now, he should have already delivered the mail to our store. I waved at him and called hello and his head jerked toward me and then away and in the next moment he vanished as if he'd fallen down a crevice and I heard a dog barking, angry and loud, and its voice coming and going as if it was running along a fence. "Mr. Simes?" I called.

Nothing.

I came to Mrs. Prior's white stucco house. All the lights were on and I could see Mrs. Prior in the living room at her piano with Lindy Thompson, a girl from my school, seated beside her. Lindy was trying to play scales and Mrs. Prior was singing *do re mi fa so* and before the *la*,

Lindy Thompson struck another "so" and Mrs. Prior sang "La, la, la," until Lindy plunked something closer to the right note.

I waited for the music to pause and knocked on the door. The scales started again and I waited for them to stop and, when they didn't, I knocked harder, because I wanted to go home and get warm again. The scales stumbled up, the scales stumbled down. Those awful sounds had eyes. Mrs. Prior loomed at the picture window wearing a print dress and the white apron she always wore when she taught piano lessons. She had on a cloche hat, which pressed her prematurely grey curls flat against her temples and made her wide round face look even rounder. I held up the basket of my mother's vegetables. The scales began again, like the slow and awkward totter of a drunk braving an icy street.

"Mrs., I have your vegetables," I said in a loud, unnatural voice. She was just on the other side of the thin, lead glass window, but she didn't hear me. I knocked on the glass. "Mrs., I have your vegetables." She stared right at the spot where I stood. She glanced down at the sack as if appraising a dismembered corpse. "Mrs.—"

"Lindy," she said over her shoulder, "that was excellent. Now start again. Do re mi fa so—"

"La," I sang the note true and on pitch as I'd done before every Wednesday after school when I went for my piano lesson with Mrs. Prior. Last Wednesday, I'd played Bach's "Prelude to the Well-Tempered Clavichord" about as well as I ever had and Mrs. Prior had clapped and said that I was ready for Debussy.

Lindy banged at the scales. The light in Mrs. Prior's

front room went out, but I could still see the dim outline of her against the far wall. I propped the sack of vegetables against her barred front door.

The light had begun to leave the world. I shivered and retreated up the front walk to the street. Mrs. Prior's front door banged open. I felt a sudden relief and swung around and smiled. Lindy was coming down the walk straight at me in her tall brown boots. She sang, "Do re mi. Do re mi fa. Do re. Mi fa. So," and as she came alongside me, she belted, "La."

"Mrs. says I'm playing so beautifully now, I can start on Bach. Mrs. says Debussy is after that. My father will be so happy when I can play Debussy. That's how he goes to sleep at night after the Great War. Listening to 'Claire de Lune.'" She pronounced Debussy "Day-boosie" and his song "Claire Day Loon." "My mother says Dad was soured by the Great War. Can't listen to anything louder than a bird. I can play Debussy soft as a down pillow. Do re mi. Do re. Mi. So."

"I have another delivery," I lied.

Lindy swung up her arm on the last "La." She had the sack of vegetables I'd left at the door for Mrs. Prior. The sack was in my hands before I knew what to do. "Mrs. doesn't want you to come by anymore."

"With vegetables?"

"With anything."

I cradled the sack in my arms and wandered out onto the darkening street. It had begun to snow, a light fluffy pall.

"Do re mi, can I have your desk at school?" asked

Lindy. "You won't need it anymore and I like being closer to Mrs. Green."

I don't remember how I got home. I was outside our clapboard fence and my hands were empty and, for a strange few seconds, I let myself think that I'd delivered the vegetables to Mrs. Prior instead of leaving them at a random door. That I'd see her on Wednesday after school for our hour-long lesson. That things would be like normal.

On the other side of our gate, I found our mail on the walk. Three of the envelopes had been torn to pieces. The last one, a letter addressed to my mother from her sister, had been sliced open. All that was left was the last page of a four-page letter. My mother's sister numbered all the onionskin pages and all I could read was her *with much love, Mei,* in her heavy Chinese script, because I couldn't read Chinese. I gathered up all the pieces of mail and stuffed them deep into the snowbank Ye Ye and I had made when we shovelled the walk.

"Was Mrs. Prior home?" Ma Ma called from the kitchen. I could smell our dinner, rice and fried vegetables with egg.

"Yes," I said. "She didn't want to come out in the snow."

"It must be the same with the post."

"Mr. Simes was nowhere at all."

"You have time to practice, before supper."

"My fingers are too cold."

"They'll warm up."

The Monkey King was seated on the piano bench with enough room for me to sit beside him.

He pressed the C key. The old upright piano sounded as beautiful and mournful as ever. The Monkey King had tuned it with the remains of his magic, as he did every time. I put my hands on the keys. Usually I would begin with scales, but the scales made me think of what had just happened with Mrs. Prior and Lindy. The cold in my fingers bled up my arms into my chest, plunged into my stomach. I pressed the C key, another key to my right. Sounds I didn't understand. I couldn't remember how Bach's Prelude began. I couldn't remember what the object in front of me was. Or what these cool, smooth things my fingers touched so lightly were. All the objects in my life suddenly had no name. Piano. Keys. Chair. Buddha. They were all gone. The government must've taken the names of things from us, so when it came time to steal them, we couldn't object. Next was our selves. When they took those, what would be left?

I was suddenly looking at my face instead of the piano music in front of me. My stupid smiling face and in the rims of my pupils the edges of my caustic little soul. Was that mine, too? Could I keep it, when the government came for us?

Ye Ye's sour face was beside mine with a weird smile on it as wide as his ears. His breath smelled like whiskey. "How does anyone say we are Japanese?" He was holding my mother's hand mirror before us. He angled it right, so it reflected just my face. "Tell everyone in mirror land we are Chinese. Prime Minister King will hear." He angled the mirror back to his own face. "I am Ye Ye. Born in Zhongshan, Guangdong province, China." He directed the mirror at the

Monkey King. "This is the Monkey King, Sun Wukong. He was born from a fat stone on Mount Huaguo, Jiiangsu province, China." My reflection appeared again in my mother's mirror. "Say your name, Edith. Where you were born."

My fists slapped down on the piano keys. The piano groaned in pain.

"This is my granddaughter, Edith," Ye Ye said. "Born in Cranbrook, British Columbia, Canada. See, mirror land, there are no Japanese here. All Chinese. All Canadian."

My mother's face appeared in the mirror behind ours. "Ye Ye is drunk again, mirror land," she said. "Forgive his insensitivity, Mr. Prime Minister." She took the mirror from him. "No customers today," she said. "Not one. Nobody. What did you do? Drink and play your little games!"

"Tomorrow there is no snow," Ye Ye insisted. "A whole store full of customers. They will buy everything, because of more rationing. You'll see. Monkey will cast a spell over everyone."

"What happens to Edith if we lose everything? If they send us back to China? This is her country."

My grandfather grabbed my mother's hand and pushed the mirror up to her face. "Look at that sour, round face. Your small eyes. Your flat nose. Not Japan, China. Nothing is going to happen to us."

My mother shook her head so fast and violently it was as if she was negating the universe. "What did Mr. Hearn say to me last week, when I gave him his vegetables and eggs? You're such a good little geisha. Me, Fang Lum born in Zhongshan with my small eyes and flat nose—a good little geisha? We need insurance, Ye Ye."

Ye Ye stared hard at my mother and then snapped at the Monkey King, "Write this down!" The Monkey King took all my grandfather's dictation, because Ye Ye could hardly read or write in English. He didn't wait for the Monkey King's pen and paper to appear from the thin air of monkey magic land. "Dear Prime Minister King. It's Ye Ye. I mean Ji Lum of Cranbrook, British Columbia. You writing this, Monkey? Mr. King, good Christmas to you and Happy New Year. I hope that the snow is not so deep like last year. Very important news. Lum family of Lum's General Store also called Happy Smiling Man General Store—we are all Chinese. Ji Lum, Fang Lum, Edith Lum, and Sun Wukong, also known as the Monkey King. We're all Chinese not Japanese. We love our Canada. Rocket Richard, Toe Blake, Turk Broda, we love all of them. We'll fight Hirohito until our last breaths. Yours sincerely, Ji Lum."

The finished letter hung in the air just above Ye Ye and my mother.

My grandfather pointed at it and said, "There is the Lum family's insurance," with such finality the matter seemed ended.

My mother said nothing. None of us said anything. One of our two oil lanterns sputtered. The room dimmed. A dog barked outside, loud and guttural. Someone yelled after the dog stopped, but I didn't know what. A call, a cry, an indictment maybe.

Something struck the window by the door. I thought it was a snowball, because sometimes the twin boys who lived nearby pelted our store with snowballs. But it struck heavier than snow, as if the boys had hardened their snowball in water for an hour or so. The glass on the window cracked and snapped as if a hot piece of metal was warping in frigid air. Something else struck the glass. Heavier than the first object. Uglier than the first object. The window pane popped onto the floor in two pieces and shattered. Half a piece of red brick came after the glass. It crashed against a pile of old gold pans and rolled against the door.

The Monkey King had his good arm raised in the air, his staff held half over head, his eyes closed and his lips pinching on words I didn't recognize. The air tingled with electric energy, shimmered before me as if I was watching the world through molten coloured glass. The piece of brick rolled backwards, flew through the air in a reverse of its initial trajectory and out the window. The broken glass pane reassembled in mid-air and sealed the window again and, for one breathless second, our store was as it was before the brick flew through the window. The dog barked. The yells of the men and women outside our store sounded like people having fun on a snowy evening. President Roosevelt had never said a word on the radio. Ye Ye was playing mahjong with the Monkey King for his gold nugget. Pearl Harbor slept.

The Monkey King gurgled and fell back on his piano stool, exhausted. His spell shattered into a million pieces. The dog barked and the brick smashed through the window again and every ugly word in the world hurtled in after it. As if the air wasn't just oxygen, and nitrogen and carbon dioxide anymore, but a swarm of slurs seeking to rend coloured skin from flesh. *Jap. Nip. Slope.* They were in our ears first and then our hearts and then the cold pits of our stomachs. They were in our futures. *Go home.*

Ma Ma shot out the door into the frozen night with our broom. I sweated cold from every pore as the barks and shouts grew louder and louder. I counted to a hundred in Chinese and backwards to one in English. I asked Ye Ye when she'd come back. I should go find her. He should go find her. Couldn't the Monkey King cast another spell?

"Ma Ma," I whispered, "come back."

I LAY in bed for three hours until the exhausted apparition my mother had become in her spent fury slipped in beside me. She felt cold against me, even through my bedclothes, and I hugged her and stroked the hair on her neck. "They hit the Chius' and the Shens'," she said. "And the Yoshidas'."

I sat up. "Is Miyuki alright?"

"I don't know. The bricks have stopped."

"The police—"

"Won't come."

"They have to."

"They never have to."

WE WOKE to the sound of a chair crashing to the floor and slaps and punches.

"Give it to me!" Ye Ye shouted. "You greedy chimp!"

Ye Ye and the Monkey King rolled back and forth on the floor, each on top of the other for the briefest moments. Ye Ye's arm snatched out to tear the little pouch that held the Monkey King's gold nugget. "Give!" he yelled again. And then the Monkey King slapped him with his good arm and snarled dust and fur at him. "We need insurance," said Ye Ye. "You're too weak."

The Monkey King set his eyes on my grandfather and rasped something guttural and ugly and Ye Ye turned into a giant pock-marked frog and then in the next second something that looked like a rotten mound of maple leaves. Ye Ye's fist tore through the leaves and grasped at the Monkey King's throat. "You can't even stop bricks. Give us your gold. Go back to heaven."

The Monkey King creaked to his feet and fell into one of the chairs at our table. My grandfather's legs were still slimy and webbed at the feet liked an amphibian's. He pulled himself up onto the chair across from the Monkey King, because he couldn't make his lower half work.

"I found Monkey in the Klondike," Ye Ye said. "You know where? In a whore house. The famous Monkey King was a coat rack in Madame's parlour. Under lady's dirty underwear." He croaked up something awful and spat into the copper pot by the table and said, "I carried him for many, many weeks. On my back like a little boy. Over the Chilkoot Pass. So high, the Chilkoot Pass. Then through swamps and rivers. Up so many high mountains, until we find help."

The Monkey King held the pouch of gold tight against his breast.

Ye Ye shook his head. The two friends had been partners on the same gold claim on the Wild Horse River. They sluiced mounds of river gravel, each day, every day. One morning, Ye Ye spotted that gold nugget gleaming in the sluice. "Then my hand became a frog's hand," he said, "A useless frog's hand. I can hold nothing, not even a pebble. Monkey grabbed my nugget." Ye Ye's eyes reddened from the salt of old tears. "You keep that gold and we go to prison with Yoshida!"

In all my twelve years, I'd never heard my grandfather speak this way. The old ape shrugged. He pulled the mahjong tiles from the rosewood box my grandfather kept them in and began to build the wall for the next game.

"Ji Lum doesn't play with you anymore," Ye Ye said. "We'll sell Lum family store for insurance."

"No," Ma Ma said. "It's all we have. It's all Edith will have."

"Last night, those dogs outside our house called us Japs. Threw bricks. The government is coming."

"Then play him."

"You say every day to Edith, Ye Ye always loses. Ye Ye will never beat the Monkey King. Now you want me to play?"

"Play for something you don't want to lose. Put up your life like you put up my husband's."

My grandfather stared at my mother as if she'd hit him across the jaw. She was the wife of Ye Ye's son, my father, and before he died from tuberculosis she'd hated that Ye Ye lived with us. It was a quiet, reticent hatred. The hate of a little morning smile as she placed Ye Ye's congee before him. Only when he'd wiped his face on the sleeve of the white shirt she'd just laundered for him as he left for our fields, only then did she hurl her whispered words at my father. Ye Ye was a pig and she didn't want me growing up to imitate him—he and his ugly ape should leave, die for all she cared. That very year, Ye Ye and my father had caught tuberculosis at the same time, lay in the same bed side by side like little broken gods, father and son swimming the same feverish ocean, coughing up bloody drops of foam into the waves that broke over them in a death dream that had no end. They clung to each other so tightly that the undertaker couldn't have pried them apart with a steel bar. They were one and the same man suffering the same deadly disease that knew no vaccine until years later and the Monkey King's magic had saved only one of them.

"It should've been you who died," Ma Ma said.

My grandfather's wheezing exhale was the exhale of the universe before it atomized into nothingness. His eyes searched the room until they landed on our laughing little Buddha. He coughed. He coughed and choked and leaned forward and said to the Monkey King, "The soul of Ye Ye for your gold?"

"I'll play," I said. "And you, too, Ma Ma, then we have better odds. One of us has to win."

My mother shook her head. No one had ever beaten the Monkey King at mahjong.

I sat down in the empty chair between the Monkey King and Ye Ye, the one reserved for the Jade Rabbit. I pointed at the last empty chair. "Ma Ma," I said.

"It's cruel," she said.

"It?"

"Him." She nodded her head at the Monkey King. "What does a little god need gold for?"

"The Qing Fish Demon," Ye Ye said. "Put very bad magic on him."

My mother's eyes rolled.

I rolled the dice to see who the dealer would be—a three. I passed it to the Monkey King, who rolled a five. Ye Ye, of course, rolled a one.

I held the dice out for my mother. "We'll get his gold," I said. "We can buy the insurance."

Ma Ma's head shook back and forth. She stared at the Monkey King with such contempt that I expected her to leap at him, to punch him. When he wouldn't lift his gaze to meet hers, she stared at Ye Ye. "If we lose—"

"We're going to win," I said, in the most confident voice I could fake. The voice I used in school, when I pretended to know the answer to a social studies question.

My mother took the dice and rolled. Six. A good beginning. A good omen.

"You're the east wind," I said. "You go first."

We shuffled the tiles in the centre of the table around and around, as if our hands and the tiles had been caught in a shallow whirlpool. Our hands brushed each other's for only the briefest instant to continue the shuffling. We built the wall: stacks of eighteen tiles, two tiles high in front of each of us. We chose tiles until we had twelve each. None of us looked at each other.

"Where did you learn to play mahjong?" I asked my mother.

My mother chose a tile from the wall, held it slightly from her and placed it with the rest of her hand. She discarded another tile, the three of bamboo. "You know it was from Po Po."

Po Po, my mother's mother. I'd never met her. She'd died five years ago and when I asked about her, my mother described her club foot and her fierce tongue and how she wrung the necks of chickens when they asked too many questions. I, by my mother's reckoning, was a little chicken with a long neck.

Ye Ye lit a cigarette and took a tile and compared it to his hand and finally laid it down in the discard pile. The six of circles.

I picked up a tile from the wall. The four of characters. I hadn't looked at my hand—there was little point. We weren't going to win. My mother was indulging me before our inevitable loss to the little monkey god of mahjong. He cheated, for all I knew, with the remains of his old magic. My hand—a crazy mix of circles and bamboos and characters—I saw as meaningless red and green and blue swirls. I didn't care.

The Monkey King struck a match and sucked on his long bone pipe and the room filled with a cloud of sweet, acrid smoke. He picked up the tile I'd discarded. I didn't care.

The copper kettle whistled from the stove. "Anyone want tea?" I asked.

"Kong," the Monkey King said and laid down four identically suited character tiles with the last tile being the one I'd just discarded.

Ye Ye and Ma Ma stared at me and then each other and their shoulders sank into their chests. The whistling kettle sounded like a bomb about to land on our store. I went into the little kitchen behind the front counter, added the jasmine leaves to our teapot, and lifted the heavy cast iron kettle from the stove. I poured the water over the dried leaves and dumped the rest of the water into the sink.

On a wooden tray, I carried the teapot and four little clay cups to the table. Ye Ye and Ma Ma looked resigned and grim. As for the Monkey King, he and his sleepy, gloating eyes shifted from the discard pile to his hand of eight standing tiles and back to the Kong he'd just laid down. His eyes narrowed, bored into Ma Ma's hands, as if willing them to move. "Go," he said.

"So you can win even earlier?" Ma Ma shook her head. "Tea, Edith, so I can throw it in Monkey's face."

I poured the tea for everyone and placed the cups in front of them and went to pour my own. "I didn't add enough water."

The Monkey King took my hand, gestured I should sit, play.

"It's one minute."

Ma Ma's voice followed me into the kitchen. "At least change Ye Ye's legs back, so he can walk into prison."

I picked up the heavy kettle, all the lighter because I'd poured the water out. I didn't breathe as I walked back to the table.

"His magic is so powerful," Ye Ye said. "Once the game is over, he'll change me back. Right? No hard feelings? No grudges like before? Ye Ye and the Monkey King, friends for all time."

Ma Ma snorted. "Powerful magic? He used to defeat

celestial armies and now he cheats at mahjong. Such friends are—"

"Cheat? The Monkey King? Ha!"

"You didn't lose 15,000 times because you're so terrible and he's so good. I've watched him, Ye Ye. I've watched the symbols on his tiles change to the ones he needs. Every game."

"Very funny. The Monkey King is my honest friend." He looked at the old ape with all the credulity of a little boy. "Right? See, he's nodding?"

"Old fool." Ma Ma looked right at the Monkey King. "You can cheat him for a thousand lifetimes, but never me."

I stood behind the Monkey King with the kettle, raised it up overhead as if inspecting the bottom for a leak.

"Edith, sit down," Ma Ma said. "Let's finish this, before the customers come."

I nodded. I smiled. I brought the kettle down with all the force I had in my twelve-year-old arms on the back of the Monkey King's head. The kettle gonged as if it had hit a rock and my arms vibrated up to my shoulders and the Monkey King turned and looked back at me and instantly the kettle turned into a chicken and I brought it down to hit him again and it was a kettle again and the second strike knocked him off his chair and he tried to crawl away but his arms stopped and his legs soon after and I didn't hold a kettle but a handful full of black feathers.

"Do you see him, Edith?" Ma Ma asked. "He said he'd come before dark."

I peered through the window up our walk. Nothing. It was only four o'clock and already the sun had set and the shadow the mountains cast over us was darkening, cooling.

"What if he doesn't come?"

Ye Ye's face appeared outside the window. The spell the Monkey King had cast on him to change him into a frog had worn off and his legs were his own again.

"How is he?" I asked. Ye Ye came inside. I'd worried from the minute I'd hit the Monkey King that I'd killed him. He hadn't breathed for minutes afterwards.

"Very comfortable with the vegetables," Ye Ye said. "Very sleepy still."

"Did you add wood to the stove?" Our little glass greenhouse, where Ye Ye grew tomatoes and peppers in the winter, froze unless the wood stove was kept stoked.

Ye Ye nodded. "Very, very warm. Warmer than here."

We'd nailed thick burlap sacks over our broken window, but still the cold seeped in.

"If he doesn't come, what should we do?" Ma Ma asked. She cupped the Monkey King's pouch of gold in her hands and blew on it as if it was a spark that might not become fire.

"I talked to Mary Lapointe, you remember Ms. Mary Lapointe?" Ye Ye said. "She guides hunters into those Rocky Mountains. Her father has an old shack on that St. Mary River. Very comfortable. Very far away from every-one. She lived there for so many years."

"You want Edith to live in the bush?"

"You want her to go with Japanese to prison?"

"Tell me he's coming, Edith."

I went outside. The snow had begun to fall again, dry, granular flakes, like pieces of white sand. There was no one coming up the walk, no cars on the street. Nothing moving. It would be dark soon, colder. Willard Lascelles said he'd head up to Kimberly to sell insurance to families there. Why would he forget us?

I listened, like I had when I'd first met him. I listened for the snow falling off the pines across the street. Tick, tick, tick. It was the snow falling. No, it was heavier than that. It was something moving. Running as fast as it could on the dry, crusted snow. Panting now, like an old bellows. Then nothing. I strained to hear it again. I willed it to come into our yard.

Two large black paws grabbed the picket fence so hard that the fence leaned towards the street. The massive head and eyes that belonged to those paws sized up our yard, the store. The heat of its breath blurred the silver dollar moon. I was standing in the shadows of our eaves and I got the feeling that the dog hadn't seen me, couldn't see me. It hopped down and paced back and forth in front of our gate.

"Mr. Lascelles," I whispered, "should I let you in?"

I couldn't make my feet move towards the gate. I couldn't.

The beast scratched at the gate handle and whined.

"Hop over," I said, a little louder. "Like you did before."

The dog peered at me through the pickets, whined again.

"Hop over, okay?" As soon as I'd said it, I knew the dog couldn't do it. Its paws went up on the gate again, but it couldn't jump. I stepped forward. I went forward in slow little steps until I was face to face with the dog.

The animal spun around and instantly I saw why it couldn't leap. There was something stuck in its flank like a screwdriver. It had a u-shaped bevelled blade, like the gouges Miyuki Yoshida's father used to carve the best burls that came through his sawmill.

I opened the gate and the dog lumbered forward past me and disappeared around the side of our house. I sucked in the cold night air. I ran after it and in the lozenge of ochre light cast by the kitchen window stood Willard Lascelles. He threw something away into the dark and it struck the outhouse door with a hollow thump.

"If it isn't my friend Edith," he said. There was a catch in his smooth baritone. "Were you waiting for me? Your mother certainly is and maybe even that grandfather of yours."

Ma Ma half rose when Willard Lascelles limped into the room. She held up the gold nugget from the Monkey King's pouch. "Ten ounces at thirty-five dollars an ounce. $350."

Willard Lascelles smiled, as if he'd heard a joke none of us could understand. "Looks like someone broke your window. That must cost a pretty penny to repair."

"I'll cut glass from the greenhouse," said Ye Ye. "Nice patch job until spring."

"It does take away a little from the value of the store, don't you think? The real estate folks call it curb appeal. A general store no one will buy anything in with a broken window. Maybe more windows get broken over the coming days. Maybe there's a fire in one of your outbuildings."

"The insurance," Ma Ma said.

"Do you understand supply and demand, Mrs. Lum? Of course you do. You're a businesswoman. You see, my insurance sales have been so brisk in this town that my company has had to raise our prices." He grabbed his hip and his face twisted in pain for the bricfcst instant and then he composed himself as if an invisible doctor had injected him with morphine.

"We have nothing."

"You have this fine store. The land on which it sits." Papers appeared from the inside of his coat. There was a smear of blood on one corner of the first paper and then, like Willard Lascelles's earlier pain, it too disappeared. "One thousand dollars with your generous deposit of the gold—let's say $350—leaves a grand total of $650. I reckon that's about a fifty per cent share in your household."

Ma Ma's eyes narrowed. "We're worth $3,000."

"You were worth $3,000 until Hirohito bombed Pearl Harbor." He smacked the table with his hand and made a noise like an exploding bomb. "The sad truth, Mrs. Lum, is that all over Canada, the price of property owned by Orientals has plummeted. It's unfair. It's worrisome. It's downright immoral. And it's reality." He pushed the papers over to Ma Ma. "I'll need your signature on page one and your signature and initials on page two. I can be your witness."

Ma Ma looked down at the papers and then at Ye Ye.

They both looked at me as if to say that they were doing this for my sake. My future. Fifty per cent of Lum's General Store. I didn't care. I wanted Miyuki Yoshida and I to move to—I struggled to think of a city where we'd be safe. Mexico City. It was warm and took foreigners. I almost laughed. There'd be no places to skate.

"Use my pen," said Willard Lascelles.

Ma Ma's fist was closed.

"It's ugly, Mrs. Lum, but it's the only way to keep what you have."

She took the pen. Removed the cap. Jabbed her finger to the nib.

She looked at the papers as if they were a bad hand in mahjong. She looked around the store that had been her home for twenty years. Where her husband had stood beside the piano and smoked his pipe, where I had lain as a newborn in a grocery crate, where Ye Ye and the Monkey King had fought over mahjong each morning. Her precious, magnificent store.

"Mrs. Lum, you're hesitant. You're afraid. You're wondering if my company can, in fact, protect you. I assure you we can. If it will help, I'll lower the percentage to 40. As a sign of good faith."

Ma Ma shook her head.

"The government will take your property and you'll have nothing for my friend Edith."

She pushed the papers back. She held the Monkey King's gold.

"We've lived through indignity after indignity to be here," Ma Ma said. "We can live through the rest."

A look of pain came across Willard Lascelles's face. He

went to say something and thought better of it. His jaw hung clicked shut. He lurched to his feet and grabbed at his hip. "Mrs. Lum."

But my mother was unmovable.

"Mrs. Lum."

The papers vanished into Willard Lascelles's heavy wool coat. "Good luck to you all."

I looked at Ma Ma and Ye Ye. "What about Miyuki?" I cried. "Won't you . . ."

Ma Ma beckoned me to come to her, but I refused. The door slammed behind me as I ran outside with tears freezing to my cheeks. "Mr. Lascelles!" I cried. I peered into the frozen night for the insurance salesman. I ran out onto the walk past our fence but already his tracks were filling with fresh snow. "Mr. Lascelles!"

I rushed back to the greenhouse where Ye Ye had bound the Monkey King in heavy manila rope. His eyes were shut and he looked worse than ever as if the tightness of the rope had squeezed more ugliness from his pores.

"You have to help me," I said. His eyes didn't even open and his breathing came in little rasps. I began to sob. "I want to be with Miyuki. Forever."

I loosened the ropes and let them fall to the floor. "I'll get the gold back. I'll bathe you like you always liked. I'll keep the water hot for hours. I'll—"

His eyes opened, found me, my tears. His hand grasped for mine. Squeezed my palm. Held me so tight I was on the verge of crying out.

I closed my eyes.

I felt cold on my face. His grip loosened, softened and

fell away. The hand that took mine felt lighter, softer, younger.

"Look," said a voice I knew and loved so well. It was Miyuki Yoshida.

We were on a small frozen pond, arm in arm, on Miyuki's skates. I was on the left one and she the right. We pumped with the skates and glided in a short arc.

"Where are we?"

"Internment," she said. "Prison. In New Denver. You never remember."

Around us were rows of small houses, each one identical to the other and in the distance a high wire fence to keep us all in until the war ended. Dogs circled and barked from the perimeter.

"And Ma Ma and Ye Ye?"

"At the store, like always."

And the Monkey King? I wanted to ask.

My skate caught a knob of ice and as I fell, Miyuki caught me in her arms.

Simon Wiesenthal, my *mensch*, my *yiddisher kop*, my *groysemakher*, let me tell you about Operation Gehenna. At least that's what Eva called our little Nazi hunting expedition of 1964. Eva read Hannah Arendt's book about the Eichmann trial and then your book about chasing Eichmann and that same July she read out her rejection letter from the FBI in this pinched voice I'd never heard before. Eva was the toughest sweetheart I ever had, but J. Edgar Hoover, well that *goy* was unrelenting. In Hoover's Bureau, no woman would ever be a special agent. *Miss Einhorn, you can best apply your natural proficiencies*, said the letter, *to an entry level position in our human resources department.* I thought that was it—the end of Eva's leaving, thank you, God. I'd wait a week for her to emerge from her tiny apartment and then I'd make the proposal I'd been rehearsing all May. I had Bubbe's engagement ring in my coat pocket, I had Coltrane ready to rock on my portable Motorola, I had my tensor bandage for my trick knee when I knelt down and asked, "Eva Einhorn, will you?"

Eva's whole life at the University of Washington had been the FBI. She went out for psychology and her undergraduate thesis was on the geographic something something of arsons in Seattle. She ran six miles a day and heaved her five foot, one-hundred-pound body up the chinning bar I attached to her bedroom door twenty times in a row, and on Saturdays she shot her father's .38 revolver at the Tacoma Rifle and Revolver Club. Eva pulled and pulled on that trigger and I lay on the bench behind her with my head beside my Motorola and listened to Chet Baker shoot at life out of a trumpet and never miss. Eva, Chet's trumpet, gun powder, that was my Saturday afternoons. I loved when it rained, too, the pitter-patter on the tin roof between shots, the clink-clink of the ejected shells on the little table when she reloaded. Sundays, Eva read the stoics—Epictetus, Aurelius, Seneca—to harden her soul to every ugliness life could throw at her. "If a schlemiel like my asthmatic brother can be FBI," she said. "I can be FBI." Her brother, for God's sake, loved Pat Boone.

After the FBI letter arrived, I counted out six of my nights without sleep, without Eva. I went around to her apartment when Mrs. Roman, her landlady, would be out playing bridge. I buzzed. I knocked. I cried out. Nothing. She didn't answer, her windows were dark. I slipped a note under her door: *Petunia, it's me, Ira, call, okay? It's 6 o'clock and I miss your kisses. Forget about Hoover—he's a goyim sexist prick. XOXO.* I called round her parents place over in Cherry Hill—Eva hadn't phoned all week. I called Rabbi

Levine over at the Temple de Hirsch. Had Eva come by for synagogue? Another three days went by and Levine phones me up and says Eva just left the synagogue's library —she wanted to look up something about the Holocaust. He didn't know where she was headed with her brain full of special-agent ideas.

The lights were still out in her apartment when I went back around at 9 p.m. I'm no Spider-Man, but I rowed for the Huskies all through university and my day job at the record store hadn't exactly sapped my strength. I climbed up eight feet off her fire escape and crawled through her kitchen window into a forest of dead geraniums and a sink full of coffee cups. Her living room was a mess of books and photostats and mimeographs and notes handwritten in her tiny serial-killer script. She'd been at the University of Washington library and the Seattle Public Library and the home office of the Seattle Swiss Society and called long distance to the Department of Citizenship and Immigration in Ottawa, Canada, and to somewhere else in deepest, darkest Berlin—she'd sent telegrams. She had her brown Samsonite packed on her bed, containing, of all things, her father's other pistol: his .25 FN Baby Browning with the three bullets still in the magazine. Pinned to the bedroom wall above her cot, Simon Wiesenthal, was your black and white photo. You were still handsome at forty: with your high forehead and thin, neat black hair and your little trimmed moustache and your eyebrows knit together only a little bit now, because some of your intensity had found its way into my Eva. Maybe even at night.

"Fuck, I hate Pat Boone," I hissed into the empty apartment. "What white guy covers 'Tutti Frutti'?"

I waited. I cleaned her dishes and put her dead geraniums out on the fire escape. I made spaghetti with olive oil, garlic, and parmesan. I tuned in the radio to Wolfman Jack and howled along with him and announced J.B. Lenoir's "I Sing Um the Way I Feel" in my bass warble. I awoke in a sweaty mess on Eva's bed and the same J.B. Lenoir song was playing again on the radio and I thought I'd been asleep for maybe thirty seconds, but it was dark and I heard Eva's key in the lock and then her slender silhouette appeared in the doorway. She cast her skeletal shadow right up to my bare feet.

"Made spaghetti," I said.

"No time for that," she said. "I'm going on the late bus."

"Going where?"

"Canada."

"You joining the Canadian FBI or something?"

"I had it with the FBI. They hate women—I hate them."

"Look, the pasta's the best I make. With garlic and olive oil. Just eat, okay?"

She vanished from the bedroom doorway. I found her cramming papers into her Samsonite. I held out the plate of spaghetti for her. "Kept it warm."

"I found a Nazi, Ira. Living right under our noses. Well, under Canadian noses. I'm catching him."

Her dad's Baby Browning disappeared under a pile of her underwear. The Samsonite smacked shut and she snapped the two locks. If I dropped to one knee, my bubbe's ring in one hand and the plate of spaghetti in the other, I knew she'd take neither.

"I always liked Canada," I said. I didn't know anything about Canada. I knew there'd be snow and mostly goyim west of Montreal and giant bears. "I got my passport at my parents' house."

"You know a thing about hunting Nazis?"

"Went duck hunting once out near Spokane. You sit and you wait and you shoot."

Eva's lips bent up into the little relaxed smile she wore when she was about to relent. If I couldn't propose to her right then I could travel with her to wherever Canada. Canada wouldn't be such a bad place to propose. Some of my favourite *prozaikers*—Twain, Hemingway, Trotsky—all of them had found in Canada the delirious beauty of a border world between peaks and sky. So why not Ira Wollman with his portable Motorola and his almost fiancée by his side? I leaned in to hug Eva, but her hands stayed glued against her hips and I pretty much wrapped myself around a telephone pole.

"Duck hunting—that's pretty funny, Ira," she whispered in my ear. "Almost as funny as those Nazis killing your aunt and her two girls at Ravensbrück. You forget about that, Ira? Over there in your record store listening to Chet Baker?"

I'D ONCE READ that Twain and Hemingway took the train to Cranbrook, British Columbia. The stylish, coal-eating, smoke-chugging train that built a frozen nation. As for the great Nazi hunting team of Eva Einhorn and Ira Wollman, we made our grand entrance on the Greyhound

—the dog bus, as this Chinese woman behind us called it. She was a hell of a lot more conversant than Eva was, bent over her sack of secret Nazi papers. This woman had to help her mother close up the family store, because her arthritis had got too bad, and she planned to move the old woman down to Vancouver. "She'll hate it," she said to me. "She's never known anywhere else."

Come early morning of dog bus day two, I was dreaming of the aunt and the cousins I knew only by a few torn family photos from the 1930s, when they lived near Lake Konstanz in Germany. My mother wrote my aunt in early '38 and said you've got to get out and my aunt wrote back that her life was with Ewald, her husband who made pews, pulpits, and communion tables for the Catholics, even Pius XI's Vatican. *Hitler won't last another year. We're coming to our senses.* But that was twenty-four years ago, I said to my dream. What the hell can I do about it now? Arrest all the dream Nazis? The voice of the woman in the seat behind us slipped into my dream. "Welcome to Cranbrook," she said with more excitement than a dry, tree-lined valley and a few old brick buildings could possibly deserve. "A big German town."

The cold summer morning smelled of clover and pine and wood smoke. A little wind blew newspapers and pulverized horse shit all over the bench outside the station. Glass from a broken pop bottle crunched under my shoes.

"Thought all the Nazis went to South America," I said to Eva.

"Hunters—that's what we call our mark from now on —a *hunter*. His name is Julius Kindler. That's not his real name, of course. He was born Reinhold Strauch. And we're not who we are either. We're Eva and Ira Smithstein and we're on our honeymoon. Put these on." She put a wedding band on her ring finger and gave me its twin. Invisible hands squeezed my throat. We had to be someone else to be married, to have a honeymoon. The smoke I smelled wasn't from the fire of *us*.

I couldn't let go of Eva's arm as we walked across the railway tracks and then down the main street of fading storefronts looking for the Mount Baker Hotel. The smoke, I overheard a woman in a white sun hat say, was from a forest fire out near Wasa Lake. Her husband's logging company had to close down operations and he was at home on the porch drinking homemade ginger beer and whittling pieces of birch into splinters, until the rains came. And then, after the tiniest pause, she added this startling phrase: "and filled up them graves." Graves? I wanted to ask her. Out at Wasa Lake Ranch, she went on, Dave Penner lost himself twenty-two head of cattle to the fire and dug a six-foot-deep grave for each and every one with his backhoe. After my twenty-four years on this planet, I knew how my brain worked. I could already feel the dream coming on. I'd dream about those dead animals and already I was telling myself that it didn't matter. They were just cows and so what anyway? Chet Baker cancelled out every evil with the meanest trumpet around.

The sweating man at the hotel desk showed Eva and me to our dim room on the second floor with a view of a red brick building that could be an old theatre. The wood on our floor was dimpled and scuffed like an old dance floor and the desk, antique dresser, and end tables looked turn-of-the-century ancient. Eva stuffed the Baby

Browning with its three bullets into her purse. I didn't let her see me smile. Yes sirree, by my bubbe's engagement ring, there was one bed, a queen, a good-old fashioned married couple's queen. It was easily as wide as Eva's cot and the single bed I still had at my parents put together. We were pretend-married, but that was good enough for now. I set up my Motorola on the dresser and realized in my rush out of Seattle that I'd grabbed exactly one LP— Jorge Ben's *Samba Esquema Novo*. I had no Mingus, Brubeck, Coltrane, Cannonball, Blakey, Evans, Getz, or Davis. I had no Chet. I had nothing. I had less than nothing. I turned on the radio and the only station was something called the CBC. Wolfman Jack didn't howl from the depths of the CBC. They played a lot of Glenn Gould. I was Nazi hunting to the Goldberg Variations.

"So, Mrs. Ira Smithstein,"—I let that one linger on my drying lips—"how do we find this Julius Kindler? This,"— I snapped my fingers in time to Jorge Ben, wrapped my arms around Eva's back and kissed the nape of her neck— "this Dybbuk of Cranbrook?"

JOHANNA, *liebchen*, it's a warm summer night and I am in my study with a new plaster cast of the creature. I can see the orange glow of the beehive burner at the northern end of town, as if a reclining giant is dragging on his cigar. These beehive burners, as they are known here, are large conical steel structures about forty feet high, which the Crestbrook Mill uses to burn wood waste and sawdust. Our valley smells of burning ash many nights and days, but after so many years here I hardly notice the smoke at all. Last winter, there was a tragedy (did I tell you?). One of the locals, an old man of eighty, crawled inside the burner (the fire was low) to stay warm and fell asleep and, in the morning, when the conveyer belt brought in another load of sawdust—but I am being morbid, Johanna. I should tell you of the perfume of the alfalfa in the local fields. Such sweetness every summer! Like the scent of your lavender soap on your skin. I kept the bar you gave me at the Hauptbahnhof in Berlin. I have it in my desk wrapped in a piece of crinoline and when I hold it against my nose, I remember our lovemaking by the castle in Gottlieben.

This is the first cast of the creature I have made in many years, for I started to lose faith that it would ever be found. How many local hunters have dragged me into the bush and showed me a track of what was so obviously the paw print of a grizzly bear and said, "Julius, it's the ape! I heard him cry out last night!" Two days ago, a woman called Molly Sickert rang me from a gas station in the town of Kimberly. "Julius, you must come," she said, "I've found a track by the St. Mary River." If it was not in my nature to bring her food or kerosene or bullets, I would never have bothered with her story. The creature had never been spotted east of Creston. Still, I drove with Michael, my youngest, in my truck to her cabin up the west fork of the St. Mary River to the lakeside where she lives alone. Molly Sickert is what they call here a home-steader. I cannot remember if there is a German word for such a person, for it is a very North American phenomenon. She cannot abide in even the smallest town, so she took what money she earned in her divorce from her philandering physician husband and bought five acres of lakeside property and built with her own adze and axe her log cabin. Her nearest neighbour is three miles away and she reads by the light of a kerosene lantern—she has no electricity.

The first time I went to her cabin was when her ex-husband asked me to deliver a mountain of staples (flour, oil, salt, sugar, bacon, and tobacco) when I next took a client out that way to hunt bighorn sheep. Dr. Sickert had delivered my three children and knew that I guided hunters in the mountains beyond Molly's home and in his joking heart, which saw past my congenial surfaces, he knew by intuition my secret, for he mocked my German accent and called me "Herr SS." He said nothing more of my past or I might have had to invite him along on a hunting trip with their myriad possibilities for accidents. Maybe his heart knew this, too.

Molly Sickert stood at the makeshift gate to her property with her ever-present ski pole in one hand and her .22 Winchester flung over her opposite shoulder in case she came across a grouse for supper. She wore a black beret and her reading glasses low down on her nose as if she'd just come from a Paris book stall after a glass of Bordeaux. "I've been reading *The Quiet American*," she said, "and wondered what you would've done in French Indochina to fight the Vietnamese." The answer, even after all the defeats caused by the betrayals of our allies, was to replace the French forces with SS divisions—intelligence and savagery under the death's head banner. But I could never utter the loyalties that remained in my heart. I pushed

Michael's long blond hair from his eyes and said, "Diplomacy. The only humane option."

"That would've made for a boring novel."

"Isn't that where we Canadians live best? In a boring novel? Think of how things were before you moved to your cabin."

I miss the man I was before I was sent here, the twenty-seven-year-old untersturmführer in the SS who had lunches with Himmler and the zoologist Ernest Schäfer in Prinz-Albert-Strasse 8. We talked of the physical evidence that the Aryan race had originated in the mountains of Tibet. Schäfer saw it—*it*, that great, physiological dilution of the gods—in the eyes, noses, and foreheads of the Tibetan nobles. Twice Himmler sent him to Tibet to find our god ancestors and twice he returned with only partial evidence. But you know this, Johanna. I am repeating myself. I am an exciting chapter in a boring novel. Where is the chapter when you and I touch again?

Michael and I followed Molly Sickert for two miles up a gently sloping trail through a thick forest of pine and larch. It was a narrow game trail that the deer and elk use to travel, for the soft, dark soil was trampled down with hoof prints, narrow and wide and an inch or so deep. After the first mile, Michael said that he didn't feel well, his spine crept with tingling cold. "Papa, something is watching us." The forest bled the silence and the stillness that presages death.

"Molly has her rifle," I said, because all I had was my rucksack of plaster, a steel bowl, some water, and a small trowel. "Papa has his knife."

What was beyond a doubt, Johanna, was that the creature was here. I could feel it as I felt it in 1939 on the outskirts of the Chehalis Indian lands before I came across its tracks, two footprints so fresh that they almost steamed in the rain. I felt that coldness in my limbs, the frigid tingle along the nape of my neck, the sense you are not only being watched but your heart scried by some living thing. An equal or maybe even a superior. It was Himmler who'd sent me here in search of our ancient superiors and what had I found so far but tracks and legends?

The forest broke open before a steep, sunlit hillock of huckleberry bushes.

"Yesterday, I was picking berries," said Molly. And then, almost as if she had to justify being there alone, she added, "To eat, yes, but to dye the wool I bartered from Jenny Fastabend."

A few steps toward the hillock lay her handmade canvas bucket, several cups of berries scattered on the dusty ground, a few random ones crushed.

"I want to go," said Michael.

His little hand was on his groin and I said, "Then go behind that stump."

"Home. Papa, it smells."

Badly. Like rotten flesh. Like it did on the Chehalis in 1939.

"I smelled it first," said Molly Sickert. "Grizzly, I thought. You know how they like to roll in carrion. But…"

I walked three body lengths past the bucket. Path. Hillock. Tree line. Behind me, the forest we'd come from. Michael with tears wetting his red-checked shirt. Molly with her Winchester tight in her hands. A million flies suddenly aloft as if they'd been born from the very ground we stood on.

"I saw the print and the bushes rustled in front of me and I just started shooting. Crack, crack, crack. Whole fucking magazine." She exhaled old tobacco smoke.

"Molly, where's Bella?"

"The thing was right there in front of me. In the bushes. Watching me. Goddamn, I got scared, Julius."

"Where's the dog?"

The first print was about thirteen inches long, the big toe splayed outward, like the prints I'd found on the Chehalis. The creature would have been facing Molly Sickert when she dropped the bucket and started shooting.

"Papa?"

"Count to one hundred," I said. "You know how counting makes you happy. *Ein, zwei, drei, vier—*"

I almost called Bella, because the white Siberian looked stretched out in mid-run. The animal had leapt into the huckleberry bushes and there it hung two feet above the ground with a blood-crusted hole where its right eye had been. Molly Sickert's bullet had gone in under its right ear when the dog leapt at the creature.

The second print, a few feet farther up the trail, was a hundred and eighty degrees rotated from the first as if the creature had spun in the air to run up the trail. Dried spots of blood led away up the trail. The creature was wounded. The gods, Johanna, could bleed.

I HUNG UP THE PHONE. "Said he'd pick us up tomorrow morning at 4:30 a.m. Best time to see game. Sounded awfully sweet for a Sha-Na-Na-Nazi."

Eva leapt off me, naked and sweaty, pungent like you wouldn't believe. "You and Hoover and all the rest—just have to be so condescending. He's a Nazi, Ira, a full-blooded SS lieutenant."

"I'm just saying, if you're going to shoot the guy, you'd better be sure you got the right one. Come back, OK?"

Eva wrapped herself in her light green bathrobe, cinched the belt so tight it'd take me hours to undo it. "You know what he did, this smart Nazi?" She tore through her stack of papers and dropped a newspaper clipping on my cooling lap. "He put ads in the *Thurgauer Zeitung. I am seeking contact with Johanna Vogel, born 1912, resident of Lake Konstanz, 1934–1939. Please reply care of this newspaper.* That was dated six months ago. You see? He thinks his sweetie escaped back into Switzerland, where her family lives in Thurgau. So, I sweet-talked the paper until I got his name."

"I just can't picture shooting someone. Even a Nazi."

"Even a Nazi that killed your aunt? Your little cousins? How old were they? Six and four. Gassed in Ravensbrück? And before you say you never knew who the killers were, do you have to know everyone for them to get justice?"

"Justice isn't shooting the perpetrators."

"Who said anything about shooting someone? I've got enough here to take him to the Canadian police."

"The Canadian police aren't Mossad."

The word *Mossad* must have been some kind of aphrodisiac in the depths of Eva Einhorn's brain, because she was all over me again, grinding me into a pleasured pulp. But I'm not even sure it was me she was riding, because she stared at the wall right where your picture would be, Simon Wiesenthal, if our hotel room happened to be Eva's apartment. Her eyes took on this crystalline gaze and her pupils enveloped the hazel of her iris and I, Ira Wollman, just happened to be along for the roller coaster ride. And I thought that this was as good a time as any, so I said, "Eva, will you? I've got Bubbe's ring in my drawer." And Eva said, "Yes yes yes yes yes," but not to me, not to me, she didn't hear me, Simon Wiesenthal. She was saying yes to your orders.

JOHANNA, my love this will be my last letter for many weeks. I found the creature. I found *her*.

HE SEEMED LIKE AN ORDINARY GUY, Mister Nazi. He picked us up off the cold summer street in this Ford truck and said, "Mister Smithstein?" and shook my hand and then Eva's hand as if there wasn't a drop of Jewish blood in us. He was six inches taller than my 5' 6" and had his blond hair slicked over in a side part and, when I asked him later what happened to his right ear, he said a wolf had bit him in the winter of 1955, when he tried to release it from a trap.

"You want to photograph our animals?" Julius Kindler asked. "No trophies?"

Eva nodded and held up her dad's Rolleiflex.

"A good German camera," he said, "but our problem will be to get close enough. Our hunting season is still over a month away, so the game will be more relaxed. That is in your favour. But they know who I am by sight, so we must be discreet." He held open the door for Eva. "This is my youngest boy, Michael."

The son of the Nazi. A miniature version of his father, but with two intact ears and the look of an adult suspicion his father didn't have. He knew what we were going to do, even though I didn't. He knew he'd soon be fatherless and that I'd feel shitty about it and Eva wouldn't. That was my crazy thought—the boy knew. The boy would hunt us down, kill us. The boy, unlike the father, couldn't be defeated.

"Good morning, Michael," Eva said. She held out her hand, but Michael stared at her as if she'd presented him with the blade of a butcher knife.

"Michael will talk when Michael will talk," said Julius Kindler. "He takes after his mother."

The bench seat of the Ford was so wide there was room for all of us to sit side by side. Michael sat against his father and Eva between me and the boy. And when we pulled out into the street the cab of the truck smelled suddenly of sawdust and then coffee as Julius Kindler opened a thermos held between his legs. He passed it to us and two little tin mugs and Eva and I looked at each other and sipped at the coffee with the same suspicion that Michael had regarded us.

"I am taking you into the mountains above the St.

Mary River," Julius Kindler said. "There we shall see deer, elk, bighorn sheep, and maybe grizzly."

"And something else," said Michael.

"Something else, Michael? A leprechaun perhaps? Or the White Rabbit from your book?"

"Papa, the creature. From last summer. Molly's house—"

"My son is talking about legend. What the Indians call the big man or the wild man of the woods or the owl woman or—there are as many names as legends. We should be more scared of this man."

We drove by a large sign on the road north to elect Charles Jarvis mayor. "It's rumoured that he was born in 1895 yet doesn't look a day over forty. That he gestated in his mother for almost four years. I do not believe a word of it. It's his socialism I fear, his love of J.S. Woodsworth. The future he wants."

The dark morning sky before us glowed the colour of a hot poker, even though the sun wouldn't be up for about another hour. Soon we were parallel with this beehive burner just off the highway out of town. Orange sparks showered the sky from its steel mesh cap. The darkness around the burner seemed to soften like a sheet of wax. The light rippled and shimmered. In the reflection of my passenger window, I caught Michael looking at me with the weirdest expression on his face. As if in the melting of the dark sky behind him the world had been revealed and he wanted me to see it. Behind the whole crazy mountain range surrounding this little town was fire, like looking into a crematorium, like the only safe place on earth from the Bomb was in the cab of this truck with this Nazi and his kid. Simon Wiesenthal, I couldn't think of a single song I liked. Everything was quiet except for the churn of the Ford's engine and the whistle of the broken seal on the window and the crackle of that goddamn fire beyond the veil of the mountains. For the first time ever, the record player in my little brain didn't know a single tune.

The highway took us into the fire.

MOLLY SICKERT TOOK Michael back to her cabin so I could track the creature. She gave me her .22 and her thermos of coffee and half a bran muffin and I said that I'd be back before dark, but I didn't know on which day. If not tonight, could she return Michael to his mother and let her know that I was alright? *If I die*—those words almost left my lips. If I died, I had the letter I wrote for you, Johanna, after the war, addressed to your parents, each year or two another stamp added to make up for the rising price of postage. It's a young lover's letter sent by a man almost old enough to be his father. Correction— Helen will send it, my Canadian wife of Ukrainian extraction. She will send the young lover's letter, unless she reads it first. *Liebe Johanna, liebchen, häschen, engelchen.* I addressed Helen with these words, too, but I never had my heart behind them. Not like I did with you.

I followed the creature's footprints, the spatters of blood, until the game trail faded into the brush. Until the footprints were nothing more than trampled impressions on the forest floor, on the long, tawny grasses and the blood, an occasional smear on a pine tree. The creature,

Johanna, was ascending a narrow valley paralleling a shallow creek. Up was a high mountain, a scree slope that crashed into the shaded tree line and beyond that a boulder-strewn, blue-grey peak. If I was in the mountains of Peru, I would say that the creature had gone to die on the mountain peak, to be sacrificed for—for what, Johanna? What is worthy of sacrifice now that the war is long over, the Reich is a figment of the political imagination, the gods are dead? Maybe you are dead. As long as I am alive you are not dead. I will be the sacrifice.

The long dark moss on the end of a tree limb waved in the wind. As I grew closer, I could see that it was a tuft of the creature's dark brown hair and on one end of it, a fine, dark crust of dried blood. Except the hair was a foot above my head and I had to stand on a stump to be level with it and I hoped it was hair from the creature's head and not its shoulder or the thing might've been eight feet tall. Had one of Molly Sickert's bullets struck it in the head, like one had her dog? It was at that moment, as the cooling evening breeze wound through the trees and the mosquitos found my damp skin, that I felt watched again, scried again for weakness or defect. Bored into. I took a drink from the creek as a prey animal takes a drink. I lapped at the water and looked around me with each drink, for the eyes, the blur of motion, the crash of the trees.

I should light a fire before it gets dark, I thought. I should lay down a bed of pine boughs, so that I can be off the cold, hard ground. I should form a defensive perimeter of sharpened sticks. But I want the creature to find me—to reach into me and take my soul and burn out my impurities with its eyes and put the fine thing back in my chest and set my life ticking again to my time with you.

Don't you understand, Johanna, I had to leave? Himmler ordered me to Canada as he had twice ordered Schäfer to Tibet? That if I had not gone, I would have been shot for insubordination? I couldn't take you. I wanted to take you. I wanted our love to—do you remember the last time we were together in that pension by the Hauptbahnhof? I looked up each time expecting the thin white door to be burst open by the boot of an SS officer and I looked down at you with your head swung over to the right side and your eyes closed as you told me how good I made you feel. And I kissed you and I looked up at the door and I kissed you and I heard heavy-booted footsteps on the stairs and they were coming for me, but it was only Frau Hennie with our coffee—and my train ticket. I couldn't tell you where I was going. That I had to leave because Wienert, the German cultural attaché in Ottawa, had come across this article in *Maclean's* magazine about the giant creatures seen on the Chehalis. "They must be descendants of the Atlanteans," Himmler had said to me a week earlier. "Some escaped to the Himalayas, but it is not inconceivable some made their way into North America. We must find them before our enemies do. You must find them, Strauch." He said this to me the morning after I bought your engagement ring, Johanna. It was in my coat pocket, as Himmler ordered me across the Atlantic. "Take Doppel with you. His English is better than yours."

We came by boat with fake Canadian passports to Montreal and then took the train to Vancouver. Old

Doppel met a grizzly at the base of Mount Fisher and I met my wife ten years later in a patch of huckleberries by St. Mary Lake. I wrapped your engagement ring in a small square of silk and carry it with me everywhere hidden in a pocket watch from which I removed the movement. I have the watch now in my fist. The creature can have my soul.

"SOMEONE LIVE OUT HERE, JULIUS?" I asked. The old Nazi had driven us along a dirt road to this lake about an hour and half from our hotel. The place had more trees than I'd ever seen in my life—the chain of mountains above us looked like one brush stroke of dark green paint. As the sun rose, a band of warm yellow light had begun to sink from the peaks towards the shaded valley where I stood shivering. Eva watched the Nazi and his boy for signs of hostility. No, watch the boy, the dad is defeated, I thought. He lost. The boy is still…his father removed his baseball cap and bowed his head. Michael bowed his head, too, but didn't stop staring at his father, as if he expected the man might give up some secret. Someone must have lived there in that cabin. Its charred roof had collapsed into the rooms below it and all the windows had a tongue of soot hanging over the sills as if the little house had tried to cough out the fire.

"Molly Sickert and her dog," Julius Kindler finally replied to my question. "She buried the dog and I buried her. Last August."

"How'd she die?" Eva asked.

"I used to bring Molly supplies and—"

"Fire," said Michael.

"She shot what she shouldn't have."

"Meaning?" Eva asked.

I tugged at her hand. Like I said, the man had lost something.

"Papa—"

"I don't know what she shot, but it bled. And it was angry."

I stepped between Eva and the cabin and said, "Take a photo of me." I threw my arms up in the air like I'd seen Bill Evans do once after a piano session, so Eva couldn't help but look at me. I wasn't visible to her, because her eyes followed Julius Kindler to the green-grey dusted brush behind the cabin and I stepped toward her and she tried to duck past me and I told her I loved her as much as I could, my heart was raging and somewhere in my goddamn pockets was Bubbe's ring. But it was Julius Kindler she heard, not me. Michael was speaking, too. "Papa, Papa, don't show her." Not *them, not me* —*her*, Eva, because the little wreck knew Eva was the one with the pistol and the sting of the FBI rejection letter and I was the one who played guys like Chet Baker and Bill Evans on my portable Motorola and smoked dope, while my parents observed Shabbat. And I smelled it, Simon Wiesenthal. The summer wind had plunged down from the mountaintop and stirred through the burnt cabin and wrung out the odour of kerosene and ash and something rotten, as if the old rusted stove pipe chimney still spewed smoke from a hidden crematorium. "Papa, Papa don't show her." Michael was running at his father with his arms swept out wide to catch or hug his father and the boy's terrified, sad face seemed to keep falling behind him and having to catch up to his rushing little body. All I could think of was black-suited Bill Evans crooked over his piano with his lolling head perpendicular to his sternum. The smell and the burnt-out cabin and the boy running and here was Bill Evans playing "Lover Man."

Michael wrapped himself around his father's legs. "No, no, no. Don't show the Jews. Don't show—"

Molly Sickert and her dog, side by side, in graves marked with hand-carved wooden crosses, the grave mounds long made level with the ground. I hadn't asked Eva when—when she was going to try to arrest Julius Kindler. It was going to be her because what did I care what Julius Kindler had done twenty-five years ago on the order of his deranged master? If someone like Bill Evans could play the piano so beautifully that the world could keep on going when it just wanted to stop and die, what need was there for revenge? Eva took out the Baby Browning by her side, barrel pointed down at the ground and I said, "Let's take a picture, okay?" and I grabbed the camera around her neck and said to Julius Kindler and Michael, "Here, turn around, so I can get you guys in the shot." Julius Kindler had this half-smile on his face and the boy was grim and posed for the camera and the wind was stirring the trees and Eva was behind me with her gun.

"What do you say to smile?" I asked. "We say *cheese* down south."

"*Käsekuchen*," said Julius Kindler. "Say it, Michael."

But Michael was pointing at me, behind me. "Papa," he said. "The lady."

I didn't want to turn around. I didn't want to look into Eva's pistol.

"Lower your arm," I said to Michael.

I took their photo anyway, Julius Kindler half-smiling and his son about as happy as a kid in an old Victorian photograph.

Eva was walking away. Her disgusted walk. Her arms tight at her side, her back flat like a tombstone, her feet half-kicking at the ground. I found her in the cab of Julius Kindler's truck. "They killed your aunt, Ira. They gassed your two baby cousins. Carla had Mongolism. She was four years old and they gassed her at Ravensbrück when you were four years old. All you want to do is take pictures of murderers."

I took a picture of Eva, upright, her arms crossed, jaw tensed shut.

"What does that mean? I'm a murderer now, Ira? Is that it? Can you be serious about one thing?"

I jammed myself beside her and looked out the window.

"What do you see out there, Ira? A burnt-down cabin that stinks of old death. Make you think of anything?"

I took her hand and she pulled it away. I reached over out of habit and turned on the radio for some music. But the keys weren't in the ignition, so the radio played nothing.

"Maybe we can listen to 'Louie, Louie'—take all the seriousness out of the world? That's the way you like it."

"It was our song for all of last May. We danced it. Remember that, at your apartment? After the wine, how long we danced?"

Julius Kindler and Michael walked back toward the truck.

"We're arresting him, Ira. He's SS. A fucking war criminal."

He has a son, two daughters, a wife. Later, I found out that he had the sweet memory of this woman he was in love with and going to marry. He had a ring picked out like I have my bubbe's ring in my pocket. But the war sent him here. Your war sent us here, Simon Wiesenthal.

"Get ready, Ira. Here he comes."

JOHANNA, I did not sleep that night I pursued the creature. I sat with my back against an old pine tree and felt the darkness press on my chest until I could hardly breathe. I sifted through every noise—the trees soughing in the wind. A branch snapping when the wind stopped. The trickle of a nearby creek, the splash of something stepping into the cold water, the whoosh of the water suddenly diverted.

I love you now, I thought. You've been on the other side of the world most of my life and I still love you as much as that last time I loved you in the pension by the Hauptbahnhof. Your absence has been my life's work. Is that too much to write in this age of love? That the aging soldier's heart has fossilized around the love he knew from 1937 to 1939? I became a stranger to myself. A fake husband. A fake father. That is not true. In Molly Sickert I felt some of the spirit I once had when I was near you. The way she lived alone somehow reminded me—I don't know anymore. I don't know what any of this means.

When the night grew the coldest, that's when I felt the creature was very near. I could smell dead fish. The stink of it. I thought, what if the creature lies down beside me and looks into my eyes and my eyes look into it? What would it see? Nothing, perhaps. There is at the centre of me nothing. *Nihil fit ex nihilo.* No, something always comes from nothing. Himmler saw in me something worth sending to Canada.

I reached out with my hand to touch the creature. My fingers trembled and then my whole arm. It was there, a dark bulk beside me, gasping in a kind of silent pain. I would touch the past Ernest Schäfer could not in Tibet. The ancient ancestor of the Aryan race preserved in the Rocky Mountain trench. Who would I tell? Every German who wanted to find the gods preserved in temporal form was dead. Their spirits had dissipated over Europe and South America and fallen as the cold rain that seeps into the fissures of the earth.

I felt warmth at the end of my fingertips. The heat of something as I stretched out my hand. The cooling heat of the old god.

Nihil fit ex nihilo.

No, something can come from nothing, Johanna. What has been between us all along.

Fire.

I PILED up branches covered with Old Man's Beard around the base of a pine tree. A mound of tinder. My hands palsied—what should I fear? That if the gods bleed, they can burn? I struck a match and soon the dried moss began to crackle and pop. In a minute, the tree looked like a candle wick. And soon the tree beside it. The hillside glowed like a strange dawn.

"THERE WAS a forest fire here last summer," Julius Kindler said, "but never mind, we are going up the side of the valley behind us."

I took Eva's camera and framed the mountain opposite our dirt road. A long oval of charred trees swept down from the top of the mountain to the valley bottom, like decay in an old tooth.

"Lightning or something?" I asked.

"A careless hiker perhaps," said Julius Kindler. "When the forest is dry even a cigarette—"

"Papa, the creature did—"

"Legends don't start fires, Michael."

"But last summer, Molly's cabin."

"Kerosene."

"It was hurting. Mad."

I'd never seen someone move so fast. Julius Kindler had been beside me as I took the photo with Michael, who was about ten feet away standing on an old stump. And before my shutter opened again, Julius Kindler had his son by the wrist and was yelling at him in German and the boy was yelling, "It's still alive!" and his father yelled back, "*Es ist tot! Ich habe es getötet!*"

"No, no. It had a husband. There he is!" The boy's free hand shot out at the mountain of burnt trees. "He's coming for us, like he came for Molly."

Slowly, perhaps, slowly. That's it, isn't it, Simon Wiesenthal? The burnt blackness of that mountain would creep down toward the town and find the boy and his mother and sisters and leave his father alive, so he would suffer loss until he, too, died. Unless—I looked at Eva. She had her thin arm stretched out, the little semi-auto with its three bullets squared on Julius Kindler's broad back. The humming came out of me, low and resonant. I couldn't stop myself. Ira Wollman would die a crazy cat fool. Out of me came Chet Baker, the soft, opening trumpet on "My Funny Valentine." I was reclining again on the bench at the Tacoma Rifle and Revolver Club. Eva was banging off .38 shells in a half-heart-shaped group on a paper target ten yards away. A paper man. A paper Nazi. *Bang, bang, bang.*

I went down on one knee on the dry Canadian earth. Oh, Simon Wiesenthal—my funny valentine! I had Bubbe's ring in my hand. Good old Bubbe! *I want you to have my ring for your girl*, she said. *Take it, Ira, and you tell that girl you love her for all time.* Oh Bubbe, I do I do I do.

"Eva, will you—?"

Ira, you've got to say it louder, so she can hear.

I said it loud over Chet's trumpet in my head.

"Ira, what're you doing? For god's sake!"

Bang, bang, bang. A paper man. A paper Nazi. His son.

JOHANNA, I had visitors this summer. A young man and a young woman. Jews. Married. Ira, the young man, loved music. He was always humming or singing jazz tunes. You knew that as long as he lived, nothing terrible in life would penetrate very deeply into his mind and, if it did, he would never hear it for all his music. I'd met S.S. men like that—immune through sheer cheery spirit to even the butcher's block that was the camps. You can accuse them of burying the horrors of the world, of distracting themselves, but the truth is those horrors pass through them, as if they, the men, were somehow insubstantial. But substantial they are—intelligent, thoughtful men who simply can't contain horror.

The young woman, she burned inside that small frame of hers. Not for the young man—it was hard to believe she'd accepted his ring. No, she burned for an idea. An abstraction, any one of the nominalizations that the politicians of the mass media have always used to subdue the heart of a country. She was dangerous, but I didn't know why. Not at first. She grimaced a little at Ira's exuberant nature. When we drove, she'd place his hand back on his lap without taking her eyes off the road, off the future she saw coming at us at road speed. "Ira, there's a child with us," she said. I knew that she didn't mean Michael. She meant her new husband, who'd proposed I imagined during a concert by this Chet Baker. In reality, he'd said that he'd taken the young woman to the top of Seattle's new Space Needle and brought his ring, his grandmother's engagement ring.

I took the Smithsteins, for that is what they called themselves at the time, out to see game on the West Arm of the St. Mary River, past Molly Sickert's old cabin, after it burnt down in last summer's forest fire. They'd chosen the Kootenays as the place of their honeymoon because the young woman wanted to see the Rocky Mountains, north of Colorado, the place she and her family often went on vacation to see the ruins of the Pueblo people built into the cliffs. She'd heard Indians lived here. "A plains people," I said. "Not a cliff people." Molly Sickert had studied them, how they shared much in common with the Salish people of the Cascade and Rocky Mountains, as far west as the Bitterroot range.

Ira was especially interested in Molly's cabin, how it had come to burn down. I told him that Molly must have been careless with a kerosene lamp, for she had no electricity out here. I could hardly keep Michael from telling him the truth, that the cabin had burnt down in the name of love. The pain of love abruptly ended. That the mate of the creature Molly had wounded and I had tracked had come to Molly's cabin with a burning bouquet. The child of the gods had brought a firebrand. Returned the favour of pain for the dead mate.

Ira photographed Michael and I outside Molly's cabin. The girl stood behind him in his shadow and that's when the pistol flashed in her hand. I couldn't believe that I'd seen it. A pistol in the hands of this small, slight woman. I said nothing. I went along with them in a kind of shock. Back to the truck with Michael, but by then the pistol had vanished. I was dazed. A pistol? I drove the four of us along the road to where the forest fire had swept down the mountain to the valley below. We'd walk up the valley opposite and spot game.

Why the pistol? The little nothing of a pistol in the hand of a young Jewish woman? It was my ad in the *Thurgauer Zeitung*, wasn't it? That was how they found out. The pursuers. Simon Wiesenthal's soldiers. Mossad or Shin-Bet. They'd snatched that paper-pushing *dummkopf* Eichmann from Argentina in 1960. I heard again those booted footsteps I heard so many years ago outside the door of our pension by the Hauptbahnhof. It was Frau Hennie then, but now this Jewish woman with a pistol, riding beside Michael in the cab of my truck. I didn't bring any of my rifles. What for? Hunting season was two months away.

I pulled the truck over at the limit of the road, a little landing where the logging company had pushed the waste into piles to be burned. I couldn't keep Michael silent. He kept wanting to talk about the creature, that its mate had come down the mountainside and burned down Molly Sickert's cabin with Molly Sickert in it. I yelled at my son, that he should forget the creature—it was dead and there was nothing that could be done about it. I had my back to the young couple. Michael cried out. I spun around. The young woman had the pistol outstretched at me again, except the young man was down on one knee as if he was proposing to her. The gold ring in his hand gleamed in the sunlight. They were fifty feet away at most.

"Ira, what are you doing, for God's sake?" the young woman said.

He was holding her other hand and asking her if she'd marry him. They weren't really married, but the boy wanted to be. At the climax of the story, the young man had elected to choose love over history, over punishment, murder, or arrest. He and I, weren't we the same? I put an ad in the *Thurgauer Zeitung* when I should have done nothing, but, Johanna, I couldn't stop forgetting our 1937 to 1939. Those two years were the only years that meant—

I left Michael and stepped toward the couple, like I did when I was tracking a deer. Slowly, imperceptibly, so the animal can't tell if you're moving towards it, looking but not looking so the beast can't feel your eyes, your predatory eyes. The boy was on both knees now, both his hands grasping the girl's right hand in the attitude of a penitent. And she was staring at me with her pistol hand extended, saying, "Ira, let go, for god's sake, let go!" The first bullet went somewhere over my left shoulder, struck the wood waste pile behind me.

And I thought I, too, am being watched again. I could feel the creature scrying again my soul. Where was it? I laughed—I meant the creature, where was the creature, but I might as well have meant my soul. Wasn't that on the night table in the pension by the Hauptbahnhof? Did you take it with you before you left? Or did Frau Hennie dispose of it with the remains of our supper?

The second bullet clipped the billowy fabric of my pant leg near my right knee.

The girl's face had turned pale blue, like the colour of an iceberg when it flips itself over and exposes what has remained hidden for so long to the air. She was screaming at the young man. She would marry him, but not right now. Later. After this thing is done. She almost meant it, too.

I was five feet away from the barrel of her little pistol. "Himmler sent me," I said, "to find the old gods."

"Under arrest." It was the only two words she could say.

What I always liked best, Simon Wiesenthal, about Eva was her tenacity. I mean the FBI won't have her, so why not you and your Nazi hunters? The secret Nazi living in the backwoods of Canada wouldn't stop for her, so she shot him with her last bullet. Right in the heinie. He turned away from her and when he wouldn't stop—bam! But he didn't stop. That little .25 calibre bullet didn't do the trick. He went and grabbed his son in his arms and started for his truck and Eva kept yelling at him that he was under arrest for war crimes and when he still wouldn't stop, she told me to get up off my knees and tackle him for fuck's sake. But there was a patch of blood blooming on his pant leg, from the little leaking hole in his buttock and how do you leap on a man like that with his son in his arms shrieking as if he were the one shot?

"You wanna marry me?" Eva yelled. "Get me my Nazi!" At least, I think she yelled that. It didn't matter, it's what I heard and if Eva wanted a Nazi for a dowry I'd get her a Nazi.

"Hey!" I yelled, as I ran after him. "Just want to talk to you!"

God, his boy was an ugly little shit. With his mouth thrown back and his accusing finger jabbing at me and "Jew! Jew! Jew!" falling off his lips like kettle corn. The father at least seemed reformed—I mean he had a wife and kids and doesn't that redeem everything? I mean, it did once, didn't it? You could get a degree in English and do nothing but work at a record store and you could marry a girl like Eva and everything would be Chet Baker beautiful.

"The creature!" the boy yelled. "The creature!"

My ears started ringing, I mean really ringing, Simon Wiesenthal, like when you run out of school past a clanging fire alarm. What could the kid mean other than me flying for his father's legs to the sound of Judy Holliday singing "The Bells Are Ringing?" I had the man around his injured leg and we fell against the side of his truck and the boy kicked me in the head and yelled, "Papa! The creature!" and I couldn't think of anything else to do so I punched Papa in his wounded cheek and he hit me in the jaw and goddammit my head snapped to the right so I was looking back at Eva fifty feet behind me and by my bubbe's ring, behind *her*, was this tall shambling hairy creature. The thing was as tall as Wilt Chamberlain and as hairy as Lon Chaney's wolfman.

"Eva!" I cried, "behind you!" She belonged to me, not this beast looming up behind her. Not this beast, not this *dybbuk* of Cranbrook.

"Papa, Papa!" Julius Kindler's boy yelled, "the creature!"

Julius Kindler's face took on the trace of a beatific smile, as if his whole Nazi life suddenly meant something. "*Gott,*" he whispered. "*Gott, ich bin hier.*"

"Ira!" Eva yelled. "Get me—"

Get you what, my love? I'm here, your ring-bearing, Chet

Baker man. I'm here under this joy-filled Nazi. I've always been here for you, my sweet.

"I-rrr-aaaaa!"

Simon Wiesenthal, it was the last thing I ever heard her say. The last beautiful thing I ever heard in the rest of my little life.

My name—not yours.

LETTERS TO ANDROPOV

J udith and Stevie wanted to build a fallout shelter for the four of us, but Joe didn't. Joe, their father by blood. Joking Joe Equinox who last Easter dangled a dead hare in front of me and said, "Brownie, I'm gonna throw this and you're gonna fetch, 'cause it's your special dinner." Woof, right? Joe didn't feed me for three days, because I wouldn't retrieve the animals he shot—ducks, coots, grouse, hares, coyotes, gophers, squirrels. A six-toed cat once. Joe called me his "hypocrite Labrador" because I wouldn't touch a dead animal, yet I'd gobble horse meat from a thirteen-ounce can. Joe said he ate everything he shot. He said he'd eat me come Armageddon with the "fuckin' gusto of a lion."

"See them mountains out the window?" Joe said from the depths of his recliner. "How they circle the town? That's our goddamn shelter."

It was March 8, 1983 and we'd just watched President Reagan give his "evil empire speech" to the National Association of Evangelicals. Reagan wanted to build more nuclear missiles to "write the final pages of the history of the Soviet Union." I tried to comfort the kids, but I only had my warm furry self and some old canine lullabies about famine and pestilence. I didn't yet have the power to bring something modern to my musical repertoire, certainly nothing about radiation or nuclear winter. Judith ate bowl after bowl of Mini-Wheats and Stevie warmed up fish sticks and tater tots for Joe's supper and dried his eyes with the heat wafting out of the broken oven door.

"The root cellar by the old barn," Judith said. "If we fix it up, it could be somewhere safe—"

"Know why there isn't gonna be a nuclear war?" Joe said. "Mutually assured destruction. Everybody dies. It's what keeps us alive."

"But what if—?"

"What if? What if a meteorite hits the chicken coop? What if your mother left Dr. North and came back? What if Brownie could talk?" Joe spat out another "what if," and settled in to watch the *The Joy of Painting*, about the only thing in the universe that soothed his cuckolded soul. A happy, titanium-white cloud filled in the TV screen. "Soviets launch everything and nowhere is safe. Say it's a limited strike. Well, I've got the address of every Mormon in town and a closet full of rifles. You know they have to squirrel away a year's worth of food—it's what they call a holy precept."

I couldn't add my opinion, that the scent of war wafted through the psychosphere and every dog from here to Kamchatka could smell charred, irradiated planet. I didn't get my full intellectual powers—sub-genius thoughts, observations, and deductions—until days after the first strikes. On that March 8 evening, with my body leaning against Stevie's thigh, I couldn't do more than whip my tail a little and whine my canine sorrow.

When Joe fell asleep in his recliner, Judith and Stevie called their first war council.

"The root cellar is our best chance," said Judith. She looked as determined as I'd ever seen her in her thirteen human years on this planet. She pulled back her brown hair into a loose bun, which she secured with a grey pencil, and her off-yellow eyes rippled with stubborn electricity.[1] She stared down at the little drawing she'd made that night of the root cellar-cum-fallout shelter. Judith reminded me of someone far more mature: Ms. Orlando, the Cranbrook public librarian, who was twenty-five and had the critical, literary powers of a staff writer at *The New Yorker*. Ms. Orlando wrote gifted 300-word reviews of the latest books to arrive at the Cranbrook Public Library, in the *Daily Townsman*, which was how I learned to read during my first weeks after the war.

"Dad said we can't," Stevie said.

"Balance of probabilities. If there's a war and we don't have a shelter, we die. If we have a shelter . . ."

Stevie set his sleepy, hooded eyes on his older sister and smiled a mouth full of dark gaps. "If Dad finds out, we die anyway."

"He never goes near the root cellar. We'll clean it out, stockpile food and water."

"And the door needs a lock to keep out mutants. And a vent like we have for the wood stove." Stevie had an engineer's mind for mechanical detail and a nerd's fascination with the imagined apocalypse he'd read about in *The*

Chrysalids. Unfortunately, he didn't have the charisma to lead the local survivors of the war to a coastal island in the west that had survived largely unscathed and which had a more temperate climate than the Rocky Mountains. That was left to me, when the burst of radiation I suffered also enhanced my leadership skills. In Stevie I found an excellent house builder and a fine, if somewhat awkward, companion when it came to talking about subjects other than technical ones.

Both children looked at their father, as he snored before *The Joy of Painting*. Slack and fluid, he looked almost harmless. His dark black goatee alternately blew from and then sucked into the ruddy well of his mouth. His thick right arm jerked and palsied at the side of his recliner like a conductor with an invisible baton. But they couldn't see what I smelled: awake or asleep, he reeked of violence. I didn't want to believe my nose, for this was the same man who'd snatched me from the SPCA's crematorium two years ago. Even when his wife left him for Dr. North, our vet, and Joe spent days cleaning and polishing his .30-06 and drinking glasses of whole milk mixed with his ex's home-made Kahlúa and talking up the stolen railway dynamite he had in his workshop, he only shot "the fuckin' hell" out of her potting shed of dahlia tubers and, not as he swore, Dr. North's "barely descended balls." The same man who worked as a porter at the Cranbrook Hospital and sat with the abandoned dying of the Extended Care facility until they ceased breathing, the same man who brought home armloads of the fruit cups his patients wouldn't eat to his children, that same man bathed in the hot, invisible star-shine of gamma rays would become the world's last, notorious murderer. I feared him then, but I didn't know until it was almost too late that I should fear another even more.

"Brownie is tessering again," said Stevie. He'd just finished reading *A Wrinkle in Time*, and concluded that when I was in deep, doggie thought that my mind was roaming back and forth through spacetime. After a tennis ball. "You'll stop the Black Thing, won't you, boy?"

The next evening, we worked in the root cellar while Joe worked a graveyard shift at the hospital. The cellar, in fact, was a ten foot by twenty foot oval-shaped cavity in a jagged limestone tooth that jutted from the small aspen-covered hill behind the Equinox farm. Whoever had owned the property before the Equinoxes had built a barn overtop the cave and secured the opening to the cellar with a thick steel door that now hung loose in its hinges. Children could stand in the cellar, but not a grown adult.

"The latrine will go in that corner," said Judith, "in the little alcove."

"We'll need a vent," said Stevie. His face had already begun to crinkle.

"It can't be seen from the surface."

"Who will fix the door? Anyone can get in."

"Think of something."

"Don't know how to drill rock."

"Then we're lost."

I stood up from the pile of old newspapers I'd been lying on.

"Brownie has an idea."

"Brownie is a dog, Stevie. He can't think or move through time. Only we can save us."

My stomach aches now as I recall Judith's remark, as if I'd eaten too much bunch grass. I, Brownie Equinox, pet license 239, somehow wasn't deemed part of humanity, couldn't save humanity. That because I couldn't walk on my hind legs or read *A Wrinkle in Time* or manipulate doors with other than my mouth, that I could never be buried in the family plot in the Westlawn cemetery alongside Grandpa and Grandma Equinox. I would be like Blackie, thc family cat, relegated to a two-foot hole beside the honeysuckle bush. Blackie, Brownie, and soon Goldie the goldfish—we'd become a lengthening row of pet corpses nourishing the heady white flowers of a non-sentient shrub that remained stubbornly non-sentient post-apocalypse.

I left Judith and Stevie and retreated into the warring winter night. I went out to our gravel driveway and padded up Gold Creek Road to our next-door neighbour's, this old man, Mr. Kindler, who lived alone after his wife died from ovarian cancer. Mr. Kindler, the hunting guide. Mr. Kindler, the hunter of Sasquatch and the keeper of strange lore. Mr. Kindler, who'd built his own timber frame house in the Bavarian style, who I'm sure would know how to fix the hinges of a steel cellar door. He had an old German shepherd named Johanna and she rose stiff-hipped from her kennel and greeted me with a nose kiss. "My children need your master to help them with their shelter," I said. "Both of you would be welcome to join us."

Johanna gazed at something behind me, through her milk-clouded eyes. "He writes letters all day and tears them up," she said. "He writes to the other Johanna. One of them, the hairless walkers, the broken-hearted-never-sleep-long. He doesn't see me anymore, Brownie. Doesn't feel my head on his lap, my weight against his body. He pushes me away to my bed, skulks through the house in search of something. What use have we of survival?"

Use? I didn't, at the time, understand her question. How could more life not be a blessing?

"You should come, Johanna," I said again, as she closed her eyes against me.

The last remaining rooster on Equinox farm crowed at 11:37 p.m. and the lights in Judith's and Stevie's bedrooms winked out. I wandered around the darkened farm to make sure that the weasel I'd chased off last week hadn't dug back under the wire to maraud the chicken coop. I could smell a bear and a coyote and, to the west, on the light, moonbeam-dappled breeze, a male cougar. I was in a strange, warm mood. They, too, should join us in the shelter from the radioactive firestorm. All the animals, crammed into that little cave cellar, because out in the open they'd die from malignant sores. Their carcasses wouldn't rot, because the bacteria would be dead, too—they'd be scorched into ashes from the little suns that the Americans and the Russians sent into the atmosphere on the backs of ICBMs. I was more dog back then than sub-genius and all these thoughts lacked the words of the human inner voice: they were images, odours, and raw, inchoate feelings. But I had them and they clawed up from my stomach into my throat and the darkness of Equinox farm was total and enveloping and I pushed through it like a stiff, pelting wind, until I collapsed on the pile of shredded *Daily Townsmans* that

Joe had stuffed into a canvas sack to make my bed on the front porch.

When he awoke for work just after dawn, Joe stepped off the front porch with his .30-06, lowered to one knee, and shot into the chicken coop. "Brownie, you piece of shit for brains." He poked at me with the smoking hot rifle barrel. "Kinda fuckin' guard dog are you?" Couldn't he see that I, Brownie Equinox, pet license 239, carried the weight of the future on my canine soul? That I could smell into the future and it terrified not just me, but the broad dog consciousness that united every mutt across the soon-to-be dead planet? That to even contemplate getting up at 7 a.m. was impossible. That—

He dragged me from my bed by my collar, down the stairs, and into the cold, slushy mud. "See what I see?" he asked.

A panel of the high chicken wire fence had been pushed inward to a low, sloping angle. There were bloodied chicken carcasses streaked across the old snow at the front of the enclosure. Henry, the rooster, still squirmed in the jaws of the dead, bloodied cougar, now sliding down the little ramp that the chickens used to access the inner sanctum of the coop. And, my god, Henry crowed to announce the start of the day, as if he wasn't clamped in the teeth of a savage predator, but bent over a microphone like an old time crooner.

Joe dragged me into the fenced-off area for the chickens.

"Stay," he said.

He pried open the jaws of the dead cougar and pulled Henry out and the bird fluttered about ten feet and pecked at the ground and then leaned up against the wire as if about to faint. Joe hauled me outside the fence again, near the honeysuckle where we'd buried Blackie, and began digging a hole through the old snow and into the hard ground.

"Get the chickens," said Joe. "Or we're digging your grave next."

I felt so ashamed of sleeping through the cougar attack that I limped back into the chicken compound and sniffed at one of the four dead chickens. Its eyes were open and its beak gaped as if its last chicken words were a scream. Its left wing lay detached beside its head, like a fan the poor thing had dropped in the heat. I took the dead chicken in my mouth and tasted dirt, mud, and feces. I dropped the cold, bloodied thing at Joe's feet. "Get the rest, Brownie. And then drag that fuckin' cougar here." I could carry the chickens, but the cougar was too big for me and I came back before Joe with my head down and my tail curled up against my stomach. Joe cursed me again and dragged the cougar into the wide hole he'd dug for the chickens.

He told me to get into the hole next.

I looked up at him, the man who'd rescued me from the SPCA. The sad, violent look to his eyes. "Get in the fuckin' hole, Brownie." He booted me into the pit. "Lie down." Beside the dead chickens, half on top of the cougar, my body so tensed I thought my legs might break from the strain. The first shovel of dirt struck my haunches and the second, my head. It was in my eyes and ears and nostrils. The third buried my leg. I smelled Joe's apple-scented pipe smoke. "Brownie, tell me one good reason that you should live. One good reason. See, I didn't get you for reasons of happiness. Can get that in a beer can. I got you to be useful." Another shovel of dirt, another. "One good reason." I was half-buried, when he said, "Nothing to say for yourself?"

I couldn't smell Joe's smoke anymore, no more dirt fell on me. I crawled from the hole, shook myself off, and limped back to the front porch. I could smell butter, the wet, dairy scent of frying eggs. Judith and Stevie shivered in their pyjamas at the front door.

"What happened to Brownie?" Judith called out.

"Come and get your eggs before school," said Joe from the kitchen.

"He's filthy."

"Brownie?" called Stevie. "Boy?"

"He's dead. Cougar attack last night. Buried'im beside Blackie. We'll get a better dog."

I went down to the little half-frozen pond and waded into the frigid water to clean myself. My reflection—I couldn't make it out in the water, as if I already suffered the myopia that would afflict my older years from too much post-apocalyptic reading. I had died, I was a ghost, I was the dog-wraith of Gold Creek Road, the haunter of Equinox farm. I was as good as dead to Joe. He walked past me outside or in, as if I didn't exist. He wouldn't fill my bowl with Gaines-Burger or scraps from supper. He'd buried me with the dead chickens and the dead cougar and there I remained under a skiff of wet humus. Judith and Stevie fed me Gaines-Burgers and kibble until the big bag ran out and, when Joe wouldn't buy anymore, I ate the extra they cooked for supper for the three of them. Fish sticks and tater tots and chili and wieners and, when

Judith could convince Joe to buy something decent, sirloin steak and couscous salad.

The next few nights when Joe was at the hospital, the children worked on clearing out the root cellar. They hid the old tires and scraps of useless metal and an old baby carriage in a broken-down outbuilding. They moved in three canvas cots that Joe had bought for summer camping trips that never happened. Sleeping bags and pillows and, from some source I didn't know, two giant boxes of toilet paper.

Johanna came that night. She lay at the sagging metal door of the root cellar and said nothing to me and looked away with her old, milky eyes. In an hour, I heard her master calling for her and, in another hour, he'd walked up the driveway and, seeing the light at the cellar, he strode up to us. "Johanna," he said, "*komm her.*" She didn't move. He stooped to grab her collar, but Stevie called out, "Oh, Mr. Kindler, it's so good to see you."

Mr. Kindler looked at Stevie as if he didn't know him. "My Johanna wandered off. It is unlike her."

"She just wanted to see our shelter."

"Shelter?"

"Nuclear war," said Judith.

Mr. Kindler tapped the floor of the shelter with his walking stick. He walked with the stoop of a tall man who lowered his head to better hear the people around him.

"Dirt," said Stevie, "over limestone."

"And above?"

"Farmhouse, dirt, limestone. Twenty feet below the surface."

"It won't be enough."

Stevie's face fell and he glanced at Judith who hadn't let her eyes leave Mr. Kindler.

"When the old gods are angry, nowhere is safe."

"Maybe so," said Judith, "but better down here than up there eating radiation."

"I will be in my study. Writing my books. Listening to Chet Baker on my gramophone."

"You could come stay with us," said Stevie.

"I will see my Johanna."

I looked at Johanna, his dog, who gazed steadily at the floor. Mr. Kindler didn't mean her, he meant, as Johanna had already told me, his lost love. A human love. A human love across decades. Johanna who fled for Switzerland before World War II.

"Mr. Kindler, we need your help," said Judith.

Tap, tap went Mr. Kindler's walking stick, like a blind man prodding for a curb. "Johanna's hair, she wore it in a long, blond braid that fell almost to her waist."

I wanted to bark at the old Nazi. Snap, "Can't you see you're making poor Johanna, your dog, suffer? She is here. She loves you. She wants to live with you!"

"We can't fix the door."

"Why would you want to fix the door?"

"Radiation."

"Mutants," said Stevie.

"What does your father feed you that you think such strange thoughts? War? Annihilation? Why fear it? They are cleansing things. They liberate. Release the human soul for its transition. Back to the gods. Back to the true life."

"If you hadn't noticed, Mr. Kindler," said Judith, "we're children and we haven't been here very long and it behooves adults to help us have a little more life, in the here and now."

Behooves. Judith had learned the word when she wrote her first letter last month to Yuri Andropov, the big papa dog of the Soviet Union.

Dear General Secretary Andropov,

My name is Judith Equinox, age twelve, of Cranbrook, British Columbia, Canada. I am the elected president of the grade seven class of Amy Woodland Elementary School. Among other sacred things, it's my job to make sure everyone in my class is safe. I want you to know that it behooves *you to stop fighting with America. You must prevent a nuclear war...*

"The here and now?" All the life left in Mr. Kindler seemed to rush out of him. He looked around as if suddenly realizing where and when he wasn't. This wasn't the German pension where he'd last seen his lost love. This was the low, empty space after the song of his life ended.

Mr. Kindler turned and wandered into the night and Johanna rose stiffly to her legs and followed him.

"Mr. Kindler, please."

"What do we do?" Stevie asked. "Our shelter is nothing without a door."

The children had no option but to go on and hope. In the next few weeks, when Joe was away at work, Judith threw herself into readying the shelter. She brought in pillows and blankets and five-gallon covered pails to hold water. Canned peaches and apricots and jars of tomato sauce and giant bags of macaroni. Vitamins: C, D, and iodine. Salt and sugar and flour and safflower oil. Cutlery and plates, cups and saucers, and a used propane stove for cooking when the little wood stove Stevie dragged out of the old, crumbling greenhouse lacked for firewood. She bought twenty-five-cent copies of the *Survivalist's Guide to the Apocalypse* by G.E. Tannhauser, *Scouting for Boys* by Lord Baden-Powell, *Self-Sufficiency* by John Seymour, and numerous books for each stage of her and Stevie's intellectual development. I cringed at the thought that there was nothing for good, ol' loyal Brownie to develop his brain, but how were the children to know that inside their chocolate Labrador was a subgenius just waiting to be irradiated out? That a dog brain, a *tabula rasa* of higher thought, suddenly kick-started into massive cerebral activity, requires introductory texts to absorb and digest slowly? The sweet, asexual dimness of Winnie the Pooh followed by the psilocybin dreamlands of Dr. Seuss followed by the macabre love of orphans courtesy of Roald Dahl? Instead, I had to begin with yellowing back issues of the *Daily Townsman*, which, believe it or not, was my starting point for literacy. But it wasn't like those newspapers were supposed to be read by anyone: Stevie had kept them piled in a dry corner if we ran out of toilet paper or needed tinder to light the cedar and aspen the children had stolen from Joe's woodpile. I began my cerebral growth, reading substitute toilet paper before moving on to a library copy of *Last of the Mohicans* and, a week later, *Darkness at Noon* by Arthur Koestler, which Stevie thought was a survival manual. But I am being an uppity dog and should really thank the children for thinking to stow away ten vacuum-sealed bags of dog kibble.

Besides the door, the other problem for Stevie was the shelter's toilet facilities. The smell, for one. Ours was a ten by twenty foot room and weeks waiting for the atmospheric radiation levels to be safe for humanity would be a fragrant affair. It was in the *Survivalist's Guide to the Apocalypse* that he read of a sawdust composting toilet. He built a rudimentary box from scrap lumber with an old toilet seat attached and below it a five-gallon pail, over which sawdust went and when the bucket was full the mess would be—and this was where Stevie's plan broke down—stored and composted *outside* to grow vegetables. I didn't know better at the time to criticize the plan or to criticize the obvious fact that I, a dog, wasn't adapted to using other than trees and the ground. Stevie stopped thinking about his plan and moved on to venting our wood stove and propane cooker through a little hole in the ceiling of the cave, which he carefully hid with a pile of rocks, so the tube vent couldn't be seen. I sniffed around Stevie's pile of rocks and peed on them to say, yes, yes this is ours, keep away, mutants, we, the children of the future, eat meat.

By May, our shelter looked almost habitable. A third of the space was dedicated to stored food and supplies, a third to sleeping, which Judith separated with an old floral patterned bed sheet, and a third, in the corner behind another smaller bed sheet, to the composting toilet Stevie had built. They kept the door propped shut with a cinder block.

"Mr. Kindler doesn't care," said Judith.

"We can hire someone to fix the door," said Stevie.

"We've got no money. All my birthday money went on supplies."

"Radiation is going to get in through the door."

"We could ask Dad for money."

"For what?"

"A school field trip."

"$200 for a school field trip?"

Joe's voice blew hurricane-like up the path to the cellar. "Kids, where the hell are you? Daddy's hurt."

We slipped out from the shelter and there in the driveway sat Joe in a wheelchair pushed by a tall man we'd never seen before. "It's my bulging disk," Joe said. The man whispered something to Joe and then loped back down the driveway to his van. "Here, get me in the house."

There was, of course, no ramp to the front door, so Stevie and Judith pushed the wheelchair to the back of the house and heaved Joe up the long, sloping path to the rear door. "Should've got me a husky," he said. "At least than he could help, instead of snortin' around and around us like a fuckin' bottle fly."

Once again, Joe misunderstood me. I went around and around them to keep the path clear of rocks and branches and the hubcaps that blew off the back wall where Joe hung them for no one to see but himself. Would a dim husky struggling to pull the deadweight of his wheel-chaired master be able to do that?

They rolled Joe into the living room, so he could watch *The Joy of Painting* re-runs and drink what he had to drink: home-made pear schnapps from a recipe Mr. Kindler gave him three Christmases ago. There he would stay for the next four months and bark out orders and try, with a telescoping fishing rod, to strike my haunches each time I edged near him. I took to sleeping in the shelter on one of the spare camping cots and dreaming that I had opposable thumbs, could manipulate a hammer drill to repair the shelter door. Could help, instead of resort to what power I had—the ability to comfort.

I couldn't even comfort Judith and Stevie. They took to whispering a lot, when they were home from school. Even if they could hire someone to fix the shelter door, they couldn't escape the fact that Joe was always home, his goatee growing to a sharp, diabolical length, that he was visited twice a week by an occupational therapist who didn't seem to do much except drink schnapps with him and talk about how close the airforce base in Boise, Idaho was to us and Spokane, Washington was only 190 miles away and a nuke would pretty much rain fallout on our little town. Not to mention Reagan was sending more missiles to Europe.

"Sound like my kids," said Joe. "Worrying about some scary future. Soviets aren't going to strike. They die, we die. Got it right here in writing." Joe read out the reply to Judith's letter from Yuri Andropov's assistant Grigory Lukyanov, the reply Judith had never seen. "*We want only peace, Miss Equinox. We vote only for peace. Our children do not want nuclear war and so we do not want nuclear war. We are collaborating with the President of the United States to secure lasting peace.*" Joe folded up the letter and put it in the chest pocket of his shirt. "See? Peace in our time." The two men drank to that and Joe sank back into his recliner and turned up the heating pad for his lumbar and on the TV Bob Ross daubed happy little clouds into an inviting Alaskan sky.

Stevie woke up Judith early the next morning. "Is it school?" asked Judith. The batteries in her Walkman had died and the music she went to sleep to—the music that I hated so much I couldn't even howl at the tinny strains of it, Def Leopard, Black Sabbath, and Judas Priest—was mercifully silent.

Stevie said nothing. He sat on the edge of her bed, folded over so his head lay in his lap. "We need a door, Judith. For the shelter."

Judith lay the crook of her elbow over her eyes, to block the wedge of light that came through her open door from the living room. "That was news weeks ago."

"I heard it on my ham radio."

"Heard what?"

"A plane was shot down."

"What kind of plane?"

"A passenger one. By a Soviet fighter."

"American?"

"Korean. Everyone is dead."

Judith sat up. "We need a door."

Judith and Stevie argued over which one of them should steal Joe's credit card. "Even if we have his Visa," said Stevie, "Dad will be here."

"Just get the card," said Judith.

The next day Louis Meekie, from Meekie's Machine Shop, pulled into our yard with his van.

"Who is that?" asked Joe from the living room.

Judith offered him a second glass of pear schnapps spiked with two of the valium tablets left behind by our former mother. "It's the mail," said Judith.

"Sort of early."

Out in the backyard, Stevie guided Mr. Meekie and his tools to the heavy steel door of the cellar, hanging loose in its hinges. "Dad wants the door fixed," said Stevie.

"Why would I want to help your father?" asked Mr. Meekie. His yellow-black moustache now hid his hairlip. "All of school he made fun of how I talked."

"Dad said he'd pay double." Stevie showed him Joe's credit card. Mr. Meekie looked at Stevie as if he couldn't believe the eleven-year-old son of his former tormentor wasn't also making fun of him.

"Triple," said Stevie.

"Triple?"

"To re-hang a fucking door? What's so hot shit important about your goddamn cellar?"

"Harvest will be soon."

"Harvest?" Mr. Meekie looked around at our dry fields overgrown with spike grass and dandelions and the wrecked chicken coop and the little graveyard of dead pets.

"Potatoes. Back field."

"A Fort Knox door for spuds?"

"Dad said the door needs to lock from the inside. With a steel bar." Stevie produced his little blueprint of the reinforced door and the iron bar that would secure it from the inside.

The next day, Louis Meekie stood in front of Joe and held up the imprint he'd taken of Joe's credit card and said, "I put fifteen hundred dollars' worth of work into that cellar door of yours. An' your card is maxed out."

Joe peered past his old schoolmate and said, "You're in the way of my show."

"You hear what I say, Joe? Fifteen hundred."

"Sure as shit wouldn't ask you to fix my cellar door, even if I wanted it fixed. I got leftover railway dynamite and I'm thinking of blowin' up that cellar and the goddamn door for that matter."

"That boy of yours said you gotta big spud harvest."

"Spud harvest? All our tater tots go in the freezer."

Louis Meekie shoved the bill and the imprint of Joe's card into Joe's hand. Joe looked down at the card. His face wrinkled. His mouth bent into a horseshoe shape. "Stevie, you come here."

"I'm just going to go out there and undo what I did," said Louis Meekie.

"Stevie." Joe's voice came out guttural and low. "What did you do?"

Stevie edged into the living room. He'd curled himself around the door jamb as if to let go of it would mean he'd be sucked into the merciless void that was Joe's wrath.

"Stevie," said Joe. "Thank you for your gumption. That cellar door did need fixing. But so does our roof. And the pump on the well. And the chicken coop that cougar raided and if you haven't noticed my take-home has dropped thirty per cent while I'm laid up. Meantime, we're fucked. Understand? Fucked." Joe closed the front of his robe over the browns and grays of his chest hair. "First thing we're cutting from our budget is extra sirloin for the dimwit mutt here. Say good-bye to Brownie. Don't look so sad, Brownie, okay? You'll find some shithole to take you in. Second thing is, you can go live with your mother.

Judith can stay. So go pack your knapsack. No, don't—just start walking and I'll send it along with Brownie. I'm sorry to all of you—I should've fixed the family fucked-ness sooner. Avoidant attachment disorder, that's what it is, you guys are just plain avoidant." His eyes blurred, moist and glistening. On the TV, Bob Ross had finished a sunset that exploded behind a winter cabin. "Good-bye, Stevie."

THE CHILDREN'S mom lived up near Jim Smith Lake in the Cranbrook equivalent of a palatial mansion. It had a two-car garage with doors that closed and when I visited with Stevie or Judith I slept in a wicker basket with a heated pad and it felt like Brownie-gets-to-go-to-the-spa. I looked back along the road from Joe's house to see if Judith was racing after us on her ten speed or if Joe was coming in his truck, because he'd found forgiveness for the theft of his credit card.

"What's the matter, boy?" Stevie asked. We trailed after the yellow glow of Stevie's flashlight bouncing ahead of us on the gravel road. "We just need to walk all night and we'll be fine."

Stevie had been crying in the way that he often cries: without tears, without mucous, with little popping sobs that came out of his throat like slow beats on a parade drum. I had been creeping low against the ground with my ears almost folded over my eyes, because I could smell what was about to happen just before it happened. I could smell the aluminum plant we once visited. Burning ashes.

The psychosphere howled like a thousand dogs baying before the sounding of a hunter's horn.

I stopped.

"Now come on, Brownie."

I began to trot back in the direction we'd come.

"Mom's house is the other way."

There wouldn't be a Mom's house or a Mom or anything.

"Brownie, not coming after you."

I looked back after him, until his flashlight caught up to me and I began to whine.

"I miss them, too. But we're this thing Judith calls exiles now. Without a home. Until we get to Mom's."

I whined so hard and so long, I thought all the glass in the world might break. Follow me, I thought, you've got to follow me, Stevie.

His flashlight left me, swung back around the other way as he trotted down the road away from me.

I howled, I bayed, I cried at the universe for Stevie to come back. The stars began to shimmer as if the air was melting. Stevie's light vanished around a corner. I dashed after him and leapt and caught his pant leg between my teeth and yanked at his leg. I snarled. I foamed a little foam for effect. Mad dog Brownie and his mad ideas uncommittable to paper until he gets irradiated.

Stevie petted my head and hurt me with his bad grammar and pop gun sobs. "Dad don't want us anymore. Settle down, okay?"

A light came the other way. "Stevie!"

Joe, Judith, somebody to save us from perdition.

"The TV fuzzed out during Bob Ross! The radio stopped working!"

Judith stopped her bike beside us, breathing like a bellows. "The shelter. We've got to—"

"But Mom, but Mom," said Stevie.

"No time!"

Judith doubled Stevie and I ran after them, alongside them, in front of them, until a shriek of pain rent open the psychosphere and my mind and the air around me rushed, ripped, and roared and a flash of light struck south of us and the night was day again, a dawn of yellow-red writhing light shooting up into the southern sky. And sparks and fire as if the very air was fire and the stars and cirrus and everything above those flames had been incinerated at once. The wave of fire was growing larger, coming closer and at the head of that savage light I saw him for the first time: the rider, the nineteenth-century legend, the dead man, the dead blacksmith on his dead horse and gripping his father's waist was the dead son. Their blistered mouths wrenched open and their laughter galloped before them and smashed at me like a drunkard's fist. Those spectres loomed up so large in the southern sky they became it, the roiling thundering flashing sky, and I thought they were coming straight for me so I sprinted after Judith and Stevie and they were already going into the shelter and I thought, no, no I can't leave her behind, so I ran over to Johanna's house and found her huddled in her doghouse and told her to come after me and her master ran after us, stooped and calling, and back on our land, I scratched at the locked steel door and my skin grew hot as if I lay near Joe's wood stove full of cedar coals.

"Open up!" My mind roared. "Open up, Stevie and Judith!"

The fluid in my eyeballs felt warm as a bath and I could smell burning hair. Was it the world that was smelling like this or us, scorched by the red light and the savage laughter of the spectral, burning sky?

I pawed at the door, I whined, I howled and yipped and already Johanna had curled up on the ground and her master, old Mr. Kindler, the lover, the Nazi, the shaman, was stroking the dog and asking her not to go, not yet, not while his heart still beat loud and true for her namesake he'd left behind in a German pension near the Hauptbahnhof.

Another flash of light to the south and I felt the ground shift and ripple beneath us. I howled one last time.

"Fucking stupid dog," yelled Joe, "just shut the hell up!" He'd pushed himself half-way up the dirt path in his wheelchair toward the shelter door and, because the path sloped on an eight per cent grade he could get no further. "Where's Judith, Brownie? Where's that daughter of mine got to? The kettle's whistling on the wood stove. You hear it? It's time for cocoa and a story. *A Wrinkle in Time*, we're only about half way through. Somebody turn down the sky."

I, Brownie Equinox, dog license 239, bore witness to the final madness of the world. My last sights. Johanna. Mr. Kindler. Joe, gone strange with repressed fright. The ruddy, roiling glow of the last known sky. The laughing sky.

I shall die like this. I am going to die. My tears are steaming on my cheeks. I shall—

I felt myself dragged backwards by my collar, dragged back into the darkness. After me came Johanna and old Mr. Kindler and then the deep slam of the heavy steel door on its new hinges.

I lay on my side panting in the cool darkness of the shelter.

Oh Brownie, you shall live another day.

It was my first epiphany about the old world about to become the new. I was thinking in words, in the words of Judith and Stevie, I knew my mortality. I knew the relief of another day.

Joe wants his cocoa, I thought. Where is Joe?

THE FIRST TWO days in the shelter I remained just a dog, not a hint of subgenius cortical activity or above-average leadership aplomb. I lay on the white quilt Stevie had spread on the floor for Johanna and me. We lay snout to snout, our paws intertwined, our tails tap-tapping in a quiet dream of floating in a canoe down the Kootenay River. I, of course, assumed that we were dreaming the same dream, because we lay in the identical position in the square bottom of the canoe. A white film smeared Johanna's eyes and I gently licked it off and each time I did the viscous liquid filled the pool over her eye from an unknown, poisoned spring. Her breathing came as wheezing gasps and with each breath tufts of her hair rose up from her torso into the candlelit dark. Mr. Kindler stroked her spine with his burnt, seeping hands. "Johanna, *meine Liebe, atme die süße luft, atme.*"

Judith announced that we would be eating just two meals a day, because she hadn't counted on there being an extra adult in the shelter. The hate-filled logic of her months of planning frightened me. She hadn't ever wanted Joe to join us—that even in the horrific moment of war, she couldn't find charity for her own father. Stevie hadn't thought any differently. Even when the metallic pounding on the steel door went on into that first night, the children inserted foam earplugs into their ears and Mr. Kindler's and put wool earmuffs on Johanna and me. It was me who thought of monstrous Joe Equinox with compassion, out there in the irradiated, burning world with his cups of cocoa instantly heated by the microwave in which humanity now lived. That pounding went on for hours. Then came the choked calling for help. For a drink of water. For the TV to work again. For *The Joy of Painting*.

For supper, Stevie sliced up a tin of Spam and beside these came a can of green beans and for dessert half a fruit cup each. I ate a third of a Gaines-Burger and Johanna took nothing but the saline Mr. Kindler squeezed onto her tongue.

I was no longer thinking in images and smells and sounds. I was thinking in words. Human words. I thought I was dreaming that I was human in the bottom of that canoe with Johanna. "Johanna," I said, "if we just make it to the end of the river. Everything will be okay. Just to the end of the river." For the first time in the short, happy life of Brownie Equinox, I could understand Judith and Stevie's talk. Not just one or two words, as I had before— my name, din-din, drink-drink, runsie—no, entire sentences.

"Sergeant Stevie," said Judith. "How are the troops?"

"One dog minor radiation burns, one dog major radiation burns. Breathing is short and stert, stert—"

"Stertorous."

"Stert-orous. Prognosis, short. One elderly human, burns to hands and face. Difficulty swallowing. Difficulty eating. Prognosis unknown. Two children, basically fine. Brief bouts of crying and insecurity. Prognosis fair."

"Threats?"

"The pounding on the door has ceased."

"Challenges?"

"We will need to move a body outside soon."

It was as if I was the only one who understood what the children were saying about Johanna. If Mr. Kindler did, he didn't acknowledge it. He just stroked his old, dysplasic dog and wept. He caressed her until her legs began to shudder and spasm. I paced around her and when I pushed in to sniff her sour, rotten breath, Mr. Kindler pushed me away and shouted something in German that even though my mind had expanded beyond the bounds of the ninety cubic centimetres of my cranium, I couldn't comprehend.

I barked twice. "She needs to be cleaned. She needs to be prepared for—"

Johanna's head shook and her lips trembled and her eyes tore open and swirled in their sockets about the room and landed on me and I knew in that moment that she wanted me to tell Mr. Kindler that it was she who loved him, she who loved him despite his longing for a long-dead woman. I slunk in to lick her face, as my father had licked my mother as she died giving birth to me, but Mr.

Kindler smacked me across the snout and Stevie yelled at the old grieving man that I was a good dog and I didn't have to sacrifice my health to save either Johanna or him, he could leave. Mr. Kindler yelled back at Stevie in German, old orders, old memories, and in the moment that the old man and Stevie shouted at each other, I slithered along the dirt floor of our shelter and as gently as I could, I licked Johanna's head and what was Johanna left her burned body as a long, trembling sigh. Like the breeze soughing through the aspens behind our house.

"Sergeant Stevie," Judith said. "We have a body to take care of."

Mr. Kindler glanced down at Johanna's corpse and cried out and pushed me away and embraced her and lay there the rest of the irradiated night.

None of us slept.

The pounding on the door grew loud and metallic, as if someone was striking it with a ball-peen hammer. "I think it's Joe," whispered Stevie to his sister from his cot. "He never got Morse code right. SOW. It's three short, three long, three short. SOS." As if the basic problem wasn't that the children's father was locked out of the only viable shelter for miles and miles around and in need of not correction but help. That pounding went on until the next day, going by Stevie's wind-up Timex watch. Finally, the boy shouted, "Three short, three long, three short" and the pounding transformed into a series of random, ugly beatings. "No, that's not it either," said Stevie and tap-tap-tapped the door with the end of his fork.

"It really doesn't matter at all," Judith said, "We're not letting him in anyway." She went and shook Mr. Kindler.

"Sir, we must think about what to do with her body. And your burns must be treated. We have saline, vitamin E cream, and plenty of gauze. Mr. Kindler?"

His back rose and fell with his breath. He, at least, could sleep through Joe's racket. While he slept, Judith and Stevie cleaned the wounds on his face and hands and wrapped his burnt arms with gauze.

"What do you think, Stevie?" Judith asked. "Will he live?"

Stevie shrugged. "We could read the medical book."

Judith retrieved a burlap sack and stretched it over Johanna. "When can we get her outside?"

I didn't want to tell them that already I smelled a hint of putrefaction and her abdomen had begun to rise like bread dough. I might've told them, but a rifle cracked and the door rang like an old church bell. And rang again, perhaps half a dozen times.

"We'll have to wait for night," Stevie said, "so Joe doesn't see us."

"Mr. Kindler should mourn first. We can't just —Brownie?"

It was at that moment that I, Brownie Equinox, pet license 239, had glanced down at the pile of *Daily Townsman* newspapers that Stevie had collected for fire starter and read the special for iceberg lettuce at Super-Valu. *Thirty-nine cents—SAVE!* I stared at the thick red letters—*iceberg lettuce*. I'd never been able to read a single thing before and didn't even know what reading was except for people sitting in chairs at the dinner table, as Judith and Stevie did for their homework, peering at books or pieces of paper. My eyes whirled around the page. Pears—twenty-five cents a pound. Orange marmalade—one dollar and ten cents. Gaines Burgers—$4.99 for a pack of twelve. Milk, Count Chocula, diapers, Vaseline, Johnson and Johnson. I didn't know what these things were or how they related to some of the things I'd seen in my life with the Equinoxes. But I could read the words, whole, unbidden, seemingly without any effort or previous training, as if merely my life in a literate world had seeped into my dog consciousness and, courtesy of a mild dose of radiation, had blossomed. What was most startling of all was what I heard: not from without, because try as I might I couldn't locate the sound outside of me; it was the voice from inside I heard when I read. The voice of the reader reading to himself, the voice that spoke to me when my eyes ran over word after word after word.

I spent half the day pouring over that first *Daily Townsman* from July 1983. But I didn't want to reveal my new skill too soon, and so I pretended to be resting on the newspaper and not struggling to read every article and make what I absorbed mean something. But as my mind grew, as I connected into what I imagined must have been the larger consciousness of humanity and its stock of knowledge over the last forty thousand years, the meanings came to me and I to them. When I glanced up at Mr. Kindler still curled up against Johanna's body, I knew in the way that humans do what it meant to miss the beloved spouse or pet or child. And I knew that Mr. Kindler had so linked Johanna the dog with Johanna his lost love that the death of the dog was the death of the love, the death of the hope that had kept him alive for so many years.

Judith shook the old man by his shoulder. "Mr. Kindler, you must get up and eat something. Stevie made oatmeal."

When Mr. Kindler's oatmeal grew cold and Judith came and reached for his burned hand and held out a cup of water, she knew what I'd known for the last few hours. That Mr. Kindler had died from his wounds but more so from the wound he'd suffered after he left Berlin—the loss of love, that the tether he had to his life had finally snapped. When none of the others were looking I went and licked his face and I thought what Steve and Judith were thinking—that we couldn't leave Mr. Kindler and Johanna in the shelter any longer. And just then a rifle cracked and a bullet clanged off the door.

"Stevie! Judith! Brownie!" It was Joe's hoarse shout, as rough as two strips of dry leather passing over each other. "Open up now for Joe. Remember, Joe, your father? Joe who raised you even though your mother wouldn't?" I whined, because I felt a sudden burst of pity for Joe, because he included me with the children. He'd raised me after he'd rescued me from the shelter. He'd—

"Why don't you let us in, all of us?"

"Us?" whispered Stevie. "Judith, are there more people out there?"

As if he'd heard Stevie's low voice, Joe yelled, "Of course there's more of us out here. We're the last known survivors of the great atomic war. The incineration of the world. But Cranbrook was spared—well, the southern end to Gold Creek. The good people. Ain't that right, everyone?"

Murmurs from whoever else was out there came from

right outside the door, as if they were pressed up against the steel, the limestone it was set in.

"They'd like to come in too. Wouldn't you?"

We stepped back from the door as if we expected it to peel back off its hinges.

"How long can you wait, Judith and Stevie? Huh? Till your dead begin to stink?" Someone or something outside laughed or tried to laugh, because that choking rasp had the ha-ha rhythm of a laugh. "See, our dead don't stink out here. We can't smell 'em over the smell of the incinerated world. Can I get an amen? I said can I get an amen?"

"Amen," came the pained, moaning chorus.

"But we bury them anyway, those that weren't cremated where they stood. We bury them with the chickens and the cougar and Brownie, my dog which died to me—was it last week? Time is so different now. Warped like the space we occupy in our unfolding story."

Again, "Amen."

"But there's someone who wants to meet you."

"We don't want to meet anyone," said Stevie. "Just go away."

"Not you he wants to meet, boy. Or even Judith. Or even that dead dog and dead Mr. Kindler, god bless his romantic, Kraut heart. I'm talking about Brownie. The Brownie that was resurrected after I buried him. The Brownie that crawled from a grave of dead fowl. The Brownie that reads the newspaper and plots your escape. By the way, you fail, Brownie."

Judith and Stevie looked down at me and I sat on my haunches and tap-tap-tapped my tail and looked innocent and a little dim, as many chocolate Labs do. How did Joe out there know that I could read the newspaper? That I devoured every word of a ten-page newspaper, mostly filled with advertisements, but all of this made up for by the columns from Ms. Orlando, our presumably incinerated librarian? And how did he know I was plotting our escape? Even I didn't know I was doing that until much later, when more of my subgenius thought poured into my consciousness.

"Isn't me that can read what's in your little head, Brownie, it's him, he's standing right beside me. He knows you better than you know yourself. He tells me what's passing through your head."

"Brownie's a good boy," shouted Stevie. And then to me in a hushed tone, "You're our special dog, don't listen to Joe."

Judith, lovely Judith, gave Stevie some earplugs and put some into her own ears and wrote on a little chalkboard slate in pink chalk *silent running*. Meaning that we had to be quiet and not listen to whomever was creeping around outside. Below *silent running*, Judith wrote *reading time for 30 minutes* and then *prep. body disposal*. Stevie nodded and went to our little card table and picked up the book he was reading on organic gardening and Judith read for the fourth time Bradbury's *Something Wicked This Way Comes*, and I went to the pile of newspapers and pawed the page over to Ms. Orlando's review of Julio Cortázar's *Blow Up and Other Stories*. And I thought, yes, yes, Ms. Orlando, I will find a copy of this book in the ashes of the earth and devour every word in honour of your fine prose. When I looked up from Ms. Orlando's four ellipses, which was how she liked to end a review, when I looked up with my dreamy dog in-love look, Judith and Stevie were staring at me from behind their books.

"Brownie," asked Stevie, "how'd you know it was reading time?"

"Don't be silly," said Judith, "he copied us."

"No, he didn't. He'd come beside me if that was his game. He read your slate."

Judith laughed. They both spoke in raised voices, because they still had their earplugs in. I wagged my tail and let my tongue loll out the side of my mouth and looked idiotic, because god knows what would become of a mutant dog in a time of scarcity. And outside the door, Joe said, "Brownie, Mister Jarvis has the only copy—the what?" He was clearly speaking to someone else now. "Don't know that word, but if you think he does." And to me again: "Mister Jarvis has the only *extant* copy of that book you want. But you gotta come out. You gotta surrender."

Outside, in the nuked world of the East Kootenays, was what Ms. Orlando referred to in her October 1982 review of *The Chrysalids* as a telepath—someone who can read minds. Someone named Mister Jarvis, a name that I felt I knew, that I knew in the soul of our decimated town, as if I'd seen the name before, but not associated with a face. Oh what a confused pup I was! Why must I surrender? What did I, an irradiated canid, mean to anybody? Some deranged telepath who sauntered up to our door post-apocalypse and now needed my adopted human father to translate his thoughts?

Judith and Stevie had pulled out two long, semi-translucent storage bags. The kind women stored long dresses in, the kind with a little zipper that caught in the plastic all the time. Stevie pulled Mr. Kindler off Joanna and lay him on his back beside the bag. He forced Mr. Kindler's arms into a crossed position on his chest. "Rigor mortis," said Stevie. Judith told him to put gloves on and Stevie nodded and they stood over the bodies in their yellow Playtex gloves.

"Should we say something?" said Stevie.

"The Lord's Prayer," said Judith.

"Mr. Kindler was a theosophist."

"You even know what that means?"

"It's got nothing to do with the Lord's Prayer."

"You have anything better?"

"My survival book has last rites in it."

"I told you not to say *my*. Everything has to be ours, because we're all we've got. We'll say something later."

Stevie sat beside me with his back to his sister, at my place now beside the door, and held his head against me. "You're mine, Brownie. All mine."

Judith loomed over her brother. "Bodies."

And from outside, Joe: "Stevie, you help your sister with those bodies. And then you open this door and let them out. Hear? Or no supper and no Atari."

Stevie's eyes filmed over with moisture. He and Judith dragged Mr. Kindler and Joanna beside the door. Stevie draped two worn Hawaiian leis over the bodies and bowed his head and said, "Great Beyond, please accept these two dead friends. Joanna loved Mr. Kindler. And Mr. Kindler loved her. Keep them together forever. Amen, Steven J. Equinox."

We waited, I want to say eternal hours, but more like

days. Stevie insisted that we couldn't leave the shelter for forty-eight hours to ensure that the level of radioactive iodine was low enough to open the door. We waited for the throng outside the door to sleep or die or at least give up. And I kept my thoughts to a minimum—my inner words—so that this Mr. Jarvis couldn't scry my plans, my weaknesses. Judith and Stevie lifted up the heavy bar that sealed the door and slid back the two deadbolts and gently, on freshly oiled hinges, pulled the door inward and revealed a strange dawn. The farm looked much as it ever did: there stood the house, the dilapidated chicken coop, Joe's F150, Joe's workshop. Except the first crisp frost of the coming winter was covered with a sooty, black dust, muting the greens and oranges and reds of autumn. I heard no thrushes or owls or our rooster. I heard nothing but the silence of the throng seated in a distant half-circle around the shelter, maybe a hundred feet away. Perhaps fifty people or what were people, half-singed rocking things wrapped in blankets or old coats or plastic sheeting. Behind them all stood Joe, before his wheelchair, wrapped in the melted shreds of his red-checked mackinaw and John Deere hat. And beside him, this older, balding man in his navy blue suit and yellow tie. The suit lacked the right arm and his right arm the ability to bend at the elbow joint, for it hung loosely at his side and couldn't move like his left arm did when he pointed at us.

"Mr. Jarvis says good morning," said Joe. "Good morning, Brownie."

"Don't listen to them, get the bodies out," Judith yelled at a whisper. They both wore the WWII gas masks Judith had found in Second Time Around on Baker Street and, for me, a painter's mask pulled tight around my snout. They first dragged Mr. Kindler's body along the trampled earth before the shelter door and, then, when the throng of survivors didn't move toward us, Judith pulled Joanna's body beside Mr. Kindler's.

"Back inside," Judith yelled.

"Their flowers," Stevie said. He bent down to grab the leis where they'd fallen off the bodies and Judith grabbed him by the arm and Joe held up a book and said, "It's that book you want, Brownie. Come and get it, boy. Just c'mere."

I shook my head back and forth not because I was saying no to the book by Julio Cortázar, but for the insult of being treated like a servile mutt. I growled at Joe and he began to laugh and down went the book and up came his rifle. "Mr. Jarvis says you have an ego now, Brownie. A goddamn child's ego and that's gonna be your ruin. Surrender now."

Judith pulled Stevie to the ground as the first shot clanked off the rock above us.

Stevie went to reach for the leis and I raked at his hand and growled at him. Judith scrambled back into the shelter and Stevie yelled that I'd bit him and another bullet struck the dirt beside us and we crawled back into the shelter and just before Judith pushed the door shut, all the survivors jumped up with what looked like clubs in their hand and slouched towards us.

"Why'd you bite me, Brownie?" Stevie asked.

"Because you behaved like an idiot," said Judith.

"They needed flowers. We can't even bury them."

Outside, those clubs struck the door again and again

and Stevie and Judith put in their earplugs. "We'll have to wait for the cancers to kill them," said Stevie. "And then it'll just be us. Anyone want bacon for breakfast?"

Judith stared at me. "What did Joe mean when he offered you that book, Brownie?"

I sat on my haunches and let my tongue hang out and looked dull and backward.

"Don't play stupid, Brownie. I can see the radiation changed you. It's in your eyes. Intelligence."

"He just smells the bacon."

"Brownie," Judith said. "Can you read?"

A little pebble fell from the ceiling of the shelter beside Stevie as he fried the bacon.

Judith held up a *Daily Townsman* in front of me. "You can read this, can't you?" She must have seen something in the movement of my eyes as I took in a welcome notice for the birth of Stewart Chisholm, seven pounds one ounce, at the Cranbrook District Hospital. The little tyke had been overdue by three weeks and the parents, history teachers, had feared that Stewart's gestation would go on for years like this other baby near the turn of century. "Stevie, Brownie is reading."

I looked down. No, she can't know. No one can know, until—

A metallic rattle came from above us and a fist-sized rock struck the kitchen table. "They found the vent!" cried Stevie.

Something boomed outside. An explosion. A spray of little rocks struck the door.

"You in that shelter there," yelled Joe. "You that were once my children and my fuckin' dog. You remember that little box of TNT I found out in that CPR shack out by Wycliffe? Well, old Joe kept it and that was your only warning. Those bodies you put out, we just sent them to heaven. You've got twenty-four hours to come out now or the next thing that comes down that vent of yours will be a stick of dynamite."

"You said you camouflaged that vent," Judith hissed at Stevie.

"They must've smelled the bacon," he said.

"Can we seal it off?"

"Only from the outside."

"We're supposed to stay in here for ninety days."

"Dad wouldn't kill us."

"We've never had a dad. We had Joe. And, if you didn't notice, he shot at us."

Joe's mutant army was still pounding on the front door, but with less vigour. I'm sure that it wasn't the children Joe wanted or even our supply of food—it was me. Somehow I, Brownie Equinox, pet license 239, subgenius Labrador, was the real prize for this Mr. Jarvis. I shook my head. No, this was my vanity. I was merely a dog. I had nothing to offer humanity accept a burgeoning ability to read and some mediocre retrieving skills. Who was I to the post-apocalyptic world?

An hour later, Stevie came and took me by my collar over to Judith's cot. Judith patted the bed and I hopped up and Stevie scratched my back until my right leg kicked and kicked. Judith gave me a biscuit.

"Brownie," Judith said. "Maybe you can read the *Daily Townsman*, who knows, it's not a sophisticated paper, but I want you to know that you're like a brother to us."

"A fun little brother," said Stevie. "Remember when I threw that red ball for you and you came back with a wild rose? Like you were courting?"

"Who had to pull the prickles out of his tongue?"

"I held him."

Stevie began to cry. "He's a good dog."

"A very good dog, okay? Granted."

Stevie threw himself against me and burrowed his head into my chest and Judith patted me on my cranium in the somewhat stiff way she petted me. Stevie wailed something I hadn't heard before, primal and endearing at the same time, like one of those howler monkeys I'd seen on *Wild Kingdom.*

"Brownie," Judith began. "Stevie and I have decided to stay in here. We thought that it would be better to die in here rather than suffer what's outside. But we don't want you to die with us. We want you to survive."

Stevie held me so hard I thought I'd gasp. "Let go now," said Judith. "Stevie!"

"He's a good dog. They'll eat him."

"They're from Cranbrook, they respect dogs. Even now in the post-apocalypse."

Stevie wailed and Judith took me by the collar and tried to pull me over to the door, but I yarded against her. I fought and snapped and growled, but she yanked my collar down until I was on my side and she dragged me to the door. "Get your slingshot, Stevie."

Judith held me down with her foot and lifted the heavy iron bar and slid back the two thick bolts and Stevie stood beside her with his slingshot pulled back with a ball bearing at the ready and she eased open the door and there in the crack of light was one of those things, its face burnt and suppurating crimson gore, and when it raised its club, Stevie shot the ball bearing into the remains of its face and Judith kicked my haunches and I yelped and shot forward and suddenly I quivered in the outside world surrounded by four of the survivors and on the ground, the writhing body of the one Stevie had shot. The door clanked shut behind me.

"Nice doggy," said one of the survivors and struck at me with its club in a slow pathetic arc. "Have a biscuit." But not all four of them were middle aged and inhibited by arthritic shoulders. A shorter, lither survivor slapped my haunches with its hand and I leapt forward and ran for the woods. Not crazy fast, but fast enough I thought that my escape was easy. And then the same creature that had swung the club at me was in front of me again, lisping through a dirty red bandanna. "Nice doggy, nice doggy." I sprinted again for the aspen grove above the house and the same stupid thing appeared in front of me out of the irradiated air and I realized that I wasn't the only one who had been changed by bursts of gamma rays. This shambling creature in a blue Air Canada jacket could transport itself through the open air over short distances and so I bolted again and again through the radioactive dusk, cool and cloudy with the first creosote smell of winter, until it grew dark and I could hide from the maddening thing.

Puffs of wood smoke left the chimney of the house. In the window I could see the yellow-orange glow of a kerosene lamp. I didn't even know what dynamite looked like, but I had to find it. And then, as soon as I thought the word *dynamite*, a picture of it came to mind and I realized that my brain could call down any image from the great stock of human knowledge that had hovered somewhere just out of reach of most everybody, man and dog. When I thought about what that meant, the image that arose in me was of an owl, one of the snow white ones calling from a high branch in a ponderosa pine and when a distant call came back to it the great bird was suddenly in flight over a bright winter mountainscape and it could see everything. A lone woman, with a rounded belly, pushing west, west—to the distant sea. I laughed. I had intellect, but an idiot in an Air Canada jacket could transport himself through time and space after me.

"Nice doggy, nice doggy, where is you?"

I kept to the dark side of the chicken coop, away from three of Joe's army bent over a barrel of burning wood popping sparks into the starless sky. If I were Joe, I would keep the dynamite in the house, probably in the oak sideboard, where his ex-wife kept the good china, because somehow the dangerous with the fragile would appeal to someone like Ms. Orlando, would be something she might write about in her review in a future *Daily Townsman* about my story. But then I thought that Joe was a simpler man than Ms. Orlando was an aesthete, writer, and librarian—the dynamite was on the little folding TV tray table with the clicker and the last published TV guide and Joe's nail clippers, Vaseline hand cream, and his dish of unshelled pistachios.

I slunk around the house to the back door. There was more of the army gathered around a large fire in Joe's barbecue pit. They spoke in whispers and I edged up to the back door and pushed open the screen door with my nose and pushed into the darker, warmer house. The foyer was dark but for a slit of amber light beneath the door into the kitchen. I could make out that the chest freezer no longer hummed, that its door was angled open. Joe must be feeding his army the moose he shot last fall, before the meat went to waste. Or he was drying it or smoking it and I was glad at least that the world hadn't descended into cannibalizing radiation scarred survivors. Or dogs. Or—Something rose from my wicker bed in the corner of the foyer and shook its choker as it padded towards me and growled. The thing loomed over me and I could smell the burnt diseased flesh of a middle-aged dog, a large dog, easily as tall at the shoulder as an Irish wolfhound, but with something else in the mix, Rottweiler maybe or German shepherd.

"Can you talk?" I asked and edged back a step away from its creosote breath.

No.

"Can we negotiate? Can we just—we're the same species. Maybe the last of—"

The hound pushed against me until my haunches banged against the screen door and behind me two of Joe's army pushed up the steps. "Got 'im, Kane has got 'im," said one of them. "More ration, huh, boy?"

In my subgenius, anxious brain, I concluded that the ration was me, that torn hunks of me would be roasted over the fire outside and thrown to this tall, stinking thing and my short life as something greater than what I was would cease before I finished Ms. Orlando's columns. What if she had somehow survived Reagan and Andropov's war in the basement of the library and was still typing columns on her old Underwood Touch-Master and that this little pecking pulse of civilization meant there'd be more reviews I'd never get to read? What would become of Judith and Stevie without me to guide them to somewhere safer than a Kootenay farm at the foot of Teepee Mountain, overrun by a nuclear family of fifty? I mean, die when Joe dropped a lit stick of dynamite down the vent into the children's shelter?

A kerosene lamp appeared in the doorway to the kitchen. "I told you never set foot in my house," Joe roared. "None of you. Goddamn, can't you listen?" The hand on my neck released and the door banged shut behind me and the dog, Kane, edged away from me and I looked into his burnt, oozing face. Where there should have been a muzzle, there was a slobber-leaking hole.

"He knew you'd come," said Joe. "He's been—he said it was scrying, scrying your mind. Like reading those reviews you like. Except you're flesh and blood to read."

Joe dragged me by my collar into the kitchen. "You want some Gaines-Burger? I saved you some."

I didn't know if I shook my head or he just saw that I couldn't eat for my nerves.

"Suit yourself. I'll give 'em to Kane."

The living room smelled as I'd left it, of creosote and birch logs and the old sweetness of Joe's pipe. The room felt warmer than the shelter, inviting for the amber glow of Joe's old kerosene lamp, the warm cedar panelling. The wood stove popped and ticked. Joe's recliner had been turned around so it no longer faced the dead and cold TV, but the wood stove rather, with the little grate open and the flames curling around the outside edge of the little door.

He was seated in the chair, the man I'd seen earlier with Joe when we put out Joanna and Mr. Kindler. I could see his suited leg, his black oxford shoe. I could smell his —I had no classification for that smell. The smell of a far older man than he looked, the smell of a newborn baby. The smell of death, the smell of birth.

"I'm so glad you came, Brownie." He spoke in a soft, melodious rasp. The voice of the young in the ancient.

"Mr. Charles Jarvis. Brownie Equinox," Joe said in a rare, deferent tone.

This thin, bald man who simultaneously looked no more than thirty and somehow old at the same time. Who, unlike his followers, had not a wound on him, except for that arm that wouldn't straighten. Who wore an ancient suit shorn of one sleeve and around his neck an unknotted bowtie. Who you imagined killed enemies with a concealed derringer, like in a western. Who commanded with a glance. Who seemed as old as the town itself.

"Joe," Charles Jarvis said, "leave us for the moment. Brownie is afraid. Close the door."

"That's not the same Brownie. The scared mutt I buried with the chickens."

That Brownie was dead. In his place was cerebral Brownie, alpha Brownie, cunning Brownie.

"He's after the dynamite."

"The door, Joe."

In my life I'd not seen Joe Equinox obey anyone and when he slid the living room door shut behind him, my hackles went up.

"He won't return until I say," said Charles Jarvis.

I looked at the closed door and then, slowly, as if I almost believed the man in Joe's easy chair, I pricked up my ears and began to search the room.

"The dynamite is on the TV tray in the corner."

There it was, five ruddy black sticks of dynamite beside the clicker and a stack of old *TV Guides*.

"Brownie."

Charles Jarvis's lips didn't move, but I heard his voice all the same—within my mind, my expanding, doggy mind.

"Brownie, do you know who you are?"

Irradiated chocolate Labrador. Stepchild of Joe Equinox. Brother of Judith and Stevie Equinox. Subgenius, burgeoning leader, servant of what was left of humanity. Murderer.

"None of those things. Can you see it, Brownie? The pictures I'm sending you. Can you see what has become? Of the world?"

I smelled it before I saw it. The razed world. The scorched, blackened earth. The flesh, not putrefied but charred. The creosote stink of our ancient, spherical crematorium. An image appeared not before me, but in me. Of the world beyond the Rocky Mountains that surrounded our town. I hadn't travelled far with the Equinox family, as far north as Radium Hot Springs and as far east as Lethbridge. Of the forested world I remembered from the back of Joe's truck there was only the burnt embers of the pines and the aspens and every built-up wooden thing. Not a single living thing moved out there beyond our mountains—not a bird, tree, or dog.

"All that is left of thinking life is here on this farm. I thought I was alone, Brownie. That I would be forever alone. Whom could I communicate with? In my long life, no one. Not my wife, not my children, not my grandchildren, not my great-grandchildren. No one could hear my thoughts, they knew me only for the crude sounds my tongue made. From the ruin of the world I heard your thoughts and you heard mine. You heard the inner life of Charles Jarvis. You are the first. It is no irony that of all the creatures that can hear me it is you—the dog at the centre of the surviving world. A beautiful dog can hear me sing."

He lifted up from his chair as if he might wrap his good arm around me.

"You mustn't fear. We are together now. We are going to rebuild this world. We are going to lead it from the ruins it has become."

He looked across the room at the sticks of Joe's dynamite.

"But you want to save Judith and Stevie."

If I scrambled across the room, I could grab one of the sticks, before Charles Jarvis could cry out. Hurl it through the open door of the wood stove.

"We will take care of Judith and Stevie. What could be more vital to the future than children?"

His thought—I couldn't name what tone coloured it, but my hackles prickled.

"We will need their food and their medical supplies. Their energy. We must take back Cranbrook. Rebuild it. Did you know that town was once all prairie and Ponderosa pine? The Indians called it Joseph's Prairie. It can never become that again. Even after war. This beautiful town has been my home for almost one hundred years and it must be reborn. I will die in what we build from the ruins. My house on 11th Avenue still stands, but marauders broke in. Stole my supplies. Attacked poor Kane. I need you, I need all of you to take back my town. My home."

The explosion shook the house, knocked a dead succulent off the windowsill beside the TV. My eardrums pounded. My nostrils burned with a sulphurous stink.

"Joe is an impatient father."

I scrambled around in a circle. I went to the window to look out, but plywood had been tacked over the cracked pane. I pawed at the door, the little wool rug in front of the door. I barked at the door like a stupid fool.

"Do I have your loyalty, Brownie? Does my town have your loyalty?"

The second explosion made my ears whine, my throat burn, my heart scream.

"You cannot lie to me, Brownie. When you learn to speak, and you will learn to speak, you will lie. But in your thoughts, your thoughts, they're visible to me."

My thoughts—I could only see the mangled ruin of the fallout shelter, Stevie and Judith buried beneath the rubble. I could smell their blood.

"Those are not thoughts, Brownie. Those pictures are your imagination."

I ran around the room and scratched at the smallest crack in the floor and barked and wailed.

"We will rule, you and I. We will rule what is left of this planet and we will make it whole again. You and I."

I scratched at the open grate on the wood stove, because it was the only open thing in the entirety of the room. My paws seared but in my agony I didn't care. I sent hot coals and a crimson-coloured piece of cedar onto the rug behind me. I howled, I scratched at the linoleum around the wood stove.

"In your grief, you will know truth and in truth you will know love for those you rule. And that love will be—"

By now a little fire had ignited on the rug and raced along the frills to Joe's recliner and beside it the settee and the polyester throw.

Charles Jarvis's thoughts, his plans for the human race, the empire he would build in this valley of the Rocky Mountains—every single image of his future came at me in a relentless stream even as fire leapt from the settee to the ottoman to the splintered wood panelling. In those leaping pools of fire I saw again the dead blacksmith and his dead son astride their dead horse parading around the room and their wail and their laughter drowned out the hiss and the crackle of the flames. Soon those riders had ignited the entire room, but still Charles Jarvis didn't move.

"Fire took my mother so long ago, but it didn't take me. Fire can't destroy those like us, Brownie."

But it could. My skin grew hot, my nostrils burnt with smoke, and my lungs ached. The fur on my hind leg began to smoulder. I crawled along the floor and yipped and howled like a terrified fool. Above me, the glass face of Joe's vintage wall clock cracked and popped and my mind screamed.

The door inched open.

"Mr. Jarvis?" It was the shambling soldier in the Air Canada jacket. "Mr. Jarvis? Nice doggy."

I bolted out into the kitchen and past Kane and out the open door into the trembling frozen night. I ran pell-mell towards the shelter. The door hung at an odd angle and smoke still poured from the shattered entrance and I howled for what Joe had done to his own children. I howled for the dead lives piled upon the dead heap of the world. Oh I howled!

The dynamite Joe had left on the TV tray in the living room, where I'd met Charles Jarvis popped and sizzled for lack of a blasting cap and I could see its bright white flare through the cracks around the plywood and a scream sounded, not in my ears, but inside my head, a long wailing scream. It was Charles Jarvis screaming in agony or delight—I couldn't tell, for my ability to make any kind of judgement had vanished when I knew what had happened to Judith and Stevie. I howled along with that scream in my head, at Charles Jarvis, as the flames that were now Joe's house touched the tips of the aspens overhanging the roof, as the dead blacksmith and his dead son hurtled wailing into the night sky towards stars I wouldn't see for years.

Joe's army was running straight up the little slope towards me. I ran into the screaming dark toward the road to town. Charles Jarvis had said others had invaded his old house on 11th Avenue, that there were still survivors. But what was the point in going on without Judith and Stevie? I slumped down in the middle of the road. I looked up at the grey-black pall vented by all the burning cities of the world. It felt like the dark velvet of a coffin lid. I, Brownie

Equinox, pet license 239, had nothing left to live for—Ms. Orlando, I'm sorry: *nothing left for which to live*. No, that sounded worse. They don't tell you in the books on surviving the apocalypse that even grammar will go. That the order of words goes the way of the disorder of demolished civilization. Ms. Orlando, I'm so sorry. I loved your column in the *Daily Townsman* and now the last known stockpile of those beautiful papers has been blown up with my children.

The march of Joe's army came to me as a vibration through the cold, frozen earth. Their slouching, shuffling footfalls dragged along the gravel as Joe drove them toward me. I didn't care. *Nothing left for which to live.*

Nothing. Johanna was dead. Judith and Stevie. The world.

Joe Equinox has already buried me once.

"Brownie?"

The word sounded muffled, as if spoken through a thick handkerchief.

A foot nudged me in the back.

"Brownie, get up, they're coming."

I looked up at an old surplus gas mask and beside it a second.

"It's us. Stevie and Judith."

I put my head back down on the cold gravel. Stevie and Judith were dead.

A booted foot poked me in the back. "Get up, Brownie. They're coming."

I felt what could only be Stevie's hand, his gloved hand, grab me by the scruff of the neck and scratch me as he always did.

I raised my head. I wagged my tail. I leapt up and couldn't stop from barking.

"Shush! They'll hear us!" Judith hissed.

I couldn't believe that they'd survived. I couldn't believe that they existed in this lonely, apocalyptic East Kootenay valley. The world had been nuked, but Judith and Stevie were alive. My children were alive.

They jogged and I followed. They were wearing thin white contamination suits and rubber boots and rubber Playtex gloves taped shut at the wrists. They each carried heavy canvas rucksacks with whatever they could carry from the shelter. Stevie carried something else, something small and squirming in a mesh bag which hung from his backpack. I can't explain how the bird had remained alive on the farm, but if he'd survived the jaws of a cougar and now the blight of the apocalypse he must be as immortal as the spirit of the ghost riders. Henry the rooster bounced along in that mesh bag, a little less feathered around his neck and chest, but glowing around his eyes, not with intelligence but with irradiated relief. He crowed a little crow when I sniff-hugged him and then somehow sensing the danger behind us fell into anxious silence.

The distant stomp of footsteps came like a violent drumbeat on the gravel.

"They're not far behind," Judith hissed.

Above it all, over the smoke of Joe's house and the stomp of Joe's army, Charles Jarvis's thoughts pursued mine.

His call to me.

His call to join him. His call to be his companion in this dying civilization. *Brownie, Brownie, Brownie . . .*

"Are you wondering, Brownie-boy," asked Stevie, "how we survived?"

Brownie, Brownie, Brownie.

"Brownie already knows," said Judith, "that we slipped out after he drew those mutants away."

But I didn't know. I didn't know my role then, but I do now.

"You should've told him our plan. He could've died. Alone."

Brownie, Brownie, Brownie . . . always alone without me.

WE FOUND much of Cranbrook destroyed and deserted. Burnt empty shells of houses. Blackened trees. The soot of winter in the valley, but not a single wood stove alight. All of the town shrouded with a layer of snow made dirty by the dust and debris that still fell from the sky. We spent our first night in the old Gilchrist house on 11th Avenue, where they say Leon Trotsky once spent a few nights en route to Mexico. But half the walls had been blown down and a cold wind kept us awake most of the night, even in our sleeping bags. The basement had somehow filled with piles of dirt as if someone had tried to excavate bodies and then covered up the holes with wood debris. The second night was in the old post office on 10th Avenue and the third in the remains of the Baker Hotel, but in each building rubble from higher floors struck the ground near us and we pushed on.

By the end of the week, we'd run out of bottled water.

The Cranbrook Mall had been ransacked of anything that might be useful—food and clothing and even, so joked Judith, lottery tickets and their promise of hope. It was the Cranbrook Public Library that seemed untouched by the war. It looked perfectly preserved, despite the nearby swimming pool and curling arena now existing only as blackened rectangles dusted over by dark snow. The front door was unlocked and a strange, sterile silence crept out from the shadows. The lights were out, as they were all over the town, but in our torch light beams I could see that the books on all the shelves were undisturbed. There was a thin layer of dust on the floor, but ours were the first footprints.

"Brownie, smell anything?" asked Stevie.

I smelled dust and the scents of the many people that had passed through here many weeks ago, before the attack. I smelled book paper new and old, the stale tobacco of old books read by electric light and cigarette. I smelled ink and the old food smells dribbled on books and magazines. I smelled the typewriter ink of the card catalogue. I smelled—

"Brownie, what is it?"

"Is it something bad?" asked Judith.

I wandered through the gloom over to the front desk. There, on a low typewriter stand, was an Underwood Touch-Master with a fresh sheet of paper in the roller and beside it, a book by Heinrich Böll, *The Lost Honour of Katharina Blum,* and beside that an orange. I leapt up so that my paws were on the desk. I recognized the opening sentence immediately. "Sometimes a thin novel comes along that leaves such a startling impression over the course of its few pages, you cannot help but see the world through newborn eyes. Heinrich Böll's novel *The . . .*" There wasn't a single word after that last definite article. What had stopped Ms. Orlando from writing any more? Had a child and her mother come along with a book to be signed out? Had the bombs started falling before she could type her next sentences? Where was Ms. Orlando now?

"Good boy," said Stevie. "Brownie found us an orange."

It was in the basement that we found Ms. Orlando's treasure. Her stack of *Daily Townsmans* with every one of her columns in them was on a low desk and beside that ten gallon jugs of water and flats of canned Campbell's soup and Premium Plus crackers and four folded Bay blankets and a pillow. Enough food and water for over a month. But there was no clue as to where Ms. Orlando had gone. There were her remaining columns in a little manila folder, which I secretly carried upstairs when Judith and Stevie were sleeping and which I read in the diffuse moonlight streaming through the now locked front door. Her last published column on Friday, March 4, 1983, just days before the end of the world, was a review of *Fifth Business* by Robertson Davies. I read all three hundred words and wondered if I could find the book in the library and hoped it was in hardcover so that I could lay it on the ground and paw the pages open.

I want to say that I loved Ms. Orlando and that it was her words that pushed me to lead Stevie and Judith to the west coast. But I knew her hardly at all, except by my imaginings. No, I knew her by her scent, too. I found her plum-coloured cardigan and I inhaled it deeply and knew that I loved her, that she was someone I could love perhaps with the passion that Mr. Kindler loved his Johanna. But Ms. Orlando's scent vanished at the rear door from which she'd left. Her scent of oranges and Earl Grey tea ended where the scent of war began.

Grey cinders snowed that night from the slate-coloured sky and for the first time since we'd escaped Joe's house, I realized that I no longer heard the voice of Charles Jarvis. I had no time to feel the loneliness of my thoughts. The sky lightened on the eastern horizon and from the top of the card catalogue Henry the rooster crowed in alarm over the distant sound of Joe's army.

"Judith and Stevie." They were the first words I ever said and I whispered them in the hoarse voice I'd always have when I spoke English. "We have to go. West."

ENDNOTES

LETTERS TO ANDROPOV

1. My description is inaccurate, I now realize, because we dogs see much like the red-green colourblind. Judith's hair, Stevie said, is orange-red like the fire in our wood stove, the pencil was violet, and her eyes are in fact a shade of light green. I hope you know what these colours are, you surviving readers.

ACKNOWLEDGEMENTS

I view the fact that I can write stories at all as a gift. I am especially indebted to my mother and father, Ruth and Alan, who moved our family to the foothills of the Rocky Mountains so many years ago. I am equally grateful to the people of Cranbrook who gifted me with so many formative experiences, when I was growing up.

Writing is a solitary activity, but not a lonely one. I am especially thankful to Zsuzsi Gartner for her mentorship and friendship, to Lenore Rowntree for her support over the years I wrote these stories and to Tessa Wright for her candlelight in my darker artistic moments.

Thanks to Michel Vrana for the cover design, to Kate Kennedy for her editing and copyediting, to Maria Hypponen for the index, to John Farrell for the audio version and to Richard Lett for his photographic wizardry. Also many thanks to John Zada, Basil McDermott, Tahir Shah, Robert Twigger, Dawn Fenwick, Isabella Wang, Erin McNeill, Kathie Gallucci, Doug Stevely, Nadir Karanjia, ManWoman and Astarte.

And special thanks to the Canada Council for the Arts whose generous support helped me craft each story.

Lastly, I would like to acknowledge the Indigenous peoples of the region, especially the Ktunaxa Nation on whose lands my stories grew.

Thank you.

ABOUT THE AUTHOR

Andrew Boden's fiction and non-fiction have been published in numerous anthologies and magazines across Canada and the US, including the Journey Prize anthology, and he has been a finalist in *The Malahat Review*'s 2016 and 2018 novella contests. He is co-editor of *Hidden Lives: Coming Out on Mental Illness*, an anthology of personal essays. Andrew grew up in Cranbrook, British Columbia, and now lives in Burnaby.

Request

If you enjoyed this book please review it on your favourite online retailer or review website.

Reviews are an author's best friend.

To keep up with Andrew Boden's work and/or follow him on social media, please visit any one of the following links:

www.andrewboden.com

 facebook.com/andrew.boden.982

 twitter.com/andrewboden2

 instagram.com/instandrewb